W9-AUE-623

Praise for *The Human Disguise*

"This near-future page-turner debut amalgamates apocalyptic science fiction, police procedural, and thematic dashes of alien invasion and vampire mythos. His self-assured, hard-edged writing style, solid characters, and wildly entertaining thriller plot will keep readers enthralled."

—*Publishers Weekly* (starred review)

"One helluva story from one helluva writer! Only a cop like James O'Neal could create futuristic bad guys like those in *The Human Disguise*. And only O'Neal could weave them into such a slick, fast-paced story—one you're convinced is the real world. This is a ride—and a writer—you're long going to remember."

—W. E. B. Griffin

"Aliens, a rotten future, civilization on the ropes . . . James O'Neal writes like an old, twisted, wigged-out Hunter S. Thompson. Al Gore, save us, please!" —Stephen Coonts, *New York Times* bestselling author of *The Assassin*

"As soon as I began reading *The Human Disguise* I was immediately reminded—strongly—of Orwell's *Nineteen Eighty-Four*. [O'Neal's] vision of a new future, in which ordinary life has taken a surreally dark turn, bears a more than superficial resemblance to Orwell's vision. Only in *Disguise*, [O'Neal] has thrown in two even more ominous wrinkles: aliens already living among us and the presence of a spaceship from another solar system making its way toward Earth."

—David Hagberg, *USA Today* bestselling author of *Dance with the Dragon*

THE HUMAN
DISGUISE

James O'Neal

A Tom Doherty Associates Book New York

This is a work of fiction. All of the characters, organizations, and events portrayed in this novel are either products of the author's imagination or are used fictitiously.

THE HUMAN DISGUISE

Copyright © 2009 by James O'Neal

A Tor Book
Published by Tom Doherty Associates, LLC
175 Fifth Avenue
New York, NY 10010

www.tor-forge.com

Tor® is a registered trademark of Tom Doherty Associates, LLC.

ISBN 978-0-7653-5977-3

First Edition: June 2009
First Mass Market Edition: July 2010

Printed in the United States of America

0 9 8 7 6 5 4 3 2 1

To Donna, John, and Emily.
Now you're in two books.

Acknowledgments

A work of speculative fiction requires an open mind about the future. I'd like to thank: my friend Jim Boyette for his engineering insight to possible innovations.

To Paul Allen for his support of the Science Fiction Museum and Hall of Fame. The idea for this novel hit me while visiting the museum in Seattle.

THE HUMAN DISGUISE

ONE

From the end of the bar, Tom Wilner could look through the cavernous main room and pool hall and still see her dark hair as she leaned back in her chair. The boyfriend, Tiget Nadovich, sat next to her, wearing that dark jacket over his black shirt and black pants that Wilner had seen him in twenty times before.

It bothered Wilner that all the databases listed him as a citizen of the United States for the last eleven years. That meant he got it just before the ban on immigration. It also meant he got it just for being in the United States when the amnesty bill passed and everyone inside the borders of the country was awarded citizenship. The Congress limited it to the first forty-nine states because they saw the writing on the wall about Hawaii. Once the independence movement started rolling, no one wanted to stand up and say that the native people of Hawaii didn't deserve their own country. Plus the fact that the United States was engaged in three wars at the time didn't help their position.

That's why the United States took in another twenty-seven

million citizens in one day, and then conscripted most of them into the military. Somehow this creep had avoided service, but he was legal and that didn't make Wilner happy.

Wilner motioned for the bartender to bring him another Jax beer. Since the government didn't get involved in much regulation of industry there were more products available in more places. Antitrust was a thing of the past. That meant a wider selection of beer and this New Orleans brew was originally deregulated to help raise money for Katrina redevelopment when the government gave up about ten years after the storm. Now everyone drank it.

Wilner slowly sipped the beer as his eyes, almost involuntarily, stayed on the woman. Her dazzling smile and her dark eyes conveyed intelligence.

"Detective Wilner," came a voice from behind him, making him jump.

Wilner turned, then shook his head. "Hey, Steve."

"Hey, Willie, I thought you were busy tonight, or were you just avoiding me?"

"Nothing like that. How'd you know I was here?"

"Your housekeeper."

"When did you talk to her?"

"You aren't answering your V-com. I called the house."

Wilner nodded, looking straight ahead. He'd turned off his video communicator, which was a misnomer for a device that did much more.

"Why'd you come way out here?"

"Just a nice change. You get a different kind of people wandering through."

"Yeah, folks that don't want to see the cops. You're not working on something, are you?"

He shook his head, too embarrassed to admit what he was

really doing. He tried to change the subject. "Anything happen on patrol today?"

Steve nodded as he sat on the stool. "Oh, yeah, riding that bike from the Northern Enclave to the Miami Quarantine Zone is so exciting I never run out of stories."

"What happened?"

"Nothing, you knucklehead. Same as every other day. Just a long ride in soggy weather."

"Lot of area."

Steve mumbled, "Damn Unified Police Force. I remember when each city could field a police department."

"That was a long time ago. No one can afford the taxes now."

They sat in silence until Wilner asked his friend, "Why aren't you reading up on the aliens?"

"Go ahead and make fun. When they finally arrive I'll be fully informed and know what to do." Then Steve scanned the room and stopped at the table with the beautiful dark-haired woman. "Oh, I get it." He looked at Wilner. "Are you crazy, following you ex-wife around?"

"We're not divorced yet."

"Has she called?"

"No."

"Has she even come by to visit the kids?"

"Once, for Emma's birthday."

Steve sighed then said, "You're not armed, are you?"

"Out here, who cares? More shit goes down between the turnpike and the Everglades than the rest of the state. No one ever investigates."

"But a gun in a bar, even by a cop, would land you ten years on a penal farm. Or worse, ten years back in the military in some godforsaken desert battleground."

Wilner nodded. "You're right, Steve. And I did leave my pistol in the car."

"You crazy? In this place? Shit, I brought in two."

Wilner had to laugh at his smaller friend's attitude. They had gone through the police academy together and joined Florida's Unified Police Force about three years after it had been established.

Besslia stood up and took hold of Wilner's arm. "C'mon, buddy, plenty of places for a couple of cops like us to drink. You don't need to be here."

Wilner jerked his arm free, still staring at his wife at a table of four men. For the first time he noticed that the men all looked similar. All in their thirties, with black hair, high cheekbones and dark eyes. For a moment he wondered if they might not all be brothers, but according to Nadovich's limited profile he had no living relatives in the United States.

The door on that side of the huge bar opened and the rain drifted in.

Wilner shivered slightly just thinking about the near endless rain out on the edge of the Everglades.

Steve said, "Global warming, my ass. I miss the days when August in Florida was warm. I even miss mosquitoes. What about you?"

Wilner settled back onto his stool, glad his friend had known enough to leave him alone about his wife. He said, "I don't remember mosquitoes."

Now Steve looked across the room. "Those two that just came in could be jihadis if they only had on their headdress."

Wilner nodded. Muslim headwear had been banned in the United States for a dozen years now. Some of the Muslims had left to seek religious freedom elsewhere. He didn't think any of them found it. But Besslia was right—with the dark hair and facial features these two did look Middle Eastern. Then, to his surprise, the men walked directly to the table where his wife, Svala, sat with her boyfriend.

The table welcomed the Middle Eastern men and then Nadovich leaned to Svala and she stood and slowly tromped toward the bar.

Wilner watched her come closer, but she didn't look up. Past her he saw the men at the table huddle and then exchange packages.

"What's that look like to you?" he asked Besslia, who had followed the exchange as well.

"Like there are too many of them and it's none of our business."

Wilner fought the urge to approach his wife. She'd never notice him all the way in the corner. That was his original intent. Now he faltered.

The door on the other side of the room opened again. This time a tall blond man slipped in quickly and settled, unnoticed at a table by the door.

Wilner made a quick assessment as the blond man scanned the bar and watched the table with Nadovich. He didn't look that interested in the quiet table's activities, but something wasn't right about him. Wilner had been a cop for six years and he was starting to believe his hunches. Now he had a hunch they were going to see some trouble.

Another man entered from the door directly behind him. He was shorter than the first man, but also blond with light features. This one marched directly across the wide floor toward the table with Nadovich and his friends.

Besslia nudged him. "That don't look good."

"Tell me about it."

"Here," said Steve, poking him under the bar.

"What's this?"

"My backup. An old Glock .40 caliber conventional handgun."

"You really did have two guns?"

Steve smiled. "Hey, we weren't all combat marines. I brought a knife too."

Wilner accepted the small pistol. "Just in case something goes down, I'll keep it." It was light compared to his duty automatic. They were issued conventional firearms, but the rounds were hot, 11 millimeter. Slightly bigger than the .40, only the military or police were supposed to have the rugged semiautomatic made by the venerable Beretta firearms company. Using superlight alloy casings and concentrated propellant, his duty weapon carried 28 rounds stacked in a long magazine.

The short blond man shouted something in an unknown language as he came to the table and whatever he said got everyone's attention. Even Svala turned from the bar and looked at the man. He spoke again and then turned and made a spitting sound of disgust.

That stirred the table as the two Middle Easterners stood up and backed away, one of them clutching the leather pouch Nadovich had given him.

Besslia said, "What's this?"

Wilner slowly stood, gripping the pistol in his hand under the bar. "Easy, Steve. No harm in just talking shit. Let's see what happens."

Before he could hear Steve's reply, gunfire erupted from that side of the room. The pops from the automatic weapon echoing in the tall, wide room like claps of thunder.

Wilner instinctively ducked and then moved to the corner of the bar to get a good view.

The big blond man by the front door leaped and drew a

knife as he fell on one of the men from the table. The others had scattered as the second, smaller blond man returned fire with a small machine pistol.

Then Wilner saw a flash and heard the crack a split second later.

Steve yelled in Wilner's ear, "Christ, someone has a flasher. I thought only the military had them."

"I guess there are some on the open market." Then he stood to take another position closer to the action. As he came up from behind the bar another flash of light destroyed a jukebox as it surged past the intended target. An energy weapon, or E-weapon, had been nicknamed a flasher by the Eighty-second Airborne since they first came into use during the third Iraq war. The flash of light beamed through a prism of gases could melt steel, destroy living tissue and cause terror among troops. As the deadly devices matured, the weapons became smaller, but lost some of their power. This one was handheld and probably only good for two or three shots. That's all it usually took. Instantly the jukebox melted and settled into a heap of glass and metal. An old country song skipped on an endless loop of a man singing "Live like you were dying," over and over. It was still identifiable, but no one would ever hear the jukebox play any other song again.

The two blond men, working together, were wading into the group led by Svala's boyfriend. The taller one used his knife to nearly gut one of the men from the table. The blade cut through his leather jacket and shirt, leaving a vicious gash where blood and internal organs looked ready to spill out onto the bar's dirty floor.

The other man fired his pistol into the center of the group and reached for the satchel sitting on the edge of the round table.

Nadovich also grabbed it and the satchel ripped apart, spilling several items onto the table and ground. He had his own pistol and pumped a bullet into the smaller blond man's chest, sending him back a step.

The noise, shouting, smoke and burning jukebox gave a level of confusion that emptied the bar at the edge of the Everglades in moments. Patrons fled out the door nearest Wilner as he and Steve started to advance toward the melee.

"Police, don't move," shouted Wilner as he ducked, knowing it would draw fire. He was mainly trying to scare the men outside. No one wanted to be caught with unlawful weapons like a flasher.

His shout did the trick, as someone threw a chair through a window and men started to flee.

Wilner looked to where his wife was standing at the bar. She was rushing to Nadovich's side and raced out the front door with him. As Wilner stood to follow, another shot came from the fight, but this one was aimed at the two cops.

Two more men jumped out the shattered window. The taller blond man fell to one knee to help his wounded friend.

Wilner and Steve advanced, their pistols up and aimed at the remaining conscious men.

"Don't move, don't move," he shouted, thinking of his last combat mission in Iran eight years earlier.

The big man slowly turned his head. It was the smaller man that surprised them. He had at least two serious bullet wounds yet he stood, turned and dove out the window.

Steve muttered, "What the hell were they firing? Blanks?"

The other man raised his hands.

Wilner looked over and saw one of the Middle Eastern men with a gunshot to his face. He was dead. The canvas satchel

Nadovich had given him was by his side. The man with the horrendous knife wound lay on the ground, but was still moving.

As Wilner heard the sirens in the distance he said, "What a mess." He watched as Besslia checked the corpse, then looked in the canvas satchel.

Steve whistled and held up the bag for Wilner.

He stared at what had to be more than a million dollars in standard U.S trade currency that was commonly called "suds."

This whole night was going to raise questions.

TWO

The paramedics had transported the knifing victim to the main district hospital and Wilner had the big blond man in custody. The crime scene guys photographed the body of the Middle Easterner and picked up bullet casings around the bar. Someone had finally unplugged the jukebox stuck on one line of an ancient song. Wilner was surprised that crime scene came to a bar fight, but because there were cops involved in the shooting, even though they didn't hit anyone, the district commander thought it was smart to be thorough. Crime scene was too expensive to send out on every case, usually the victim's family had to be wealthy enough to pay the expenses. But every once in a while the state showed good judgment.

Besslia was searching the area around the table while Wilner waited for a detective to take charge of the scene. He looked at the big man and said, "You're in one load of trouble."

The man remained silent.

"You feel like telling me what it was all about?"

The man just stared at him. He had blue eyes and looked

to be in his late twenties. His blond hair was cut so close to his head that it resembled a pale fuzz.

"One man dead and the one you stuck with your knife won't survive."

"He will live." He had a deep monotone voice and a slight, unfamiliar accent.

"What?"

The man repeated, "He will live."

"I saw the wound, pal. His intestines were exposed."

The man just stared at Wilner.

Wilner knew people occasionally survived catastrophic wounds. He had seen it himself, up close and personal. But flukes like that didn't happen twice. The man he saw with the knife wound was as good as dead.

Steve walked over with something he had recovered from the floor of the bar.

"Look at these."

Wilner inspected the little electronics boards. There were five small, sophisticated circuit boards with high-end metal guides designed to fit some specific device. He wasn't much of a technical guy, but he saw that the boards slipped into slots and were probably military in origin. They looked too expensive to be for anything else. He turned toward the blond man. "You guys were fighting over shit like this? Or was it the suds?"

The man stayed quiet.

Wilner shrugged as he stood, then his V-com beeped. He stepped away from the man and mashed the receive key. A small video screen appeared with his boss's face and he was obviously not in the office.

"Willie, what the hell happened?"

"Just fell into it, Chief. These guys started shooting and I was present."

"And your moron friend, Besslia?"

"Yes, sir."

"Look, Willie, I don't care if you guys were in that dive with your weapons. All I care about is that it looks like someone is involved in the case when the media calls. You got it?"

"But, boss, I was a witness and . . ."

"C'mon, Willie, it's late. Spit it out."

"My wife might have been with one of the groups."

The older man sighed and thought about it, then asked, "Does it bother you?"

"You mean her involved in the case?"

"Yeah."

"No, I guess not."

"Well, Detective Wilner, this ain't the twentieth century and the realities of a short staff and one police force have eliminated any need to worry about conflicts of interest. It's yours. Find out who's dead, who killed them and what the fight was over. Then move on. Got it?"

"Yes, sir."

"And Willie."

"Sir?"

"There's no overtime for this. Good luck." The screen went blank before Wilner could respond.

Tiget Nadovich leaned back in his favorite chair, a monstrosity from the late-twentieth century that had been reupholstered six or eight times just since he'd had it. It reclined back and had excellent padding. None of the electronic devices or electrical work that was standard in relaxation chairs of today. He still appreciated the old comforts. He liked the fact that technology had slowed down and invention had stagnated since the catastrophes of the last twenty years. The terror attacks had done almost as much as the lawyers' suffocating lawsuits to kill corporate development of new ideas. Now research and development cost too much and companies needed revenue immediately, not after years of development. Innovation was left to the individual citizen.

The world's developed nations were now too focused on conflict. With the jihadist states, an aggressive, unified Germany and with the vast military power of India, threats were all around. India had been left relatively untouched by terror attacks or epidemics and had started to flex its military muscle. The Indians' odd mix of culture, diet and technology had left them well prepared for the back-to-back flu pandemics, the man-made bioplague as well as the resurgence of the new strain of bubonic plague.

Now Nadovich considered how things had gone so terribly wrong back at that dive of a sports bar off the old highway they used to call the Sawgrass Expressway. He looked across the living room of his spacious home in the Eastern District. The New River ran directly behind his house. He even kept some grass on his yard. The houses on either side of him had been demolished due to their age and the need to clear out structures in the housing community. Nadovich had lived in the house on and off since the area was called Fort Lauderdale.

Nadovich stood up to pace as he said out loud, "Did you recognize those men?"

"The two Hallecks?" asked one of the men seated at a table near the kitchen.

"No, I realized they were Hallecks. The tall one was Johann and the smaller one is one of Dag Halleck's sons." Everyone in Nadovich's family knew what the members of the Halleck family looked like. His own family name was Simolit and the bad blood between the massive extended families went back longer than anyone knew. It clearly had to do with a rivalry between the families to dominate European politics and acquire power, but had transformed into something much more personal and visceral. Even the name Halleck could cause his heart to race. Their superior attitude and belief that they had been designated as "protectors" of God's creation mocked the Simolits. Nadovich could hardly stomach the thought of them.

He felt this way even after a long period of extended peace. The last several decades had not seen the violence and animosity that many of the elders had known. Nadovich sometimes wished he had been around in the real heat of the conflict. That would've been a good way to become a leader of his people. Everyone followed a warrior.

Nadovich snapped out of his thoughts and turned to Svala on the couch. "Did you recognize the two policemen?"

She shook her head.

Nadovich picked up on his paramour's silence. "Svala, your former husband is a policeman. Maybe you had met them. I have never bothered to commit your husband's face to memory."

Svala looked up at him, hesitated, then shook her head. "No, I didn't know them."

Nadovich nodded silently as he moved back and forth across the room like a cat in a cage. He wondered why the police were in the bar like he wondered why Svala was lying to him now. There would be time to figure it out later. But he knew she was hiding something. He had purposely never met the man she had married. He didn't stoop to looking at his photograph or learning anything about the lowly police officer.

He looked up and said, "What're we missing from our transaction?"

The man at the table said, "We lost five important components to the device and of course we still don't have enough radioactive material."

"I realize that, Alec. But what about the parts? Can we get new boards?"

Alec shook his head. "I doubt it. We would do better to find where they were taken."

Nadovich considered this, then said, "The police have them."

"Better than the Hallecks."

"We're also missing Demitri, but I know he'll return once he leaves the hospital."

Alec said, "I don't know if our suppliers got the cash."

"It is not our concern if they're wealthy or not."

Alec hesitated. "No, not really except . . ."

Nadovich slapped the kitchen counter as he stepped toward it and shouted, "Spit it out, Alec. What worries you?"

"We may need our friends in the jihadist movement later. And they may think we engineered this whole event in order to cheat them out of their money."

Nadovich sighed and wiped his face. Although he had never been sick he sometimes felt like he had a headache. He could feel pain, like he had felt it a thousand times in his life. But he had never felt disease. Yet Alec's unending stream of logical concerns seemed to be causing him to become ill. It was surprising because his younger cousin generally worried about nothing other than his vintage Harley-Davidson motorcycle.

"Are you saying we need to pay them more than one and half million suds for material we didn't receive?"

Alec just shrugged.

"Perhaps we should try and recover it all from the police."

Alec brightened. "And tell Mr. Hammed what happened. He might work with us."

Nadovich shook his head. "This is why we must act soon. We're now worried about how one of his kind might treat us? No, he'll help us or he'll die. That's how things must be from now on."

He plopped back into his chair, wondering if aspirin might help him with his imaginary headache.

Demitri Nadin, as he had been known for a very long time now, opened his eyes to bright, institutional lights. He had been concentrating on healing and didn't know how long he had been unconscious. He thought he'd wake up with Tiget, Alec and the others, but realized quickly that he had been taken from the scene of the fight.

He turned his head slowly and saw another bed with an old man in it. There were tubes in his nose and an IV in his wrinkled arm. Demitri had an IV too. It ran into his left arm.

He tried to recall all that had happened, then remembered the big Halleck slicing him with a knife. A big combat knife that the Saudis had developed for their army before the jihadists had overthrown the royal family. Fancy knives were of no use once Israeli bombs stated falling. But the knife had done the trick on him. A few more slashes and that big oaf of a Halleck might have done him in permanently.

He sat up in the comfortable bed, pulled his cheap hospital gown up and saw he had at least sixty stitches across his abdomen, but the scar was already fading. He picked at the stitch on the end with his long, neat fingernail. After a few seconds he had pulled it loose. He played some more with the next stitch and then grimaced as he pulled the surgical string through the small holes in his stomach. He continued as it became easier the more string he had to play with. After fifteen minutes he had a wad of thread and funny-looking holes on either side of the long, light scar on his abdomen. He touched it and winced. That Halleck would pay for this.

He swung his legs to the side of the bed. The old man across from him turned his head slowly and looked at him. He said, "They told me you'd probably die during the night."

Demitri smiled. "I've heard that before." He yanked out his IV. "What's wrong with you?"

"I was born in 1960, that's all. Just running out of steam."

"What month were you born?"

"November."

"The month John F. Kennedy was elected."

The old man coughed, then said, "You know your history, young fella."

Demitri smiled. "Yeah, I do, but I knew that because I voted for him." He stood, found his jeans in the closet, pulled them on and tucked in his robe. He nodded to the man in the bed as he headed out the door.

THREE

Tom Wilner could hardly focus his eyes as he prepared breakfast for Tommy and Emma. Mrs. Honzit, his housekeeper and nanny, usually got up a little later and worked late so he didn't have to rush home from a case. He wasn't sure about the Turkish housekeeper, but he thought she spent a lot of late nights out.

He had slept for a few hours after booking his large, silent prisoner for attempted murder, assault, possession of a weapon in a drinking establishment and failure to comply with questioning. The revised penal code of Florida, which was established in 2020, made all of those offenses punishable by up to life on a penal farm or military service. His prisoner was too fit to avoid the military. They'd drop him in with a special "penal unit" and then let him fight his way out of wherever the United States was at war now. As long as it wasn't Germany, he wasn't too worried about himself.

He could hear the kids laughing in the bathroom as he broke open the heat sticks on two separate, self-contained egg and bacon breakfasts. Since there were very few pigs left in the world he didn't dwell on what the bacon was made of. The eggs were probably reptilian, although the chicken population was coming back from the last avian flu outbreak.

He had the flat video broadcaster on the wall tuned to the local news for south Florida. Since not that much happened anymore and few news stations could afford their own camera crews, most the stories were just regurgitations of national stories broadcast the night before. He wasn't someone who used his computer to search news archives. He liked to hear and see footage on a big screen.

There was a brief mention of Unified Police Force action at the Big Cypress Bar, but the announcer didn't mention E-weapons, a dead man or anything else that might be accurate. Then Wilner looked up as they broadcast photos from one of the Jupiter orbiters of the massive spaceship, carrying emissaries from the planet, orbiting the small star mu Arae outside the Milky Way galaxy. The space travelers were generally referred to as Urailians due to the fact that a scientist in the former Russian Republic named Uraille who had lived near the Ural Mountains had first heard the ship's message. No Earthling seemed to think that an entire civilization that was intelligent enough to travel through space would mind being named after some backwater astronomer who happened to hear them.

The message that they were coming five years ago had sent shock waves through an already shattered world. A brief cessation of hostilities occurred as the governments of the Earth debated if they should unite and prepare for another foe. But that all ended when the next message from the aliens talked of peace and brotherhood. Their goodwill had cost another hundred million human lives.

Now the ship was still years away and people's interest had faded or shifted to more immediate threats like war, famine and plague.

Wilner knew more than most about the aliens because his best friend, Steve Besslia, was a living encyclopedia of everything about them. Besslia had become obsessed with the story and his fondest dream was to be present when the aliens finally arrived on Earth.

"Hi, Daddy," said his daughter, Emma, as she gave him a quick hug before settling down at the table.

A few seconds later, a sleepier Tommy shuffled in and plopped in the chair next to his older sister.

Wilner smiled. "Hey, sport, rough night?"

The six-year-old boy raised his dark eyes to his father. "Mrs. Honzit is teaching us French."

Wilner smiled. "Excellent. You never know when you might need it."

Emma added, "And she reviews our work from school and makes us study ahead."

Wilner nodded. "I'll talk to her."

Both young faces brightened.

Emma said, "Really?"

"You bet. I'll tell her I appreciate what she's doing and to keep it up." He contained his smile at the outraged looks of his children.

Emma kept her dark eyes on Wilner. "Where were you last night?"

"I had to"—he paused—"work late."

"What about tonight?"

"I'll be here." He marveled at how much his young children looked like their mother with their dark features and high cheekbones. Svala had captured his attention while he was posted in a devastated Belgrade just as the latest Balkan war had ended. In those nine years, eight as a married couple, she had not aged one second. She still looked like the fresh-faced college student whose English was already perfect when he met her.

Tommy said, "Daddy, Mrs. Hall said for you to call her."

"Are you doing okay in your skills level?" School was nothing like when he attended the Corazine Elementary School in Ocean Grove, New Jersey. Now kids were grouped by intelligence instead of grade. Both his kids were in the same skills level. The highest. The parents of the kids in the other levels were constantly screaming for their children to be promoted so that their kids would be eligible for all the benefits associated with the high achievement. It came natural to his kids, unlike him.

Tommy said, "No, I think it's something else. She asked about Mama and gave me this for you." The young boy dug in his backpack next to his chair and pulled out a small white envelope.

Wilner took it and ripped open the seal. Inside was a perfumed note that said, "Call me for dinner, Janice Hall." Her V-com code was written below the message. He smiled, imagining the teacher's pretty face on the screen of his own V-com. Then he pictured the face of his wife, Svala. At least, his wife for now, and looked back at his kids.

Emma asked, "What's she want, Daddy?"

"Just says that Tommy's a good student."

"So am I and she didn't write about me."

"She will, don't worry, sweetheart."

Tommy said, "Daddy, when will Mama come by and see us?"

At that moment Thomas "Willie" Wilner felt a pain in his

gut worse than any bullet ever fired by an Iranian soldier. He looked at his son and said, "I wish I knew, sport."

Johann Halleck sat silently in the corner of the huge holding cell at the edge of the Western District. This was where everyone who ran afoul of the Unified Police Force or violated the Miami Quarantine Zone ended up. Now the auditorium-sized floor with more than one hundred bunks lining the walls looked empty with only twenty prisoners.

Johann knew that only fifteen years ago this facility would have been crammed with loud, raucous prisoners awaiting all sorts of pretrial hearings and sentencings. Now, with less people in the southern tip of Florida, not only had crime dropped off, but also the manpower necessary to operate the jails was hard to find. Courts acted merely as a waypoint between arrest and sentencing to one of the massive penal farms where inmates raised crops, made furniture and generally stayed until they died. The other option was the military, where they received minimal training and then were sent out in special units that raided and disrupted the enemy behind the lines. In the case of one small African nation, the criminal combatants managed to unseat the government and take over the country. Then the United States found itself in the awkward position of having to fight its own convict-soldiers.

Johann was not worried about his fate. He had already spoken to one of his cousins who was an attorney. He'd get Johann in front of a friendly judge later in the day. That was weeks sooner than most inmates would even appear before a judge.

Johann's cousin hoped that the cop, Tom Wilner, had charged Johann with attempted murder or maybe even jumped the gun and charged him with murder, thinking the slashed man from the bar would, in fact, die. Johann knew better. He thought the man was Demitri Nadin, but it had been many years since he had last seen him. That part of the Simolit family had migrated to the United States as the world descended into World War I. The Nadovich side of the family had trickled over from the Balkans starting in the 1950s. God knew how many were still in Eastern Europe and Turkey. Enough to drive out all the Hallecks who had tired of the constant fighting and moved back to Norway, Sweden and Denmark. A large segment of the family had come here to America to keep the Simolit expansion in check.

Johann had suffered many personal insults from the Simolits over the years, but it was his father's stories of the old atrocities that had shaped his early years. He intended to use all the resources at his disposal to stop whatever Tiget Nadovich planned to do.

Now Johann looked out from his bunk, the most comfortable spot in the smelly holding facility. Only two guards watched the main door and passed out the boxed meals, which consisted of surplus military rations of dehydrated meat and fruit. Each prisoner also received one bottle of water to use to rehydrate their food as well as drink. There was very little trading that occurred. The food provided calories and nutrition, not taste.

Johann noticed a younger man of African heritage attempting to keep two Latin men, obviously from the Miami Quarantine Zone, at bay. They were harassing him in Spanish, which the young man apparently didn't speak.

The guards did nothing, if they even noticed the growing threat to one of their charges.

Johann recognized that this conflict did not involve him or his family's pledge to protect those who couldn't protect themselves. To keep humanity safe from the Simolits. These were equals arguing among themselves so he had no role in their dispute. But he couldn't help himself. The younger man, perhaps twenty, was smaller than the other two and was offering no resistance other than to keep himself separate from the men who wanted either his food or sex. Neither sounded fair to Johann.

He slowly stood from the small bunk and stretched his six-foot-three-inch frame, then started to walk directly to the three men, hoping the two Latins would notice him and just give up. Johann took a quick look over his shoulder at the guards who were now busy watching a small screen video broadcaster in the corner of their area outside the bars. Everyone was fascinated with the slow approach of the aliens. He knew that the small screen held images of the giant ship coming past Jupiter on its rendezvous with Earth. He smiled at how narrowly most people thought.

He stopped a few feet from the men. The two Latins were taunting the young African man as they eliminated any escape route he might have. One of the Latin men had a homemade weapon he had fashioned out of a metal brace. It looked like a blunt, short bayonet with a cloth handle. He just showed it to the frightened victim, allowing him to imagine worse things than what he might really do with the weapon.

Other inmates had already slid away from the potential assault. They now gazed up at Johann who stood silently behind the attackers.

Johann said in a low voice, "Why do you act this way?"

The attackers froze and swiveled their heads to the taller blond man. They ignored their victim and turned to face Johann. Both men smiled slightly.

Johann looked at their dark hair and thought of all the Simolit family members he had faced down in his life. These men's faces had different shapes to them. They didn't have the high cheekbones or oval eyes. These men were from the south. Cuban, maybe, but more likely from one of the South American countries devastated by war. They had flooded the southern tip of Florida after the ban on immigration and were largely responsible for the quarantine zone the United States had established in the old Miami-Dade County.

One man said, *"Mira, más carne."*

Johann smiled, knowing the man had said, "Look, more meat." Johann answered in English, "Leave him be." It was the only warning he was prepared to give.

The men stepped apart, obviously practiced at attacking people together.

Johan realized they would now come at him from opposite directions. He held up his hand to make sure the young African man stayed by the bunk and out of the line of fire. The young man seemed relieved that he was not needed in the conflict and scooted down the wall away from Johann.

The first Latin man feinted toward him. Johann did not react.

The other man slashed at him with his homemade knife, causing Johann to bob his head back and pivot to face him. That's when Johann learned the other man also had a knifelike weapon. Unfortunately he didn't realize it until it was too late. He felt the pain radiate up his left side as the metal blade punctured his skin and plunged several inches into his back. He could only imagine what internal organ had been affected by the attack.

He didn't want to twist to confront that man only to be struck by the weapon he had already seen. He grimaced slightly and allowed the man in front of him to swing the knife in a deadly arc. Johann caught his wrist well away from his body. He didn't have time to waste as he felt the knife removed from his back and knew another strike was imminent.

Johann squeezed his hand and immediately crushed his attacker's wrist, causing him to drop his crude knife. He yanked the man around as he turned to face the second attacker.

The second attacker looked shocked as he paused before his next strike with a slightly more sophisticated homemade knife. God only knew how they smuggled them into the holding cell or made them inside, but the knives were deadly.

Johann looked back toward the guards who were still glued to their small video broadcaster.

The second attacker thrust his weapon out, aiming for Johann's stomach. Johann dropped the man with the broken arm and parried the blow with the knife, knocking the weapon to the floor.

The second attacker, now realizing he was outmatched and alone, turned to flee, but Johann grabbed him by the collar of his durafiber shirt. Of course the garment didn't rip. He wondered how a refugee like this could afford such an expensive shirt.

He spun the man around to face him, grabbed a fistful of the front of the shirt and lifted the man off the ground with one arm to look him directly in the eye.

Johann growled, "Is it fair to pick on one man like that?"

The terrified man started to jabber in Spanish, *"No inglés, no inglés."*

Johann said, "Leave him alone." A simple, direct command not to bother the young man anymore.

The man nodded furiously, looking down at his friend who was whimpering as he held his right arm. The man's hand hung loosely where his wrist had been turned to crumbled bone.

Johann set down the man and tugged at his shirt, motioning him to take it off. He also waved the young African man over to them.

He had the men exchange shirts so that now the Latin attacker had the old, dirty standard shirt made from some blend of synthetics and had a few rips in it as well as stains under the arms.

When they were finished, the African man stood taller with the durafiber shirt looking brand-new. The synthetic fabric was virtually indestructible except to open flame. It never ripped, wore out or even stained. Anything that came in contact with it slipped off harmlessly. A four-year-old durafiber shirt looked identical to a brand-new one, if you could find a new one.

The African man touched Johann on the arm and turned him slightly, looking at his back.

"You're hurt, man."

Johann felt where the crude knife had torn into his back, looked at the thick red blood on his hand, then smiled. "Nothing to worry about. He just nicked me."

He turned and eased back to his bunk.

The Latin men had scurried across the wide floor of the holding cell and cowered on the far side. All the other inmates just stared at Johann as he carefully sat down on his bunk and closed his eyes.

He'd have to concentrate to heal up this wound before he was supposed to appear in court that afternoon.

FOUR

Tom Wilner shook his head for the fourth time while speaking with the young doctor on duty at the largest district hospital.

Wilner said, "I saw this guy last night, Doc. There's no way he checked himself out today."

The dark-skinned doctor was obviously in a hurry, but didn't want to risk offending a detective with the UPF. "Technically, he didn't check himself out. He just left. We got no one to bill and no way to collect."

"Did anyone see him leave?"

"His elderly roommate spoke to him. He said the guy pulled on a pair of jeans, and wore his hospital gown as a shirt."

"He say anything else?"

"That the guy was a little loopy, babbling about voting for John F. Kennedy."

Wilner stopped, not that clear on history. "When was he president? In the 1950s?"

The doctor shook his head. "Hell, I got no idea. I went on the rush medical track at the Military Medical Training Center in Kansas. They specialize in getting you an M.D. and into a field combat hospital in less than two years. We didn't have time for any subject but medicine."

Wilner reassessed the young doctor now that he knew he wasn't some rich kid whose parents had whizzed him through school. "Where'd you serve?"

The doctor looked at him. "The Balkans. What about you?"

"Iran, then the Balkans."

"Iran, that's rough. Before or after the new shah?"

"After, so they were mighty pissed off that we had installed a leader. Even if it was only for a couple of years."

The doctor paused and said, "I saw this kind of thing in Serbia a couple of times."

"What kind of thing?"

"Someone comes in with a massive wound and the next day seems fine."

Wilner thought about it and said, "I even saw it once with a gunshot to the head." He shuddered, slightly remembering the whole event. "How's that possible?"

The doctor shrugged. "The two guys I'm thinking of looked a little like that John Doe they brought in. Both had been shot and looked dead. The next day they were screaming to get out and start killing some Bosnian Muslims."

"Any medical explanation?"

"Some people are really fast healers."

Wilner snorted and nodded. "Thanks," he said as he headed down the hallway. As he neared the wide door, a young woman with light brown hair and startling green eyes passed him and smiled. He turned as she passed because he had the feeling she knew him. Her steady, confident stride showed off her athletic build under functional, if not fashionable, clothes.

Two hours later as Wilner waited at the first appearance court he had an odd feeling. How had the tall blond man, identified as "suspect in assault #19333," managed to get brought before a judge so quickly? Wilner figured the man would be in holding at least a week before anyone even noticed him.

Wilner also wondered how the disappearance of the victim would affect the case. He didn't think it would. Once a judge saw a big, healthy man, she'd find a way to send him into the military, at least for a couple of years.

The new president pledged that once the country was out of the Balkans and fully withdrawn from Syria and Iraq, the United States would not engage in any other conflicts. That's what every president had said. Both Democrat and Republican. That's what had led to the collapse of the two-party system.

Wilner liked the choices they had now on the ballot. Just names with a one-page bio and campaign pledge. Since the penalty for bribery and misuse of office was death, most of the current politicians were pretty straight. And there wasn't any partisan bickering like the early part of the century. But that was before Wilner could vote. Now politicians were actually judged by what they had done and how closely they had stuck to previous promises. And God help the candidate that hadn't served in the military. Only the oldest politicians had not been in the service. Anyone under fifty-five had done a stint where someone shot at them.

Wilner sat in the uncrowded gallery watching shackled prisoners march up from a small cage. On the far side of the public seats he saw someone enter the room and sit in the same row as him. He had to take a second look to confirm that it was the same woman with the green eyes from the hospital.

Was this coincidence? He couldn't see how she'd have business at the hospital and here in a courtroom attached to the district jail ten miles away. When he saw her at the hospital earlier he thought she might work there. Now he knew that wasn't correct.

He waited as one prisoner after another appeared in front of the judge. They stood before the small Asian woman in a black robe. The giant African man standing in front of her now glared around the courtroom to see if anyone had sent a lawyer for him. It appeared no one had.

The judge called out, "Robert Morris."

The man nodded.

"It says here that you were arrested for shoplifting and that when the UPF officer stopped you, you struck him in the face."

The man was silent.

The judge continued. "The attached photo shows a uniformed officer with a black eye and swollen cheek." She held up the photo so the prisoner could see it. "Is this your handiwork?"

The large man mumbled, "I hit the officer."

"Why?"

"I was scared."

"Did you shoplift meat product?"

The man looked up and started to cry. "It weren't no steak or nothin'. Just the synthetic stuff. The Chub."

The judge nodded and looked at the bailiff.

Wilner could see the older man stiffen as if ready for a fight.

The judge said, "Have you been in the military?"

The prisoner said, "Yes, ma'am. I was sentenced to three years in Iraq back about ten years ago."

"And what happened?"

"The war ended and I came home. I was out before the next war started with them."

The judge took on a formal voice. "Very well. I hereby sentence you to military service in Syria until the conflict is concluded." She banged her gavel.

The big man wailed, "Until it's over! I could be an old man by then."

"You will be an old man in the service of your country then." She ignored his pleas, banged her gavel and called out, "Next."

Wilner waited as three more men were sent to the military. Sometimes seeing these sentencings he wondered why he had volunteered. But he knew why. Anything was better than having his old man beat on him. The funny thing was that he had been wrong. He would've taken a beating from his dad every day of his life in exchange for missing his four years in Iran and Serbia. He'd have fewer scars, fewer nightmares and might even have gone on to college.

Who was he fooling? His father, a mechanic who didn't understand the new engines, never could've afforded school. And Wilner had been desperate to leave New Jersey. And that was before New York City's population had fled and flooded northern Jersey and Philadelphia.

Occasionally, during the proceedings, he glanced over at the pretty woman with the green eyes. She was still there, but seemingly uninterested in anyone who had appeared before the judge so far.

Finally Wilner's suspect stood and walked defiantly out of the cage and stopped in front of the judge. He moved precisely, like a soldier in formation.

The judge looked over the sheet as a man stood up in the front row.

"Your Honor, Mark Hanson representing the defendant."

The judge looked over at the young attorney and said, "And your client's name?"

"Johann Halleck," said the attorney.

The judge looked at the tall blond man. "Is that correct?"

"Yes, Your Honor. I am Johann Halleck."

Wilner couldn't place the European accent. It wasn't German, but had a hard edge to it.

The judge said, "And do you want to explain why you slashed the man with a knife and what you think will happen when he dies?"

Johann said, "It was self-defense, Your Honor, and I do not think he will die."

The judge turned to a young woman. "Miss Ball, is the victim still alive?"

The petite young prosecutor, who was rarely required to speak, stood up, cleared her throat and said, "Your Honor, I've been informed that the victim has left the hospital."

"Under his own power?"

"Yes, Your Honor."

"But according to the affidavit written by"—she looked at the bottom of the page—"UPF detective Tom Wilner, the victim had 'a severe laceration across the abdomen with massive trauma.'"

The prosecutor cleared her throat again. "Yes, Your Honor, I know."

"Is the detective lying in this affidavit?"

"No, Your Honor. Even the admitting doctors didn't do much because they thought the victim would bleed to death and they didn't want to waste the resources."

"And where is he now?"

The prosecutor shrugged.

The judge banged her gavel. "Case dismissed." She paused, then shouted, "Next."

Wilner bolted from the gallery, racing out the door and then identified himself to the security officer at the rear gate. A few minutes later, Wilner saw the tall man he now knew was Johann Halleck.

Wilner waited in the breezeway as a light rain started to fall. His thin jacket was waterproof and kept him from getting a chill. He unzipped it so he could also reach his duty weapon if he had to. The big Beretta Millennium model fired 11-millimeter rounds made of depleted uranium that penetrated any body armor. The pistol also had a biometric safety, which kept anyone but Wilner from firing it. Either his right hand or left was configured to activate the weapon. In his left rear pocket he had an electronic stun baton, which his son called his light saber. He didn't think he'd need either weapon, but he had seen the tall man in action. He wasn't going to take any chances.

Johann walked toward him, then Wilner stepped out into the walkway so the man saw him.

Wilner said, "Why not tell me your name last night?"

The tall man slowed and assessed him. "I was unsure of your role in it."

"My role? In the fight? What're you talking about? I identified myself."

"But we never know who is in the employ of the Simolits."

"The who?"

Johann just looked at Wilner as if he were trying to decide if he was trustworthy. "Let it go, Detective Wilner. You have no idea who you're dealing with."

Wilner stepped back so he didn't have to look up so much at Johann. At six feet Wilner wasn't used to bending his neck to speak to that many men. "What were you guys fighting over?"

"Did they leave with everything?"

Wilner hesitated, not knowing what to disclose. He had a feeling this guy wasn't a criminal. There was something about his manner. "No, not everything. If I knew what everything was I'd be in a better position to work the case."

"Where are the parts?"

"Safe."

"Why were you in the bar, Detective? If you're not on the Simolit payroll then how did you end up there at the wrong moment?"

"I was there for personal reasons." Then Wilner added, "Who are you? Internal affairs?"

"I'm the man who is trying to keep you from getting hurt."

"I appreciate your concern but I can take care of myself."

Johann chuckled and said, "Sure you can."

Wilner had a lot of questions but most concerned his wife. He didn't want to compromise the case but he had to know more about Svala's involvement. He intended to ease toward those questions. "Where'd you get the Saudi combat knife you used on the not-so-dead guy? Were you in the service?"

"I have been in the military."

"Where'd you serve?"

"All over. Some places you've never even heard of." He looked down the hallway toward another blond man standing by an old conventional-gas Ford. "I'm afraid I have to go now."

"Where can I reach you with some more questions?"

"My lawyer." He started to walk away then stopped and turned. "If you don't let this incident drop we'll run into each other again. But watch your back, Detective. Things haven't even started to heat up yet."

Wilner was about to follow him when he heard a woman's voice behind him say, "Detective Wilner?"

He turned and saw it was the woman with the green eyes. He hesitated; interested in catching Johann Halleck before he left, but found that once he looked at her face he couldn't turn.

FIVE

Tom Wilner sat across the small table with his protein and caffeine drink in front of him. He was mesmerized as he listened to Shelby Hahn. She not only had an interesting story to tell but she retained a slight accent from Tennessee. No one in Florida seemed to have an accent anymore. Since the migration to the state had nearly stopped, people from the other parts of the country had not brought in their own influences. Not even displaced New Yorkers had ventured as far south as Florida after the September eleventh anniversary attack that shut down the city. Once Manhattan had been completely irradiated and the government had declared the city one of the six quarantine zones, most of the residents had invaded northern New Jersey, eastern Pennsylvania and, for some reason, Atlanta. There had even been an initiative to rename Atlanta New Manhattan, but the longtime residents were able to defeat the measure pushed by the new arrivals.

When Shelby had finished her personal history, with that light, breezy voice tinged with phrases that Wilner had not heard since he shared a barracks with guys from the old Deep South, he just looked at her and said, "Wow, artillery, really."

She had a dazzling smile as she nodded her head.

Wilner, like most Americans, knew the various wars the United States engaged in through history classes and the news. But the two Iranian wars had affected the largest number of U.S. military personnel and he often found other soldiers who had taken part in the bitter combat of the desolate desserts and hills.

Wilner said, "Where were you in Iran?"

"Hameadan and Zahedan."

"You might have bailed us out in Zahedan. We called in a barrage that scattered some of the Revolutionary Guard and gave us a chance to regroup. Then we crossed the border into Afghanistan."

"Maybe, we got those calls all the time."

"And now with the Department of Homeland Security."

"They were recruiting out of my unit after the war."

"So you cover the whole state?"

"And southern Georgia."

"That's a lot of territory."

"This is the first time I've had to come all the way down here. I've been to the Northern Enclave a few times, but most of the people and action are still in Orlando. The whole country still goes to see all the amusement parks. With the taxes and fees Disney provides, DHS is not about to allow a terrorist to hit any of the parks."

Wilner nodded, just wanting an excuse to keep looking at her. "Makes sense, even though I don't like it. We may not have as many people down here but it turns uglier everyday."

"Our jurisdiction is only federal. If it's not terrorism or treason we pass it on to you guys anyway."

"By the time I was a cop with the UPF there were no federal agencies except you guys. I would hear the older cops talk about the FBI and see them in old movies, but they'd been disbanded more than three years when I came on the job."

"A few of our really senior guys were agents with the FBI or ATF. They said that no matter what they did the public was unhappy. When they were aggressive and monitored phone calls they were accused of invasion of privacy, but with every new attack they were called incompetent. There have still been some big attacks since DHS has been in charge, but now everyone realizes that there has to be a federal law enforcement agency to hold things together."

She had a fire and intelligence in her eyes that radiated energy. It looked like she wore contact lenses and that they gave her eyes that darker green hue. He knew better than to ask.

She sipped her juice from an unknown fruit.

Wilner said, "So now I'm waiting for your interest in Johann Halleck."

"How do you know that's why I'm here?"

"The hospital and now his hearing, I *am* a cop."

"Well, Detective Wilner, you're wrong. I'm here because of who I think he slashed with a knife."

"The John Doe who left the hospital?"

"I think he's part of a family named Simolit."

Wilner remained silent, recognizing the name that Johann Halleck had mentioned and now interested only in what the lovely federal agent had to say about the case. After a moment he asked, "Why?"

"They've made some unusual associations across the globe."

"Such as?"

She hesitated.

Wilner said, "Oh, come on, you're not going to pull 'it's classified' bullshit, are you?"

"Well, it *is* sensitive and if I told you I would technically be violating the treason statute. I'd find myself back behind an artillery piece lobbing shells at Syrians or, more likely, Germans."

Wilner flinched at the last comment. Once interest had died in the slow approaching aliens, the German chancellor's remarks about reexpansion had captured the world's attention.

Then Shelby sighed and said, "The dead man at the bar was Amir Abbas. He was an amnesty citizen, but still had family in Lebanon and Syria. We believe he was meeting with the Simolits but I wanted to confirm it by a DNA swab from your victim."

"But you were too late."

"I was just curious to see what his alleged attacker looked like."

Wilner thought carefully about what he was going to say, then finally just blurted out, "One of the men this Abbas met with was named Tiget Nadovich."

She grabbed her pen and scrawled his name on her page of messy notes. "How do you know his name?"

This was harder to say. "He is my wife's boyfriend."

She looked him in the eye. "Excuse me?"

"Well, my soon-to-be ex-wife."

Now Shelby's tone was different. More interested. She smiled and said, "Really, almost divorced."

Wilner noticed her slight smile.

Svala Wilner brooded on the rear porch of the beautiful house off the New River. A light drizzle seemed to reflect her mood as she remembered every line of her husband's face as she saw him for the first time in months the night before. He still looked dashing, but not like he did the first time she had seen him in his U.S. Marine uniform in the plaza in Belgrade. She remembered looking up at him as he flirted with her that September day nine years ago. She had told him she was only nineteen and a college student and snickered at the outrageous lie even now. She'd been able to have realistic paperwork showing her as seven years younger than the handsome marine and claimed to be a war orphan whose parents were killed in the first, devastating attack by the Bosnian Muslims or Bosniacs as they wanted to be called. She had had her name listed as Svala Klatic after a family of furniture makers whom she was very close to.

Although Tom Wilner had shown her kindness and love, her instinctual and longtime attraction to Tiget Nadovich had proven to be too much. She had tried to resist his pull the year before when he showed up out of nowhere in south Florida, which was considered nowhere. She couldn't believe her eyes. He had visited twice before and she had spent that last passionate night with him in Belgrade, but she had not expected him on that wet July evening. It was right after Tom had left for a night shift that he just walked into the living room of her comfortable Eastern District home and literally and figuratively swept her off her feet.

She realized he was completely self-absorbed, despite his claim of concern for the whole Simolit family. Although there was no doubt she was in love with him, she knew he could only truly love himself. Yet she could not escape his power. His energy. She reveled in his vision of the future and even his false promises of reuniting her with Emma and Tommy. She knew that for now they were safer with Tom and although she missed them she wasn't worried, they had a long lifetime to get to know one another. She wasn't limited in the view that "life was short, you had to make the most of it." Her ancient culture taught that time was their friend and all else would crumble from it.

She still missed Tom. But knew there was nothing she could ever do about that.

SIX

Tom Wilner sat across from Steve Besslia under a covered walkway outside the main UPF office on the edge of the Eastern District. It was a little late for lunch but Steve had to drive his Hive-cycle down from the Northern Enclave, which contained the old city of West Palm Beach and the surrounding communities. He had brought the sandwiches, which were made with actual cow meat. No synthetics or supplements.

The name "hive" was short for hydrogen-powered vehicle and applied to the newer vehicles that operated on the water-based fuel cells. Originally called Hydros, the HiVe quickly became Hive or, if a motorcycle, "Hive-cycle" or "Hive-bike." Occasionally, if someone owned an early, buggy version of the hydrogen fuel cell vehicles it was called by the derisive term "Hindenburg."

Wilner said, "Catch anyone speeding?"

Besslia let out a laugh. "Only saw five cars on my way down. No one can afford Hives and gas is too hard to find for conventionals."

"I see plenty of drivers on the news in other places."

"What other place is like this? All spread out. Nobody moving down. Not everyone can live in the Eastern District like you."

"I got it because of my combat veteran status."

"Just because I was a clerk all I get is a condo at the south end of the Northern Enclave."

"You're not married either. And have no kids."

Besslia smiled. "That I claim."

Wilner laughed at his goofy friend.

Besslia said, "C'mon, Willie, what else did the big blond guy say?"

"I already told you. Just warned me not to get involved."

"That's some balls to tell a UPF detective to lay off."

"It wasn't that way. It was like he was concerned."

"And now the Department of Homeland Security is involved."

"An agent asked questions that's all. She was actually very nice."

Besslia gave him a sly smile. "What'd she look like?"

Wilner wasn't going to dignify his question but had to say, "She's not bad." He added, "The whole thing is weird. I mean DHS, the blond guy. Just a lot of questions."

Besslia nodded. "Yeah, I sure would like to know what all that shit was about."

Wilner glanced over at the side window to reception and saw the image of the German chancellor on a video broadcaster next to the receptionist. The head of the German government had spent billons expanding the military even though Germans had never been involved in the traditional jihadist wars. Now the nationalistic fever was running high as the fat bastard barked about everything from European resentment toward Germany to the limited land available for the German people. "That sort've puts our problems into perspective. That asshole could kill millions." Then he added, "No one much cares what a UPF cop does when that's headed our way."

"Ain't that the truth."

Wilner heard a shout from somewhere inside the building. The holding area was usually quiet but maybe they had a loud prisoner. Then he heard a hollow pop then another.

Besslia jerked his head up and said, "That's gunfire."

Wilner nodded as he stood up, unzipped his jacket and drew his big Glock from his hip.

Besslia reached to the duty belt of his uniform and pulled out an identical-looking pistol.

Wilner could see the receptionist scramble at the next round of pops and then the window burst out. He felt a shard of glass cut into his cheek as the force of the blast knocked him and Besslia off their feet.

Wilner lay on the ground for a moment, his ears ringing, his mind drifting back to a similar blast on a plaza in Belgrade. Only this time there weren't any dead children around him and there wasn't a lady's detached arm draped across his chest.

It felt like he heard someone in the distance. It was a hollow shout. Then he realized it was Steve Besslia checking on him.

"Willie, Willie, can you hear me?"

Then the combat training kicked in and Wilner sprang up to a crouch. He assessed the terrain tactically, shaking his head to clear it then reached down and picked up his pistol.

There was no movement from inside the building.

Wilner started to advance in a crouch toward the shattered window, motioning Besslia to follow him. They slipped through the window frame. In the corner of the reception area a small, frightened African woman huddled in the corner. Wilner held up his hand to keep her there in relative safety.

He held out his pistol as he started to hustle down the hallway, which led back toward the administrative section of the building. This was the path of the explosion, which had broken the reception window.

As they traveled down the hallway the destruction got worse. With the rooms closest to the blast blackened with fire and shrapnel damage.

Besslia said, "What the hell happened?"

Wilner was too busy looking ahead to answer.

At the last door, which led to the evidence room, Wilner saw two bodies. Neither was identifiable, but by the uniform Wilner recognized the evidence custodian who also administrated the crime scene unit and anything else the UPF could throw at the poor guy.

The evidence room was a shambles. But in the rear of the room two men were rooting through the newest boxes of seized items.

Wilner and Besslia raised their guns and took cover on each side of the shattered doorway.

Wilner called out, "Don't move."

The two men didn't turn. He saw their long, dark hair sway for a second as one turned with lightning speed and raised a weapon.

Both cops squeezed off several shots as Wilner saw the flash.

He shoved Besslia one way as he dove the other as the blast from the flasher molded through the door and traveled down the hallway, finally settling on a tall window and melting the glass and frame in an instant. The heat fused an electrical circuit box and the explosion from it threw a piece of metal at

Wilner. He tried to shield his head but felt the sharp impact. The blast wave rattled his stomach in addition to his head.

Wilner rolled into the doorway with his pistol already aimed and started shooting at the forms of the two men.

They separated with the packages in their hands and disappeared from view.

A second later they both bounded through the doorway, over Wilner and down the hallway.

Wilner and Besslia turned and emptied their voluminous magazines at the fast, fleeing men.

Wilner stood, somewhat unsteadily and followed the men down the hallway as he reloaded on the run. He came through reception and turned his head to make sure the receptionist was still safe in the corner. She was.

He leaped over the counter then out the front double doors only to see a vehicle turn the corner onto the main road. He couldn't tell anything about the car except that it was dark colored.

As he turned to go back and call for help, his legs went weak and he collapsed on the ground. The world spinning, then turning dark.

SEVEN

Tiget Nadovich felt his neck and back tense as Demitri and Alec told him what had happened at the main UPF office where they thought the parts for their bomb were stored. Again, the more he heard the more he felt his head might pop. He had recently started taking aspirin and even a codeine tablet to seek relief from the headaches caused by his idiot cousins. He realized he might be the first of his kind to ever use a drug like that. As he suspected, the pills had no effect but he had continued to use them.

Demitri said, "No, Tiget, we searched the room well. There was a box with the other parts but not the main initiator and the circuit boards that connect the arming device."

Nadovich looked at him. Demitri was older by some years, but they looked similar in age. When Tiget was a child, Demitri taught him the secrets of stalking deer. He also showed him how to use the old weapons like the bow and short spear. Tiget still preferred the edged weapons as did many of his kind. They didn't run out of power like a flasher and had more honor than a lead projectile fired from a great distance.

Tiget said, "But you found the money." It was a question but he was afraid to phrase it that way.

"We found some money in one of the locked drawers."

"How much did you find?"

Demitri looked down and it caused more pain in Tiget's head than if his older cousin had struck him with a blunt object. "A little less than fifty thousand suds."

"Fifty thousand? That's a fraction of our satchel."

Demitri couldn't look him in the eye. Instead he picked at the bloody bandage on his chest and shoulder.

Tiget softened, not losing sight of the fact that both men had been injured during their assault on the UPF station. He touched Demitri's shoulder gently. "Hurt much?"

"The tall cop. The one from the bar. He's a good shot and has seen some combat."

"Did he know you were coming?"

Demitri shook his head. "No. He wasn't inside the building when we arrived. We came in the side and the only resistance we had was from the evidence clerk and a uniformed officer who never had a chance to draw his weapon. The gas ball blew them both to pieces then the flash fire charred the whole entry area. The evidence guy fired a few rounds from a conventional pistol he had in the room. But he never hit us."

Now Alec hobbled over from the couch. "The cop hit us seven times. Me four and Demitri three times."

Nadovich wiped his face. "I can't believe Svala didn't know him."

"Maybe she didn't get a good look at him."

Nadovich nodded. "Perhaps." Then he looked at Alec, the

slicker of the two men. "Find out his name. We will see what he knows and deal with him appropriately."

Demitri said, "What about our plans?"

"They can't wait. We have to be ready in a little over a month or we lose much of our reason for timing and location. With any luck the Germans will do something crazy again and everyone will be focused on Europe and another big war."

He looked at his injured comrades and wondered what had happened to his own ability to heal quickly.

Tom Wilner heard an Iranian tank up close and knew that if he moved he'd attract the attention of the heavy gunner in the turret. He had five men of his squad laying flat along the wadi near Bandar Abbas. Three others had been killed by a portable E-weapon that someone on a fast-moving converted Hive-jeep had fired thirty minutes before. The blast had incinerated the three men before anyone realized the gunner had seen them. The Hive-jeep moved so quickly that no one had gotten off a shot. Now he didn't want to lose the rest to a single Iranian tank. Unfortunately the only weapons they had were conventional firearms and a few grenades.

The tank swerved toward them and dipped as it closed the twenty yards between it and the trapped American marines. Wilner didn't want to wait to be found. He knew if he jumped up now and ran at the tank at least it probably wouldn't find his men. He yanked a grenade from his shoulder strap and didn't hesitate as he sprang up and darted directly at the tank, leaping onto its lower deck before the gunner even saw him. He mashed the arming button on the grenade, and then stuffed it through the open visor. These surplus Russian tanks didn't have grates or shields to protect the driver and gunner.

Wilner also pulled his assault rifle around from his back and stuck the barrel through the opening, grabbing the pistol grip and squeezing the trigger, emptying a few rounds into the interior of the tank. All he wanted to do was distract the occupants from the grenade.

He could hear the bullets ping inside the tank, then the blast from the grenade forced debris and fire out of the visor. The blast also knocked Wilner off the tank and onto the sandy ground of the Dasht-e Lut Desert.

He was dazed but heard someone say, "Willie. Willie, can you hear me?"

When he opened his eyes the bright light confused him and so did the surroundings. He jumped slightly at the sight of a dark face in front of him. The face looked familiar. Where had he seen this Iranian soldier before? Then it hit him. He'd been dreaming. The dark face belonged to the doctor he had spoken to about the slashing victim who had left the hospital on his own.

Wilner turned his head and saw Steve Besslia as he said again, "Willie, can you hear me?"

Next to Besslia was someone else. He closed his eyes then tried to refocus them on the other person. He saw long, dangling hair then the delicate face came in clearly. It was the eyes that confirmed it.

Shelby Hahn's green eyes looked down at him and he realized he was in the hospital. Then he recalled exactly what had happened.

Wilner tried to speak then cleared his throat. "Did either of them turn up with gunshot wounds?"

Besslia shook his head.

"How'd we miss them?"

"I don't know about you, but I was scared shitless. I don't even remember aiming."

Now the young doctor stepped up to the bed. "Detective Wilner. You had a shard of glass in your leg and have had a nasty blow to the head. You're gonna be all right, but you need to rest here for the night."

He shook his head. "Can't."

Now Shelby stepped up. "Don't give us that tough marine bull. You need to rest. Your duty can wait."

"No, it's my kids. I need to get home to them."

Mrs. Honzit looked shocked to see her employer, supported by a uniformed cop and a beautiful woman, enter the front door of his Eastern District home.

Emma and Tommy raced from the kitchen table where Mrs. Honzit had laid out one of her typical phenomenal feasts that somehow always included a piece of fresh fruit, a nonprocessed vegetable and often real meat. And she never needed more money to shop than the relatively small allowance that Wilner provided each week.

His head pounded as he was barraged by loud, quick questions from the kids and Mrs. Honzit.

Finally, after giving hugs to the kids, introducing Shelby and then settling in on the shiny, synthetic leather couch, he said, "Just a little problem at work. I'm fine."

Emma touched the lump on his hairline gently.

He flinched but appreciated the little girl's interest in his condition. There was a time when Svala would've shown it too, but now he doubted she would have even asked how he was feeling. He thought about that for a moment and realized that a thought like that hurt more than the bump on his head or the cut on his leg.

Tommy said, "If your head got hurt, why can't you walk good?"

Wilner turned to his left side slightly and lifted the end of his hospital gown he had worn home.

Tommy stared in amazement at the long gob of bioglue that the doctor had used to close the wound that Wilner probably cut crawling through the shattered window of the UPF station.

Besslia bent down to look at the wound more closely too. "Man, that shit is gross." He poked the greenish glob with his finger.

Mrs. Honzit cleared her throat loudly at the sound of an inappropriate word.

Besslia straightened up and looked over at her but didn't even realize his error.

The housekeeper let the kids snuggle next to their father as she offered drinks to the guests.

Shelby smiled at Wilner and the kids from across the living room.

After a few more minutes, Mrs. Honzit ushered the children back to their giant plates of food.

Besslia leaned in close to Wilner on the couch and said quietly, "That's a fine-looking woman. A little extra cargo, but pretty."

Wilner was going to ignore his friend but remembered catching a glimpse of Mrs. Honzit when she had left her bedroom door open.

"I think it's more the clothes. She's not nearly as old as I thought she was and she's got a good shape to her."

"How do you know that?" Besslia's leering smile said more than the question.

Wilner ignored him and smiled at Shelby as she sat at the edge of a large antique chair across from the couch.

"You gonna to be okay?" Her tinge of a Tennessee accent making Wilner smile.

"Yeah, Mrs. Honzit was probably a surgeon back in the old country."

"Where's she from?" asked Shelby.

"Turkey. She doesn't talk much about her past but she has some family down here because she visits and calls them once in a while."

Shelby looked over at the housekeeper and the kids and said, "She's devoted to your children."

"That's my only requirement."

Then, as if hearing them speaking about her, Mrs. Honzit joined the adults, making the children eat more than they wanted to like she did at every meal.

She gave a definite "look" at Besslia and then walked to the other side of Wilner to sit on the couch. She sat straight and proper, looking at her employer.

"What did happen, Mr. Tom?"

He didn't want to worry her. "Just a little trouble at the UPF office."

"Your friend's cuts on his face make it clear it was more than a little trouble."

Besslia touched the several small biopatches the emergency room nurse had put over cuts on his cheek and chin.

Wilner sighed and said, "The UPF office was attacked."

"Why would someone attack a police office?"

"To get something from the evidence room."

"Did they succeed?"

Wilner shrugged and looked at Besslia.

"When I called they said only a few things and a little cash had been taken."

Wilner asked, "What was taken besides the cash?"

"The stuff we seized from the bar fight."

Wilner stared at him and now so did Shelby.

Mrs. Honzit asked, "What did you seize?" Her very light accent only affecting a few words of each sentence.

Wilner said, "Electronic parts we couldn't figure out." He shook his head. "And someone got all that stuff back."

Besslia smiled a little.

"What?" asked Wilner.

"They didn't get it all. I kept a few of the circuit boards."

"Why?"

"To try and find someone who could identify them and what they did."

Wilner let a smile creep across his sore face. "Where are the parts?"

"My apartment."

Wilner smiled and said, "You amaze me sometimes."

Besslia looked over at Mrs. Honzit and said, "I can do a lot of amazing things."

EIGHT

Johann Halleck frowned as a video broadcaster showed footage of the damaged UPF station and heard about the two dead UPF officers and missing evidence.

He looked at his cousin, Sig, who still had a prominent mark on his neck from the gunshot wound at the bar. "This can't be a coincidence. The Simolits had to be the ones that attacked the station."

"But did they retrieve all the parts they need?"

"I have no idea but we must be certain." Johann looked out the window at the rain falling against the clean pane of glass. "We must find out exactly what they intend to do. We know they want to make a bomb, but what kind?"

"Could be a bioweapon."

"Too hard to get the weaponized plague. Besides not even they would sink that low. It could be radioactive."

Sig said, "They don't have any radioactive material."

"That we know of. There are too many places for them to

get it, especially with so many of them living in Eastern Europe and at the edge of the Arab nations. God only knows what's floating around some of the jihadist states."

Johann sat at his wide workbench next to the wall of the extra room in the giant old house he had taken over near the forgotten highway that led toward the Everglades. The entire neighborhood had been closed due to the fungus and mold that had grown when sunlight became a premium. Many of the houses had lost roofs in the last of the hurricanes fifteen years earlier. Now with the much cooler weather, the worst they got was a winter windstorm and the very rare tornado.

Mold and fungus had no effect on Johann or his cousin, or any of their family, so they had staked out several of the houses. No one seemed to care.

On the workbench lay several good, sharp knives that Johann had collected in his extensive travels. The Saudi combat knife he had lost to the UPF had been his favorite. Now he decided the old U.S. Marine K-Bar was the one that fit his needs and would cause the most damage if he needed a weapon again.

He knew the Simolits and Tiget Nadovich, in particular, wouldn't abandon their plans and the attack on the UPF station was proof that they intended to move ahead. If that was true he'd need at least a good knife.

The V-com sitting on the workbench buzzed. Johann looked up as Sig picked up the small unit and activated it.

Johann could hear a little of what was said over the small, directional speaker in the unit, but still looked up at his smiling cousin as he ended the short communication.

"The Simolits don't have all the parts back from the UPF."

Johann smiled broadly.

"Excellent."

Svala didn't know what was going to happen, but she had never seen Tiget Nadovich so angry, even in one of his legendary furies over the Muslims in Bosnia he always seemed to be in control.

Now he had smashed a lamp, a mirror and the screen of a video broadcaster as he screamed obscenities at her.

She pushed herself back on the end of the long couch, not willing to let Nadovich kill her without a fight. She had heard many stories of how her grandmother had fought off villagers of a small town in southern Hungary who were convinced she was a witch. Even after being beaten, burned and stabbed, Grandma Hessa had killed six of her attackers and managed to escape. To this day the older woman chuckled when she recounted ripping the eye out of the village mayor's eye socket.

Those were the genetics that were inside Svala. Although she had played the helpless college student from Belgrade and perhaps still looked the part, she knew that Nadovich realized it was all an act and wouldn't risk taking his tirade too far.

Svala saw the fear in the other men's faces as they stayed back from the encounter. Alec and Demitri were still healing from the wounds they had received at the UPF station.

Nadovich stood back and took a deep breath. He looked at Svala and said, "Why didn't you just say he was your husband?"

"I-I didn't see him clearly in the bar."

"Svala, do not lie anymore. What's done is done. We must move forward with our plans and he is in our way."

"You cannot hurt him. For the children's sake, I will not allow it." She was firm, but tried to hide the fear in her voice.

Nadovich leaned onto the couch now, facing her and slowly moving closer. "You won't allow it. You won't allow it. Why do you feel you have a choice in plans that affect us all? We should abandon our hopes to flourish here because of some sentimental attachment you have to this cop?"

She swallowed, not interested in running away or trying to get off the couch. "Tiget, there is no reason to kill anyone and attract attention to us. Not now."

He leaned back and looked like he was considering the advice.

Tom Wilner felt a little stiff when he sat up from bed. He could see it was daylight out but he heard the constant drizzle on his window. Glancing over at the luminous clock on his night table he realized he had just slept almost fourteen hours.

He stood a little too quickly and felt his head throb then had to sit back down on the king bed. As usual only the sheets on one sliver of the bed were disturbed. He had gotten used to sleeping on army bunks and mats and even during his marriage to Svala had never been comfortable sprawling in a big bed.

At the height of his marriage, which ended abruptly, Svala would often slide all the way over to him on the edge of the bed to feel his body heat. Now he slept alone and fitfully with most of the giant bed untouched.

He tried standing again and this time slowly made his way to the bathroom to brush his teeth and start his day.

As he stumbled back through his neat bedroom he heard his V-com beep from his nightstand where he always left it.

He took a second to gather his thoughts and pull on a T-shirt then held out the unit and activated the receive mode. He could tell the communication was on an official, secure UPF channel, he just didn't know who it was calling.

The screen came up and Wilner saw his boss behind his desk at the office.

"Willie, how're feeling?"

Wilner took a second and said, "A little rough, Chief."

"You should. You and Besslia played heads-up ball yesterday."

"Didn't help the evidence room guys."

"No, but we found some blood on the exit. You guys hit someone. We're doing the DNA lab work now."

Wilner nodded, knowing that the collapse of the DNA databases when expenses got out of control had not helped solving cases like this. They needed a suspect.

The district commander said, "Willie, you need to take a few days and rest up."

"I'm all right, boss—" he started to say.

"Save it. I need you back to your old self. God knows what'll happen if you get called back to the marines if Germany isn't stopped. And that doesn't include this alien bullshit."

Wilner just looked into the little video screen of the V-com.

The commander said, "Just see what you can find out about your bar killing. Some DHS agent was poking around and said the dead guy was a jihadist. I don't want us skunked by DHS."

Wilner nodded.

The chief said, "I'll talk to you Monday. Until then you're off duty. Understand?"

"Yes, sir."

The screen went blank before Wilner could add anything else.

He slowly got dressed, checking his leg wound before he pulled up some good utility pants. Stepping out his door into the hallway and past the empty rooms of his children, he called out for Mrs. Honzit but got no reply. It was the middle of the day and the kids were in school and the housekeeper was wherever she went to during the day. Wilner couldn't remember the last time he was home in the middle of a weekday.

He flipped on the video broadcaster on the kitchen wall as he rummaged for food.

Mrs. Honzit had left him a plate of pasta, some kind of meat and mixed vegetables. As he ate it cold with a bottle of water from Montana, now called the "spring water state," he watched the endless loop of news on one of the worldwide channels.

The alien ship had continued its trek toward earth. More messages had been exchanged between the aliens and the scientists at several observatories. All seemed to be in order for man's peaceful first encounter with a nonterrestrial species. Although Wilner was interested, it was the news from Europe that had a more immediate impact on him and his family.

German and Polish troops had skirmished on their border as Germany screamed about Polish and other European aggression.

The United Nations and the European Union had not been in operation for more than ten years and Poland was dependent on individual military aid from England and France, if it wasn't too terrified to take action.

The last part of the story was an interview with an army

general who said he thought things would be decided diplomatically, but if not the forces in Serbia could be shifted and units of the National Combat Reserve might be called up.

"Great," mumbled Wilner, knowing his old unit was part of the National Combat Reserve.

He finished his meal watching a weather report that said most of the country would be cool and sunny while Florida would be, surprise, wet and cold for the next four days.

Wilner looked up at a clock in the living room. He had about three hours until the kids came home and no pressing matters, but still felt like a truck had hit him.

Then he heard the front door and saw Mrs. Honzit with a large sack of groceries.

The housekeeper leveled her eyes at him and said, "You should be in bed. I will bring more food and then bathe you in a few minutes."

Wilner wasn't sure how to deflect that statement so he said, "I'm fine. I have to go out for a while anyway." It seemed safer on the street at that moment.

NINE

Mrs. Honzit loved this time of day. The house was quiet, the kids safe in school and her employer was usually at work. Today he had stayed late and just left the house near noon when she had returned from the store. She was surprised he had been up and about at all. The wound on his leg and the lump on his head looked serious enough, but judging by the news reports of the shoot-out and attack at the UPF station he was lucky to be alive. The event must have been very stressful to the dedicated detective.

She had changed the sheets on his bed because he had leaked blood on them from his head. He had resisted her insistence on checking the wound when he woke up, but in the end she got her way. She had offered to give him a bath but just cleaned the wounds with antiseptic spray. The newest generation of antibiotics, developed by the military in an isolated lab in response to some distant war had been very effective. The scientists couldn't do anything about the seemingly continual flu pandemics or that awful bioplague that had sent infected victims all over the world, but they had managed to find a way to keep combat wounds from becoming infected.

Mrs. Honzit sighed as she sprawled on the comfortable couch. Sometimes in this safe, pleasant house she forgot about the world and its problems. She didn't think about how the bubonic plague, once thought conquered, had spread through the streets of Istanbul near her own parent's home and killed one hundred thousand people just a few years earlier. She didn't worry about the people of Africa who had abandoned all contact with the West to avoid the vicious wars waged by the West and much of the Islamic world. Now the Africans starved and operated without much electricity or running water, even though some of the old European powers were moving back in to reap the benefits of the continent's natural resources.

She felt guilty knowing that for the next few hours she had basically no responsibilities. She had the run of this fine house and nothing to do but relax or eat.

Mrs. Honzit thought back to her first aid on her employer, Detective Wilner. He was younger than her by a good bit, but he was definitely a good-looking man. His muscled shoulders and chest aroused her as she leaned in close to him to inspect his wound. He didn't seem to mind her breasts pouring onto his shoulder or her breath on his neck as she leaned in close to get a better look at him.

She had allowed him to see her without her baggy outer garments a couple of times, knowing that her full but still shapely figure had to surprise him. He was used to the feminine-looking Svala with her small waist and big boobs, but she had broken his heart. Surely he could appreciate a woman under his own roof. It might even work to her benefit.

She thought she heard a noise from the front of the house and sat up on the couch, pulling down her dress to make sure she was presentable if someone walked in. She didn't know what she'd do if her employer walked through the front door at that moment. Maybe she'd show him other ways to relax and heal.

Instead there was a knock on the front door. A heavy, almost official, knock like the ones she would hear when she lived in Romania and the security police did not care if they were polite or not.

Standing, she walked toward the wide front door. She was apprehensive, her intuition telling her that a knock in the middle of the day in the Eastern District could not be good news.

She paused and straightened her long dress one last time before opening the door.

As the door swung out she saw the two men standing quietly and couldn't help sucking in a quick breath. She knew what they wanted. Her afternoon just took a serious turn for the worse.

Tom Wilner drove in his personal car, a Honda UK GUV or general-use van. The Hive, built by the newest Honda factory in England and designed to operate on hydrogen-rich fuel injected into fuel cells would go five hundred miles between fill-ups but at a top speed of only forty miles an hour. It was designed for local driving and vital in Florida, California and Texas. Just about everywhere else relied on public trains and buses to get people around.

He was driving the van that he and the kids used to run errands because his chief had made it perfectly clear that he was not on duty. He was not to go on duty until at least Monday, which was four days away.

He knew he couldn't just sit at home and he wasn't technically working the case. It was more of a coincidence that he intended to see his ex-wife and she just happened to be close to one of the suspects in the shooting at the bar. He was waiting until he had more before he confronted Tiget Nadovich. He wanted to know he could arrest the creep if he had enough evidence and realized he should get someone else to make the actual arrest, but he could dream.

He pulled down the street where Svala shared a house with Nadovich. It was not too far from Wilner's own house. Especially now that there was virtually no traffic on the roads anymore. That was one of the things that upset him the most. Svala might have left him for another man, but she could still see the children if she wanted to. Apparently she didn't want to.

He slowed his small van as he came down the street and pulled in behind a nice, older Hive. It was a standard utility car with no shape or style; just an aerodynamic box with dark blue paint. Simple but useful.

Before he could look past it toward Nadovich's house, the door to the car opened and a woman got out. She turned and marched toward Wilner in his van.

As she reached his short hood he realized it was Shelby Hahn, cutting in between the van and her car then opening the passenger door.

As she slammed it behind her, she turned and said, "What the hell are you doing? You're supposed to be resting."

Wilner looked into her fiery green eyes and delicate, angelic face and couldn't help but smile.

"I came to make sure you were all right."

She looked at him and instantly softened. Then lost her comforting expression. "You lying jerk. You didn't even know I was here."

He nodded. "I'm not actually working."

"Then what are you doing here?"

"I came to speak to my wife."

"Why?"

He just looked at her. "Because she's my wife."

"But she treated you like dirt. She left you."

Even though somewhere inside him he knew she was taking his side in the overall situation, he barked, "Hey, watch it. She's my kids' mother."

Shelby lowered her head and mumbled, "You're right, I'm sorry."

Now Wilner settled back and looked down the street toward the house. He let the odd silence hang between them and then said, "How long you been here?"

"Since about seven this morning."

"All by yourself?"

"Since I'm the only DHS agent within two hundred miles, yeah, I was on my own."

"Wanna break to go get something to eat?"

"I'm fine."

"Have you seen anyone?"

"Yeah. Nadovich and another guy left about fifteen minutes ago. I think your wife is still there."

"You didn't want to follow Nadovich?"

"That's not my goal today. I just want to see who's coming by the house."

Just then the front door opened and he saw his wife, Svala, as she casually walked to the small German sports car in the driveway.

He turned to Shelby, thinking of how to politely tell her he had to follow her.

The federal agent surprised him by saying, "I'll get back

to my car. God knows I don't want to stand in the way of you making a colossal mistake."

She was out and he was headed down the street toward the faster black sports car in less than thirty seconds.

TEN

Wilner stayed back several aisles from Svala as she strolled through the only large grocery store in the concentrated business area of the Eastern District. The large retail chain stores had pulled out of Miami before the quarantine went up and out of the Eastern District several years later. The farthest down the peninsula of Florida any chain still had a presence was in the Northern Enclave in the old city of West Palm Beach. That city had a Wal-Mart, but it was heavily defended and had been the subject of several terror attacks. As the last recognizable symbol of corporate America in the area, local environmentalists, political radicals and even the occasional jihadist tried to disrupt the store's operation.

In this store, Wilner watched as his estranged wife picked through vegetables shipped down from central Florida. Her face had not changed one bit since that first day he saw her in Belgrade. She still could pass for a nineteen-year-old college student. The birth of two children had not left a mark on her perfect form. He sometimes had thought of her face as "angelic" even though she had such dark eyes and features. Her nearly black hair had curled slightly and framed her face like an artist's drawing of an angel. Her smile unleashed dimples and a radiance that had pushed a young marine sergeant from New Jersey to propose to her after only knowing her a month. She had seemed so thrilled with the prospect of marriage to a U.S. Marine and moving to America.

Now, as he watched her reach for a jar above a bin of onions, her shirt lifting and exposing her hard stomach, he felt like he had lost his breath. He knew that she wasn't coming back. Even if she did, he wasn't certain he'd be able to trust her again. He'd forgive her. He had already decided that. He'd be happy the kids could see her again. But what would happen if she left again? How would the kids recover? Still, he felt an ache to talk to her and hear that soft voice with the slight Slavic accent.

He hesitated then stepped out into the aisle leading toward her as she continued to look through the vegetables, not noticing him slowly draw near. Then, when he was almost close enough to call out her name, he turned toward a shelf full of spices sent back from one of the countries the United States had occupied. He needed another minute to work up his nerve.

Shelby Hahn had no trouble slipping the sliding glass door off its track and entering the house. She had watched as the occupants, Tiget Nadovich and his two cousins, Alec and Demitri Nadin, had left in the Hive-utility vehicle that looked like it had just come from a showroom in Atlanta. She had also seen Svala head off in her sports car with Tom Wilner following along like a puppy.

She grudgingly admitted to herself that Nadovich was an

attractive man, in his own way. God forbid she ever uttered something like that around her own family; the prejudices they carried with them had developed long before her branch of the family settled in Tennessee.

She crept through the house knowing that she was violating one of the major tenants of the Federal Law Enforcement Act of the new century. It was invasions of privacy like this that had caused the vaunted FBI to be dismantled in a most public and debilitating way. Although it was ten years before she entered service as an agent of the Department of Homeland Security, she recalled her own confusion that the media screamed for something to be done to stop the terrorists, yet when the FBI took action it was criticized at every turn. She recalled one public televised meeting, where a congresswoman from somewhere out west had shouted into the microphone, "I'd rather face terrorists from abroad than fascists from home." Ten seconds later a bomb planted under the stage detonated and shredded the congresswoman and a dozen people sitting behind her. The timing was such that some conspiracy nuts thought the FBI was behind the attack and helped push reforms, which eliminated the agency. After several years it became clear that it was just good timing on the part of jihadists, who had reaped the benefits of a gutted federal law enforcement presence in the United States ever since.

Shelby knew that there'd be no question she'd be fired for entering this house, and if it was proven that she did it because she was surveilling members of the Simolit family, she'd probably get sentenced to ten years in the military.

She shrugged off her crime and continued to look through the house, not knowing exactly what she was hoping to find. The garage held only some tools and a black conventional-gas motorcycle. She recalled when the big, loud bikes had been a status symbol, but the cold, constant rain in Florida had reduced their appeal.

The main bedroom had one unmade king bed. She saw woman's clothing spread across a chair next to one side of the bed and knew this was where Tom Wilner's beautiful wife spent her nights with Tiget Nadovich. She didn't know how a man like Wilner coped with something like that. It even hurt her and she had never spoken to Svala. Wilner was such a decent guy, and she had met many that weren't, that she hated to see him treated like this.

In the bathroom attached to the bedroom she found no cosmetics or other personal items she thought a woman would have, but wasn't surprised. Looking in the mirror at her own reflection she was thrown by her contacts that she had grown used to, but hid the natural light color of her eyes. The darker green gave her face a harsher look, which she didn't mind after all that time looking like a little Nordic doll. It was a nice change and she was happy that Tom Wilner seemed to appreciate her appearance.

She worked her quick search out into the dining room and then the rear bedrooms. Any sound made her jump as she factored in what might happen to her if Nadovich returned and learned her identity and intent.

Then, in the last bedroom, where there was no bed but a desk with some notes and several boxes on the ground containing different instruments she wasn't familiar with, she found something. On a side table, sitting by itself, was a photograph and a small news article in a frame. Shelby picked it up and examined the display. She read an English translation next to the news text written in Cyrillic script. She froze as she realized the significance of the story and accompanying photo. She stuffed the frame and its contents in her jacket, then considered it and pulled it out again. She took another look at her find as her heart started to pick up its pace.

Tiget Nadovich had everyone out on different assignments while he and Demitri considered their position. Nadovich was frustrated that they had failed to find the parts they needed. He thought he had overcome most obstacles to have a plan like this in place.

His timing also seemed to be good. The world had been focused on the approaching starship until the Germans moved troops into Austria. Now the focus had changed from anxiety about meeting a race from a billion miles away to killing a race that had caused untold misery in the last century. If any other country had been this aggressive there would only be talk of diplomacy. Every major power had been so sapped of strength by wars with the jihadists and, in Russia's case, wars with their former satellites, that no one wanted a major ground war.

But twice in the last century people tried to handle German expansion that way and twice the world regretted it.

Nadovich shook his head, thinking of all the possibilities the humans had created to destroy themselves. He wondered if his little act of war would even draw a glance if Europe was engulfed in a large-scale conflict.

He looked at Demitri. "If it wasn't at Svala's cop's house, do you think the other one really has it?"

Demitri shrugged. "Couldn't hurt to check."

"And if he is home at the time?"

"Then we'll sneak away. He'll never even know we were there." Demitri added, "What about the other problem?"

Nadovich scowled. "I don't know. Svala is hiding something."

"Maybe she loves the cop?"

Nadovich glared at him. "It is her desire to remain separate from our activities. She insists that we not inform her of our endeavors and I think she feels like she shouldn't tell us everything either. It's frustrating."

"As all women tend to be."

He nodded at his cousin.

"Perhaps we could work better without her around for a few weeks. She could come back when our plans are completed."

Nadovich stared at him. There were no words that could convey his feelings on this idea.

Demitri held up his hands in front of him and said, "It's just something we need to think about. This is bigger than you and her. I know you have a long history, but part of that history is her running off to America with the marine who became a cop."

Nadovich felt the blood rush to his face and his head start to throb. He almost wondered if he had an allergy to his cousin. If he could even develop allergies. Then he realized his most trusted advisor had just told him the truth and sometimes the truth was uncomfortable.

ELEVEN

Tom Wilner had let Svala leave the produce section of the small store without speaking to her. He knew he couldn't let the opportunity slip away completely and stepped out, then turned down the aisle that she slowly strolled up with an old grocery cart that gave a steady, rhythmic beat as one wheel failed to spin smoothly. He stood behind her, the closest he had been to her physical presence in months.

She reached for a bag of wild rice on the shelf and then saw him. The rice slipped from her hand, opening on the edge of the shopping cart and spraying out onto the floor, but she didn't even look down.

"Hello, Tom," was all she said in a subdued, detached tone.

He wanted to scoop her up and feel that rich, smooth hair against his face but caught himself and nodded. "Svala, how are you?"

She stared at his face then reached up and lightly touched his bruised cheek and black eye. "What happened?"

"I was at the UPF station that was attacked."

Her eyes grew slightly wider but she didn't say anything.

Wilner searched her face for clues to her knowledge of the incident. "Svala, why are you with Nadovich? What's he involved in?"

She stepped closer and his heart rate kicked up a notch. "Tom"—she started slowly and placed a hand on his arm—"it's very complicated between me and Tiget. I'm very sorry that I hurt you. I didn't want to. But he's not a man that you should bother."

"What'd you mean? He was part of a bar fight where someone was killed. He might have had something to do with the attack on the UPF station."

She just stared at him.

"Svala, this guy is bad news."

She cut him off. "You don't understand him. His worst fears are persecution. That's all he wants to avoid."

"No one is persecuting him."

"Please, Tom, don't harass Tiget because of me."

"I'm not." He paused and said, "That's just a bonus."

Tiget Nadovich had no more time to waste tracking down parts for which he had already paid one and a half million suds. Not only did he not have the parts, the madmen he had been dealing with didn't have the money. This was not the sort of issue that would end up in the chaotic court system. A state system where civil trials were all held in Orlando and allowed to run a maximum of two days. And the loser ended up paying all fees related to the case. Nadovich knew that if Mr. Hammed and his assorted thugs were not satisfied they'd make it a personal issue. Nadovich smiled, thinking about how sorry they would be coming after him or any of his family on this matter.

He turned to Alec, the youngest of the group, as they stood outside the large utility vehicle. Alec's generation had missed the great world wars and the near rise of China. He knew only the panic of the first flu pandemic that swept the globe twenty years ago and changed many of the structures, which had allowed certain nations to dominate others. Then the bioplague, which was so strong it had stopped the Russian-Georgian war.

The bioplague was sometimes referred to as the Gleason-Raab disease after the brilliant American scientists who had figured out what was happening and that the sickness spreading so rapidly was of a man-made origin. A slang term for the illness was that a victim was a "growler." It started as the first initials of the two scientists, Robert Gleason and Eric Raab, G-R, combined with the sound many of the victims made as their throats swelled closed. The growling sounds spooked people around them not only by the noise, but by the knowledge that if you heard the growl you'd been exposed to the bioplague. Growlers were universally feared and avoided.

Finally the bubonic plague had sprung up again in China, forcing India to show its might by sealing off its massive border and displaying the ability to call up three million military reservists almost instantly. The tactic had worked as millions died in China, Vietnam, Korea and the unified kingdom that used to be Laos, Thailand and Cambodia.

Alec had seen changes, but not the human conflict of World War II. He had not known the terror of the Nazis. That was what had convinced Nadovich that one day he and his kind might need to separate themselves from humans. If they could act like that, willingly enslaving millions and murdering them, what would they do to outsiders like the Simolit family? It was his experiences fighting the Nazis that had started him thinking of a homeland; a place to call their own. The experience also taught him that he was a leader and liked being respected. This plan not only would ensure safety for his people but they would all look to him to lead and he would be ready.

The attack on New York by jihadists had created a small sanctuary. The nuclear weapon, smuggled in through the port, had destroyed much of the business district in and around Wall Street. The lingering radiation had forced the evacuation of all of Manhattan and some of the other boroughs. And his kind had learned that radiation had no effect on them. Unless they were incinerated in the blast, a nuclear weapon was useless against them.

He smiled at his younger cousin. "Alec, I will leave it to you to get the boards that this other cop has."

Alec smiled. His teeth were as perfect as the other members of their family, but somehow they looked better on his angular, fresh face.

"I don't care how you do it. I don't care if the cop has to die. I don't care about anything but getting the last two boards back in our possession." He looked across at Demitri. "We'll need to start gathering the other material. Our friends in New York claim to have enough to spare."

Demitri nodded and said, "Mr. Hammed will have what we need. The only problem is that they have already accused us of stealing their parts and keeping the cash."

"You've told them about the police?"

"They don't believe me. They could come after us."

Nadovich smiled again. "Let them come."

Shelby Hahn stared at what she had found, then placed the small frame and old photograph inside the large pocket of her jacket.

She looked around the little office inside Tiget Nadovich's house one last time, both to make sure she hadn't left anything out of place and to make sure there wasn't something else she needed to take. The discovery of the photo and document had thrown her off and she wasn't mentally prepared to look for anything else.

As she started to move into the other room she froze, cocking her head and listening. There was somebody in the house. She had a small pistol on her but didn't know if it would even do her any good. The last thing she needed was to be captured inside the house belonging to a member of the Simolit family. He may have gone by the name Nadovich, but she believed his full name was Tiget Simolit Nadovich. He was clearly one of the new leaders of the family. If that's what one chose to call them.

She backed up to the rear wall and instinctively crouched, listening for more clues. How many were in the house? Were they all in one room? Did they know she was here? She felt her heart start to race and regretted her decision to enter the house without letting anyone know where she was going.

Footsteps sounded on the hard floor in the next room and she could see a shadow as a lone figure walked in front of the sliding glass door in the next room.

She pulled her small Fonda pistol named after an actress from the twentieth century and pointed the short barrel of the gas-powered automatic pistol that made a noise like someone coughing, at the door to the office. The shadow of the person in the other room shifted and she could hear the footsteps carefully coming toward her. She raised the gun, thinking she would fire and run, hoping that the gas-powered projectile might distract the person coming toward her.

A crouched figure darted into the office and was in the same room as her against the wall.

She raised the gun, about to fire, when she heard a male voice say, "It's Tom Wilner, don't shoot."

She lowered the pistol and he stepped out into the light. She said, "What the hell are you doing here?"

"Looking for you."

"How'd you know I was here?"

"Your empty car down the street tipped me off. Now let's get out of here before we're both found. You can explain how you weren't breaking the law when we're a safe distance away."

She couldn't help smiling at his dry delivery and subtle rebuke. This cop was okay.

Steve Besslia was dead tired as he rode his big Hive-bike down the Northern Enclave Expressway toward his condo in the old city of Boca Raton. It had been a long shift working traffic on the main highways from the Miami Quarantine Zone all the way to the far end of the Northern Enclave then back to his house. The patrol area was essentially the old Broward County, now called the Lawton District after some governor that everyone loved, and the combined counties of Palm Beach, Martin and another one he couldn't remember, which were all now referred to as the Northern Enclave. His rain gear kept him perfectly dry but that didn't make talking to annoyed drivers in the constant drizzle any easier. Especially when he didn't see too many. At least in the Lawton District. The Northern Enclave still had a decent population, but nothing like central Florida.

He had stopped one older pickup truck around lunch and thought he'd write a ticket for a change, but it was just three national guardsmen late for their tour down on the quarantine zone. Those guys took enough shit manning checkpoints and patrolling the wide canal the federal government thought would keep out all the illegal aliens that had flooded the old city before the amnesty. He didn't want to add to the guardsmen's misery.

Once the rumors about a bioplague settlement going up in Miami spread, the quarantine was locked down tight and no one got out. The idea of growlers running around terrified the government. Occasionally officials and some businessmen and humanitarians could go into the zone but no residents came out. At least not legally. There was a healthy illegal traffic flow of U.S. residents going down to gamble and chase whores and smugglers bringing in everything from the illegal drug Baht to old-style moonshine.

So Besslia gave the speeding guardsmen a break and let them go on their way without even a warning. He was just glad he didn't have to stand a post.

He turned into his development, slowing down, but not much because no one parked outside if they could help it. He approached his building, noting an odd car parked in the street. A nice Hive-utility car. He shrugged and drove past.

Beyond the open parking lot for his building he pulled the big motorcycle into the garage for his unit. He left his helmet with the bike and then looked at the wide, weatherproof saddlebags. He had stashed one of the circuit boards he had taken from the bar fight in them. Besslia had shown it to a couple of tech friends of his who didn't know what the board could be used for. The best they came up with was "some electronic thing."

The garage barely had enough room for his bike anymore because of the crates of old newspapers and magazines about the approaching aliens he had saved. They weren't indexed, but he could find things if he had to.

Besslia locked up the garage and climbed two flights of stairs to his unit. He looked up the remaining six flights and was glad he lived lower.

At the third floor he walked out onto the breezeway and turned down the short hallway to his door. He reached for his key, but the door was unlocked.

He pushed it open slowly. Immediately he saw some of his stuff on the floor of the living room. He stepped inside quietly and listened.

Someone was still in the house. Then he realized there were people in his bedroom.

He pulled his service pistol from his duty belt.

Someone was about to get a nasty surprise.

Tom Wilner pulled up to his house exhausted. This was the most tired a day off had ever made him. He had scolded Shelby Hahn for her venture into Nadovich's house, but had liked getting a look at where Svala now lived.

Seeing her had worn him out. He had not been as prepared as he thought he would to be close to her again even though she'd been civil, but that had seemed worse than angry. She didn't seem to have any passion for him at all.

Now he dragged his feet to the front door and reached for a key.

Instead, a crying Mrs. Honzit opened the door.

Over her shoulder he saw that the house had been searched and not by anyone who cared what it looked like afterward.

He stepped inside and then saw the kids, eating sandwiches at the kitchen counter and his heart started to beat again. They jumped off the stools and rushed to greet him. He looked around and didn't care about his stuff all of the sudden.

Mrs. Honzit said, "The men, they say they want their property or they won't be as nice next time."

Wilner quizzed her about if she had ever seen them and their descriptions then he thought of something. He had to warn Besslia in case they tried his place too.

Steve Besslia was silent as he crept closer to his bedroom with his gun drawn and pointed at the open door. He had the drop on the burglars and he was going to use his advantage. He was still fifteen feet from the door when he heard the beep of his V-com on his duty belt. He fumbled with one hand to shut it off, but it was too late.

Two figures darted through the doorway. They moved with a grace and speed that shocked the uniformed UPF patrolman. But he didn't hesitate and started to jerk the trigger of his big automatic; the sound inside the condo was deafening. The two men charged him as he fired then they passed right by. They bounded out to his balcony as he turned and fired a few more shots then dropped the magazine and loaded one from his belt in two seconds.

He let a slight smile creep across his face; he had them now. They were trapped three floors up and he had a full magazine of heavy 11-millimeter bullets.

He crouched with the gun up and made his way toward the terrace, expecting to see the men behind the heavy curtain blocking his view of half the large balcony. As he covered more distance he sped up because he didn't see the men. How was that possible? The balcony was empty.

He stood and ran outside into the light rain that blew in from the side. He swept the balcony with his pistol then looked over the side. The cop froze. Both men were on the ground. Alive. They were running toward the first-floor covered breezeway. The second man was limping and slower than the first.

Besslia lined up and shot and squeezed the trigger this time. One easy shot echoed between the buildings and he saw the second man clearly fall against the wall. Then, after a moment of sitting on the ground, he stood and disappeared under the cover.

Besslia had to sit back against the wall and take a breath. He needed help and needed it now.

TWELVE

Sitting in a bar at the far southern edge of the Lawton District, Tiget Nadovich may have been ahead of himself, talking to his contact about more items for the device he planned to make. He knew he still needed the circuit boards to construct the "easy-to-assemble" bomb kit he had acquired and had only received one, a short V-com call from Demitri saying that they had one of the missing boards but not the final one. He didn't go into details but it was obvious to Nadovich that his two cousins had run into trouble.

He had no appointment to meet Mr. Hammed or any of his associates but he knew they watched this bar closely and thought if he stayed long enough someone would show up that he could talk to. The UPF and national guardsmen left the place alone even if there was the occasional dispute that ended in violence, for it was always considered self-defense. Anyone coming into the small, freestanding, block building knew what they were risking.

Nadovich nodded to a man he had hired several times to

take messages to some of his people inside the quarantine zone. They liked living in the free, chaotic society. Since they were not subject to some of the diseases down there they fit in well. In fact, it was their counsel that had made Nadovich choose the Lawton District as the site of their new "homeland." He could've chosen the quarantine zone and the U.S. government wouldn't have even cared. But his people there didn't want it to change.

All he planned to do was to scare the current U.S. residents out of the Lawton District, then use the radiological fallout from his bomb as a way to keep the residents from coming back. Simple and effective.

Nadovich sipped a local beer at a corner table as he looked around at the patrons coming and going. The windows were open to allow the cold August Florida breeze to sweep through the simple establishment. He knew the owner, who was now tending bar, and the man understood not to bother him.

After nearly an hour, Nadovich noticed a burly young man with dark, wavy hair enter the bar and glance around. His eyes fell on Nadovich and he stopped, turned and went back outside. A minute later he returned with two more men, who marched directly toward Nadovich. One of the men was Mr. Hammed himself. They were serious.

All three men sat without preamble or invitation.

Mr. Hammed opened right up with "Where is our money?"

"To what money are you referring?" He kept his voice low and calm.

"You know what money. The one point five million for the boards."

"Which we delivered."

"No. You showed it to Amin and Samir. You never delivered it."

"I'm afraid we did."

"No, they never touched it. They gave you the requested boards and then the fight broke out."

"Which we did not plan or initiate."

Mr. Hammed, about fifty-five years of age, had grayish eyes that did not waver from Nadovich. "I did not say that you planned it. But I do insist on payment of money never delivered." He leaned in slightly and said, "Believe me, my friend, you do not wish to upset me."

That struck Nadovich as funny and he started to laugh. Belly laugh.

Mr. Hammed leaned back in his chair. His two muscle-heads looking to him for guidance, sensing they were going to be asked to silence Nadovich. The older Lebanese man said, "What is amusing you so?"

"You. You want me to fear you. You're an amateur. You have no idea who has threatened me in my life." He cut his dark eyes to Mr. Hammed. "You're not in the top fifty scariest people I've met. Now I will say this one last time. We owe you no money. But . . ." He paused for effect. "I might be interested in working something out if you could find us another initiator board."

"To match the others?"

Nadovich nodded.

Now it was Mr. Hammed's turn to chuckle. "You have no idea how hard it was to find the first set. It is unfortunate you can't keep your equipment together." He scooted back the chair so he wouldn't be in the line of fire once his two men started in on Nadovich. "We want our money."

"Go see the UPF. They have it."

"I heard someone already visited the UPF. My guess is

that you got the money back as well as most of the boards." He smiled, revealing a gold tooth on the side of his mouth.

"Mr. Hammed, it is not my wish to hurt you or your men. But make no mistake; I am through speaking with you." He started to slide back his chair, aware that the two younger Arabs planned to strike together.

Nadovich controlled his smile as he saw the two men start to move in unison. This was gong to be fun.

In a rear UPF detective's office in the UPF building closest to Steve Besslia's condo, Tom Wilner and Shelby Hahn sat with the very shaken Besslia on a hard, wooden bench. Shelby offered the traffic cop a paper cup of water, which he took, splashing half of it onto his pants with his shaking hands.

Besslia was still speaking in a fast, high-pitched tone. "I'm telling you guys, I hit them both a couple of times at least."

Wilner said, "Look, Steve, in combat it sometimes feels like that."

"Bullshit. I know I didn't see any combat in the service but I've been in a couple of shootings with the UPF. I tell you I had the drop on them. I nailed them at close range, then made a good open distance shot that knocked one of them off his feet. The blood is still there. You can check."

Wilner nodded. He already had Besslia's keys. "I intend to once you calm down a little."

"I'm calm, I'm calm. But they were after the boards. That's what it had to be."

"Did they get them?"

"One of them. I still have one in the side bag of my bike."

"Did you recognize them?"

"They had dark hair. They could've been the ones from the station and the ones with Nadovich at the bar, but I couldn't swear to it."

Besslia started to speak, then hesitated. He cut his eyes to Shelby.

"What is it?" asked Wilner.

"I don't want you guys to think I'm crazy."

"Too late. Now, spit it out."

"It's just that there's something odd going on around here. I mean this is a lot of effort someone is putting out. And I haven't pulled the trigger this much since I tried out for the SWAT team." He stopped again and looked at Shelby.

The federal agent said quietly, "Maybe if I left you two alone he'd feel more comfortable." She stood up. "I have a lot to do anyway." She turned and both men couldn't help watching her walk away.

Wilner turned to his friend. "Okay, now what the hell are you talking about?"

Besslia grabbed his arm and said, "I've seen more seriously wounded guys walk away in the last week than in my whole life. And I think I understand why."

"Why?"

"They're not human."

"What?"

"I'm totally serious, Willie."

Wilner just gave him a look.

"I know you laugh at me about my obsession with the aliens but maybe, just maybe, there's a reason I was compelled to learn about them."

"All right, I'm listening."

"I think we stumbled into a group of aliens. Maybe an

advance party for the ship on its way. They could've been on Earth for years."

"You think the guys in your condo were aliens?"

"Yeah, I think maybe I do."

"I think we may need to get you checked out by a doctor."

THIRTEEN

Tiget Nadovich had faced down Nazis. Mr. Hammed and his two flunkies were more like a sporting event. As the two young men reached for him he leaned back and allowed his chair to tip over completely, then he rolled away from them into a standing position. He allowed a smirk to stay on his face.

The burly guy he had seen first stood and charged him, allowing Nadovich to easily step to one side, sending the man into an empty booth.

The other man, taller and leaner than the first, drew a Saudi combat knife like the one that the big Halleck had used to cut open Demitri several nights before. The man advanced but with a tactical precision the first attacker had lacked. This man had seen combat. But Nadovich was sure he had never seen anything like him before.

The tall man feinted with the knife one way then the other. As Nadovich was preparing to strike the man in the neck he felt the first burly man crash into him from behind.

The man with the knife slashed him across the face, then

delivered a brutal hacking blow to his head with the razor-sharp knife. Nadovich felt it cut into his skull and split open the skin on his forehead, pain shooting down his body like electricity and blood spurting into his eyes as the man wiggled and worked the knife out to deliver another blow, no matter how unnecessary he thought it might be.

Nadovich shook off the big man and then faced the man with a knife. Just the fact that he still stood, with blood pouring down his face and two serious blows fended off, scared the attacker. Nadovich could see it in the man's eyes as he faltered, then looked to Mr. Hammed for guidance.

Nadovich glared over at him too and said, "I would say we were even now, wouldn't you?"

The calm voice and simple statement sent all three men scurrying for the door.

Nadovich picked up a napkin from a nearby table to stop the blood from staining his clothes further. He turned, reached in his pocket and threw a one hundred-sud note on the bar for the inconvenience, then walked out the door without anyone saying a word.

Wilner had to admit that Steve Besslia was right; there was blood in his apartment and on the wall in the courtyard just like he had said. There was so much blood even Wilner couldn't believe there wasn't a body lying around. As undisciplined and wacky as Besslia could be, Wilner didn't think he could get so confused as to miss intruders with a Beretta Millennium from such a short range. The blood confirmed it.

The condo was a wreck, with drawers dumped out and clothes piled on the floor. Besslia had said the board was in the top drawer of his bedroom dresser and it was open with most of its contents still inside. The intruders must have seen the board, retrieved it and left the dresser intact, unlike much of the rest of the furniture.

Wilner had taken the last circuit board from Besslia's Hive-bike in the garage and had it in his jacket. He didn't care what happened; he'd keep this one safe.

He looked around again at all the bloodstains, then took the small, eight-vial, plastic tube from his light, all-weather jacket. He broke one of the swabs stuck inside the first vial and then wiped a sample of the blood. The chemical embedded in the tip of the swab moistened the blood and gathered a sample. He continued until he had one vial left empty. He looked out Besslia's balcony to see if he could tell where the traffic cop took the shot on the runner. Sighting down his finger he lined up the shot that matched the blood pattern on the wall. It looked like Besslia was right on about his experience. Wilner closed up the condo then went down to the stain on the wall, took a sample and then sealed the tube. He hadn't liked his past experiences with the only operational UPF lab in all of south Florida. He knew he'd have to do some fancy talking to get someone at the lab to look at the blood samples he'd collected.

Wilner worried about Besslia. Neither of them would be on duty for the next few days. While the chief recognized that Besslia was upset by the intruders and shooting, none of the UPF administrators wanted to believe it was a conspiracy or organized effort. Wilner's boss did tell him to put in a little extra effort on the bar fight in case they were related. He told Wilner he had every confidence in him, but that things were still tight and he was on his own.

Great. The more danger it seemed he was in, the less help he received. That seemed to be the American theme the past few decades. He didn't like his personal experience with it.

On his way through the parking lot to his Hive he caught someone moving out of the corner of his eye. He let his right arm brush against his gun on his hip under his jacket just to feel it there. Then his hand slipped behind him to feel the grip of his stun baton.

Whoever was wandering around near his car wasn't trying to conceal themselves. Wilner could see a man's head as he came closer. It wasn't until the tall blond man stepped out from behind his car that he realized it was Johann Halleck.

He had seen the big man in action and didn't want to give him the opportunity to cut him like he had the dark-haired man from the bar. Without warning or telegraphing, Wilner grasped the stun baton from his rear holster, yanked it out and flicked it open so it extended to its full length. Slightly heavier than a standard baton due to the powerful electrical jolt it delivered, the baton was good for about five man-stopping jolts before it had to be recharged.

Johann Halleck did not seem surprised or concerned by the sight of the handheld weapon.

That made Wilner nervous.

Shelby Hahn nodded as her supervisor from Atlanta spoke to her over her V-com. She had explained some of what she had accomplished.

Her supervisor said, "You're sure they're part of this terror group?"

She looked at the screen where he had placed the camera so close to his face she couldn't see any background but knew he was in his comfortable office. "I'm not entirely sure yet, sir. I'm working with a local UPF detective and I think this group is causing some problems."

"How many members have you identified in the cell?"

"Maybe three and a female associate."

"This group has a lot of female members, right?"

"Yes, sir. Most are related by blood."

"How long will you be stuck in that hellhole?"

She noticed he retained his disdain for the wrecked southern tip of Florida even though he had been forced to flee New York. Sometimes she got frustrated that everyone looked at their little world without seeming to care about everyone else's.

She answered his question. "Maybe a few more weeks."

"That's good. It makes them think that the Department of Homeland Security is interested in what goes on down there. Just wrap it up so you can get back to the comforts of Orlando or Atlanta soon."

His screen cut out like it always did when he was done talking. He didn't want to hear from anyone else. She was doing her job, or so he thought, and she wasn't causing him a problem. She was a model employee.

Shelby considered what the situation looked like here on the ground, closer to the investigation. She knew that things were not as they appeared to the local UPF cops and feared that Steve Besslia, despite appearing to be a little goofy, might have figured out a few more things than he should know. She could tell by the way he wanted to talk to Wilner alone and his agitated manner that he knew he had hit the intruders with a few of his shots earlier. They should have gone down. There should be bodies. But there weren't.

She didn't like keeping secrets from everyone. Even her boss. She hadn't told him about entering Nadovich's house or finding the old photograph. The DHS supervisor wouldn't have appreciated her methods and wouldn't understand or necessarily believe the significance of the news article and photo she had found.

For now she'd live with her secrets even though she wished she could tell Tom Wilner all she knew. It would make her feel better knowing a man like that was aware of the bigger picture and it might save him a little heartache later. But that was her problem. She had a mission and couldn't tell anyone what was going on.

FOURTEEN

Tom Wilner swung the baton hard, even though the idea of the electrical charge was to avoid having to swing it hard. It arced toward Johann Halleck's head as Wilner stepped into the blow. He intended to have the big man in cuffs before he knew what had happened. It was a good plan until Halleck reached up and grabbed the moving baton midair with an open palm.

He twisted it out of Wilner's hand and stood there with the stun baton in his own hands now. Instead of striking back, he took the baton in both hands and flexed, snapping the straight metal baton in half, spraying springs and small electrical parts in random directions.

Wilner flinched, calculating how fast he could draw his pistol.

Johann Halleck tossed the remains of the baton behind him harmlessly with both hands.

Wilner knew he couldn't just stand there, so he threw a right cross to the taller man's face as a follow-up.

Halleck caught Wilner's fist in the palm of his other hand and then squeezed his fingers together. The pain that shot through Wilner was brilliant, causing him to see lights and suck in air. Then it was over as the big man released him.

Halleck said, "Are you done?"

Wilner, holding his injured hand and panting, huffed, "Yeah, I think so."

"Ready to talk?"

Wilner stepped back and said, "I still have a gun."

This made Halleck chuckle. "Haven't you learned anything yet?"

Wilner shrugged and decided maybe it was time to just talk. He left the pistol holstered and leaned back against a car parked next to his in the tree-lined lot. He just stared at the man, wondering what he knew and how easily he could kill Wilner if he wanted to. The UPF detective felt lucky he hadn't been beaten. When someone loses a fight so convincingly they usually have scars to prove it. He owed Johann the courtesy of hearing him out.

Finally Johann said, "You're here for the missing boards."

Wilner nodded slowly. "And you?"

"I heard about Officer Besslia's difficulties and was curious if he had the boards too."

"How'd you hear about Besslia?"

Johann smiled, his large, thick white teeth seemed to fit in his mouth perfectly. "I have many friends and some are connected with the UPF. They tell me things."

"That how you got a bail hearing so fast?"

"No, that was my very fine attorney."

Wilner kept staring at the large man. "If I answer your questions, will you answer mine?"

"I doubt it. I told you not to get involved. Tiget Nadovich

is my problem. I'll handle him." He paused and added in his odd, clipped accent, "I will not harm your wife."

Now that shocked Wilner. He started to ask more questions, but caught himself. Instead he said, "You *are* well connected."

"And I'm not working against you. I just want to ensure that no one gets control of all the circuit boards and the other material they need."

"Why? What are they making?"

"I'm not positive but I have my ideas."

"Why not get us to help?"

"Because, for my own reasons, I cannot have the authorities involved with Nadovich or his family. They will be stopped, but quietly. You must believe me when I say I have nothing but the best intentions. I mean you no harm."

Wilner said, "The burglars got one of the remaining boards."

Johann sagged slightly.

"We have the last one now."

"Where?"

Wilner tried not to think about the board tucked in his jacket. "It's safe."

"I'm sure you thought that when they were stored at the UPF station."

Wilner flinched at his point. "No, this one I will keep safe personally."

"But they know where you live."

Again Wilner flinched at how much this guy knew.

After a few moments Johann said, "I am not your enemy."

"My friends don't threaten me."

"It's a warning. You're in over your head. There's a much bigger picture we must consider."

"Believe me, I'm considering it right now." He didn't want to have to fight to get in his car. "I have to be going."

Johann backed away. "We'll meet again soon. Very soon."

Wilner didn't like that idea one bit.

FIFTEEN

It was completely dark by the time Wilner got home. All in all, a busy day for a guy who wasn't on duty. He was sore from the UPF station attack, his head hurt from all the things he had to consider and he felt emotionally ill after his talk with Svala. He wished the kids got to see her more. She was a good mother, he didn't understand why she hadn't visited them more.

Once inside the house, he was surprised by how much Mrs. Honzit had straightened up. Not only did the house look to be in order, the housekeeper had seemed to regroup well. The kids were studying after eating what was, in all probability, a fine meal.

Tommy and Emma darted off their stools at the kitchen counter with their books spread out. They hit him like the old-time football players, wrapping small but strong arms around him, and squeezed. It was a little more than he usually got and figured it was a combination of coming home banged up the night before, the house being tossed and his general absence from the house due to work. He took them in his own arms and squeezed. It was little moments like this that made him glad he had made it through Iran. He held on to the children, almost feeling as if he might cry. He caught Mrs. Honzit out of the corner of his eye and saw that she was wiping tears away. He kissed Tommy and then Emma on the forehead, then stood, leading them back to their homework.

He turned to the housekeeper and said, "Mrs. Honzit, you're amazing. The place looks good and I appreciate your care for the kids."

She smiled and said, "These kids," she paused then added, "and you, are all I have here in America."

He knew what that meant. With the ban on immigration her family could never come over from Turkey.

Wilner said, "You've saved me. And not just tonight."

She smiled again and turned into the kitchen. "I save you dinner." She picked up a full plate from the food stabilizer. The plate still steamed as it came from the small box that kept food fresh, hot or cold, for up to twenty-four hours.

He looked down and smelled the plate. "That's great. Is it"—he was almost afraid to ask—"lamb?"

She frowned slightly. "Synthetic lamb. All the market had was synthetics. But the butcher, he says that next week they will be getting real beef. All parts of cows from out west."

Wilner nodded. "Yeah, the mad cow scare is over so they'll start moving cattle."

"I'm still worried. It killed a lot of people in Minnesota."

"Yeah, but it was probably meat from the same herd. And I thought only two hundred died."

"That's enough."

He nodded as he started to cut the realistic synthetic lamb that was made from soybeans, tiny polymers, often wood products and flavoring. Usually synthetics were also coated with vitamins and extra protein. That was for the soldier in combat to get a little boost.

The way he felt right now, *he* was in combat.

The next morning Wilner was up and making breakfast for the kids very early. He wasn't supposed to be on duty according to his boss, but he had several plans for the day that were at least related to his investigation.

He whipped up a half-a-dozen reptile eggs and heated some synthetic bacon in the food utility processor, a combination of microwave, dehydrator, bacteria killer and, when needed, freeze-dryer.

By the time Emma and Tommy stumbled out from their bedrooms he had their breakfast on the table.

Mrs. Honzit padded out in a thick bathrobe only to see that all was taken care of and turned to shuffle back to her room in the rear of the house.

The housekeeper had definitely earned a day off.

He leaned toward the kids as they started to pick at the eggs. "I'll be waiting when the bus drops you off today."

They both brightened but sleep was still muting their reactions.

After he had everyone off and ready for the day he slipped on his jacket and grabbed the circuit board and blood samples. Once in his UPF Hive, he retrieved his pistol from under the front seat and strapped it on his hip. Thanks to Johann Halleck he was short one stun baton.

He drove north up the old Florida turnpike, which was now free of tolls and called Charlie Christ Boulevard after a popular governor from the turn of the century. Wilner knew the name but not much else, like he knew some of the twentieth-century presidents. Clinton and Reagan were the two well-known ones that seemed to have had an impact on American life. The others were harder to remember and then there were the two that had been virtually stricken from the history books. But he wasn't a scholar and never pretended to be. That was the kind of stuff his kids would learn. He was just a cop and former marine. You didn't have to know who banned immigration to be a cop.

His first stop was Steve Besslia's condo at the southern edge of the Northern Enclave. Someone had told him the Northern Enclave used to be several counties, two of them named Palm Beach and Martin, but after the 9/11 attacks of the early twenties they consolidated the counties and formed the Northern Enclave where people with a little more money who still needed to live in south Florida would have a place that was quieter and safer than the District.

Wilner parked in nearly the same spot as he had the night before. He saw one of the pieces of his stun baton that Johann Halleck had destroyed on the edge of his parking spot. He made his way to the elevator, then up to Besslia's condo. He knocked on the thick, secure door and waited. After a minute he heard shuffling from inside and then Besslia's voice through the door. "Who is it?"

"Me."

"I'm not that stupid, who in the hell is 'me'?"

"You're not serious." But Wilner waited in silence until he said in a loud voice, "Wilner, Thomas J. UPF detective, badge 5662."

The door opened and Besslia didn't smile. "I'm sorry you think I'm paranoid, but I've been through a lot."

Wilner looked at his friend, draped in a thick bedcover

with his big service pistol in his hand. The condo was in the same shape as he had seen it the night before when he had collected the blood samples. Besslia needed a Mrs. Honzit.

Wilner said, "You should've spent the night at my house last night. You okay?"

"Yeah, why? Do I look funny?"

Wilner stared at his friend in the bedcover. "No, just worried."

"I thought you were off until Monday."

"Yeah, same as you, I'm just checking on you."

"Then where are you goin'?"

Wilner paused then said, "The lab in the middle of the Northern Enclave."

"What for?"

"The blood samples I took from here last night."

Besslia perked up. "You do believe me. You think they're aliens too."

"No. I think there's a chance, although remote, they might be in the old DNA database."

Besslia flopped into a large, padded chair. "You want me to come?"

Wilner looked around and said, "No, I think you need to clean up."

"Willie, be careful. We don't know what these guys can do."

"The aliens."

"That's right."

Wilner nodded, hoping his friend would get some much-needed rest and start to think a little more clearly.

Tiget Nadovich and his cousins, Alec and Demitri, sat in the small compartment of the fast-moving Delta train. Since nonessential commercial air travel had been curtailed by the government, several of the prominent air carriers had switched to trains and buses. The trains were modeled after Japanese bullet trains and could travel, at least through sparsely populated Florida, at more than two hundred miles an hour.

The private compartment of this train could seat up to six and the trip to Philadelphia, with stops and restricted areas, would take about twenty hours. Nadovich didn't mind the lull in his schedule. As he looked at his cousins he knew they both felt the same way. All of them had injuries for which they needed quiet and concentration to heal. Nadovich had stopped the bleeding from his massive head wound inflicted by Mr. Hammed's man, but he still had an inflamed and annoying scar.

Alec had four bullet holes in him from the cop's, Besslia, pistol. One of the holes was visible on his forehead. The others were in his torso. He needed more than twenty hours to heal.

Demitri's wounds were less severe; a bullet in the leg and then two in his left side. One of the bullets had struck from the long distance, but passed through him without hitting any bone or organs. The problem was that he had not fully recovered from the knife wound the big Halleck had given him in the sports bar. It was the combination and cumulative effect of wounds like those that had killed several of his family members over the years. Especially during the Nazi onslaught when they pounded areas with artillery and attacked with infantry. They would always check the wounded and shoot them to ensure they were dead. Sometimes they might have to check a Simolit several times, but their thoroughness and persistence resulted in the death of several good men.

That was why Nadovich worried about his cousin now. He didn't want him in a position to be severely injured again.

Alec, the most youthful of the three, seemed excited by the trip. "I haven't been to Philadelphia since the New Yorkers moved into town."

"It's crowded now," said Demitri.

Nadovich said, "This isn't a social visit."

"But we'll see Borislav and Eliza, no?"

"We will and many other family members, but we have work to do as well. Some of them have the material we'll need for our plan. Especially the ones still living in Manhattan. They have a great deal to show us."

Demitri added, "We must also see how living in the radioactivity has affected our people who stayed. They say they're fine, but this is a rare chance to test Tiget's theory."

Nadovich gave him a hard look. He didn't realize his theory needed testing. He had considered his plan based on fact, not theory. But Demitri liked to talk and it didn't undermine him in public, so he let the comment pass.

Then Demitri said, "It won't matter if we get the radioactive material now if we can't get the last circuit board back."

Nadovich smiled. "Don't worry, Demitri. I already have someone handling that for us."

"Who?"

"Freddie Rea and his little band of quarantine zone smugglers."

"The Puerto Ricans?"

Nadovich nodded.

"Aren't they considered terrorists by the U.S. government?"

"They *are* terrorists. If they hadn't done the things they did Puerto Rico never would've gained independence. Who better to do some dirty work?"

"If they gained independence for Puerto Rico, why aren't they living there?"

"When its economy and social structure broke down a lot of the freedom fighters came to the quarantine zone to profit from smuggling." Then he added, "And doing messy jobs for different people."

"I don't like using someone else. We can get the board back."

"Apparently we can't." He didn't smile. Then he said, "Besides, it will make Svala easier to live with if we're not the ones that kill her meddlesome husband."

"When are they going to do it?"

"While we're up here. It covers us with Svala."

"One less thing to worry about. If they can get it."

"Why wouldn't they be able to get it?"

"Svala's husband is a combat veteran and tough. Even for us. Against other humans he'd be very hard to stop."

Nadovich considered this. Maybe they would have to step in, but for now he decided to give the Puerto Ricans their chance.

Nadovich said, "We should use this time to heal. Look at us, we could be corpses we have so many wounds."

The others laughed weakly, no doubt because they realized they could be dead if the cop had been a little more accurate up close and had a few more bullets.

All three men took in deep breaths and leaned back in the comfortable compartment. The rocking of the train seemed to relax Nadovich as he drifted into a calm, almost comalike state that allowed his body to concentrate on healing injuries. He faintly knew his forehead was tingling as the process started to work. On the inside of his head a dull ache pulsed with the beat of his heart. This wasn't an injury, this was one of his new headaches. He took another deep breath and relaxed, knowing he'd be out for at least ten hours and would probably have to keep an eye on Demitri to make sure he didn't overdo it for a while after he awoke.

It was an awkward life to be stuck between human and outsider; to not be completely accepted but not singled out either. Nadovich knew that would change once the humans discovered their presence among them. He had it seen before. The Nazis persecuted the Jews. The Turks attacked the Armenians. The Iraqis treatment of the Kurds. It was a pattern Nadovich did not want his family to experience. This was his chance. An opportunity to provide security to all his people. And God would have to help the human that got in his way.

SIXTEEN

Tom Wilner had crossed onto the old Interstate 95 as he continued toward the only UPF lab in southern Florida. It was located in a low building off the interstate in the old city of West Palm Beach. I-95 was down to two serviceable lanes here but that seemed to be more than enough for the limited number of cars that traveled it every day. On the far two lanes of the highway from the Miami Quarantine Zone north, until it passed out of the Northern Enclave, were piles of old, twisted vehicles. For the past ten years every time there was a wreck, it was more expedient for a big truck with a bulldozerlike scoop in the front to just shove the cars and trucks involved in the accident to the side. They were crammed against the guardrails, most rusted and degrading, but every few miles a Hive or nicely kept conventional lay pushed to the side.

The lab was only a few blocks from the highway and not surprisingly Wilner had his choice of empty spots in front of the building. He walked inside and pulled out his identification after ringing the bell at the empty reception area. Thick protective glass covered the receptionist's desk that would stop a bullet but would be an oozing ball of heat if struck by a flasher.

After a minute wait, an older, cadaverous man with almost no hair walked into the reception area behind the glass and pressed the intercom button.

"What do ya need?"

Wilner held up his ID.

The man answered, "Yeah, so? I work for the UPF too."

"I have a blood sample to drop off."

"Why?"

"I wanted to see what DNA testing could tell me."

The man started to laugh then poured it on a little thick.

Wilner felt his blood pressure rise. He hated this kind of bureaucratic laziness. He had seen it in the service and couldn't tolerate it in the UPF.

Wilner kept his cool and said, "I have a blood sample from a police shooting."

"Which one?"

"At the edge of the Northern Enclave last night."

"I didn't even hear about it. How many were killed?"

"None."

"Is the cop in hot water?"

"No."

"Then why would we want a blood sample?" He straightened his sticklike body up and continued in that annoyed tone. "I'm the only one here. Not the only DNA tech, but the only person in the whole building. They cut our budget so much I have to answer the phones, act as receptionist, do the lab work and even sweep up in the evening. I don't have time for noncritical lab work."

Wilner looked at the man. He had a point even if he delivered it poorly.

Then the man said, "Now get back to your patrol zone before someone misses you."

That was unnecessary. Wilner said, "For one thing, I'm a detective and don't have a zone. For another, you don't need to talk to me like that. And for a third, you're cruising for an ass-kicking."

"Oh, yeah, and how would you get through the glass? It's three inches thick and bulletproof." He rapped the partition with long, bony fingers.

Wilner stared at the lab tech. Then he looked at the door, which was not nearly as strong as the glass. He threw a medium kick into the door, just to see how thick it was, and it buckled off its ancient hinges. He stepped into the lab and only a few feet from the stunned lab tech.

Wilner looked at him. "You were saying?"

"Well, I was, you know, maybe talking out my ass a little."

Wilner reached in his jacket pocket and pulled out the glass container with the blood samples. "Unless you want to breathe out of your ass, I'd like you to look at these."

The man picked them up with a shaky hand and said, "Tell me what happened so I know what I'm looking at."

Wilner waited a second to determine if the man was sincere, then said, "Officer Besslia caught some burglars in his condo last night."

The lab tech said, "The traffic cop?"

"Yeah, you know him?"

"Everyone knows Steve. Why didn't you say it was for him?"

"Anyway, he didn't get a good look at them. There were

two men. I tried to get samples from different areas so I hope I got one from each."

The man held the container up to the light. "I'll be able to get a profile from this, but the weak point is the DNA database. Since we lost funding for it, the damn thing has been almost useless. No one has added a sample to it in nine years. Your burglars would have to be old men to even be in the database."

"How long you been here?"

"I've been with UPF since it started and the old Florida Department of Law Enforcement before that. I've worked with that database for almost twenty years."

"See what you can do."

"It's not often I take cases that I don't get paid for privately." The man let it just hang out there so Wilner would have to choose to bribe him.

"I have a weird payment offer."

"What's that?" The man smiled in anticipation.

"If you don't do this, I'll force you to spend some of your privately funded money on a stay at the trauma center in the Northern Enclave hospital. Fair enough?"

"That'll work out well. I'll get right on it."

On his way back down to the Lawton District, after his talk with the obstructionist lab tech, Wilner decided, since it was his day off, to stop at one of the few remaining libraries in the southern tip of Florida. There were none left in the Lawton District but the Northern Enclave still had three and one of them was gigantic with archived newspapers and magazine articles. A perfect place to do a little research.

A light drizzle had started to fall and the temperature had dropped to about sixty. He huddled into his jacket more as he ran across the parking lot and under the overhang to the entrance.

He shook off the water that hadn't been wicked off his jacket.

There was no security at the front door. The government had decided it was cheaper to deal with incidents than to try and prevent them. Wilner didn't mind, but he wondered if people who didn't carry guns felt the same way.

Inside he signed up on a list to use the available computers. It looked like it would be a couple of hours until he checked to see if there was an "official use" computer.

The librarian looked skeptical that he would qualify for the isolated, fast and unoccupied computer until he showed her his ID. She was surprised, then friendly, after looking at it.

The pretty, sleek librarian leaned a little closer to him. "I don't get to meet many UPF officers."

"You must stay out of trouble." He smiled.

"I could be bad if you came to arrest me." She had a soft, subtle sexuality that surprised Wilner.

He thought for a moment and held up his left hand and wiggled his ring finger with the wedding band still on it.

"You don't look married."

"I don't really feel like it either, but I still am."

The librarian shrugged and led him to a computer in a small glass room near the main desk.

She said, "I'll check on you in a half hour to make sure nothing's changed."

Wilner let out a laugh at the flirtatious librarian then got down to work logging on to one of the news archive sites with his password from the UPF. To his surprise he landed right in the archive for news. It supposedly contained the text and some photos for magazines and newspapers from all over the world. Many of them added old articles as far back as World War I.

To try out the system, Wilner entered his own name. After a few revisions and narrowing the search he found a few articles that listed his name. There were three from the newspaper his father still got back in New Jersey, the Newark *Star-Ledger*.

The first article had his name as wounded in the battle for Bandar Abbas. The next one was on his medal ceremony where the senator from New Jersey pinned two of his decorations for heroism when he took out the tank and then led the charge that turned the battle of the oil fields in favor of the Allies. That was one of the bloodiest days of the second Iranian war and the fact that he was even mentioned was an insult to the 2,900 Americans and 650 British soldiers who had died in the fight. The article also neglected to mention the nearly 20,000 Iranians and jihadists that were also killed.

The last article was short. It covered the police-type blotter of soldiers in the Balkan conflict. It said that Sergeant Thomas J. Wilner of Ocean Grove was under investigation for attempted murder in an incident that involved a Serbian civilian. That was accurate for the time. But there was no follow-up article on his exoneration or at least that the U.S. government hadn't pursued charges.

He had made a snap decision and thought he had delivered swift justice where it was called for. The U.S. government had disagreed and arrested him for his actions. If it had not been for the victim surviving the gunshot and fleeing the area, Wilner might still be in a military prison somewhere.

Now, as a cop himself, he realized how frustrated the military police had been with his clear-cut crime and then a victim who refused to testify. A victim who is still probably roaming around Europe and causing pain and fear among any women he comes into contact with.

He then started entering Tiget Nadovich's name into the computer. Through some side searches and following similar names he found a number of references, but many had to be of relatives because they were from as early as 1935. Three were in Serbian newspapers and there was no translation. Three more were originally in Serbian papers but translated. One article was about a Tiget Nadovich who had been accused of terrorism against Croatian citizens of Yugoslavia in the mid-1950s. That could've been this Tiget Nadovich's grandfather. The next article talked about a Nadovich who was running for parliament in the newly formed Bosnia in the 1990s. Perhaps this one's father.

The last was older and came from a wire service story in 1945. The story claimed that a Tiget Nadovich had been a leader of Serbian resistance to the Nazis. The article talked about how the fervent resistance had tied down a division of crack Nazi storm troopers and had helped the Allies get a foothold in Europe.

Wilner searched the scanned article and found a photo in the corner of the scan. It showed a handsome, dark-haired man raising a U.S. Army M1 Garand rifle and shouting with joy as an end of the war is declared. Wilner did a double take at the photo. He enlarged it only to see a grainy photo of a man who looked disturbingly like Tiget Nadovich. There was a female's arm next to him in the photo with the edge of a dark skirt and the hand gripping a German pistol. This man had to be related to this Tiget Nadovich. The resemblance was remarkable.

Wilner printed out the article and folded it, then stuck it in his jacket. The photo and text had unnerved him as he thought about Besslia's contention that they were dealing with aliens.

SEVENTEEN

Tom Wilner sat across from Shelby Hahn at the table with a real cotton tablecloth and smiled at her as she took a sip of a nice Mexican red wine. The vineyards, which had sprung up in the mountains of Mexico, had replaced coffee as a chief export in the past few years. Wilner didn't care one way or the other about the quality, he was relieved Shelby had ordered one of the cheapest bottles on the nice restaurant's short wine list. The Italian restaurant just inside the Northern Enclave was the closest sit-down dining establishment to Wilner's Eastern District house.

Wilner had heard that once this area, what used to be called Fort Lauderdale, was filled with fine restaurants and bars. He had a hard time believing that now when he roamed the empty streets of the business area. As one traveled farther north on the peninsula, restaurants sprang up with more frequency.

This restaurant looked good, with real meat in most of the dishes and seafood offerings as well. Granted the fish was expensive, but with so few left in the ocean it was a rare chance to see one on the menu.

As he looked at Shelby his pulse picked up. Not like in combat, but not too much unlike it. He looked away for a moment to gather himself. The broad windows looked out over the parking lot. On one of the cement islands in the middle of the lot Wilner noticed two young Hispanic men standing a few cars down from his personal van. One man wore a plastic rain slicker with the Puerto Rican flag sewed across the chest. Some people were sensitive about that flag. Since the series of bombings and killings on the island and their vote for independence, many residents of the island nation had sought to return to the status of a U.S. Commonwealth. The pain and sorrow caused while the United States was engaged in the first Iranian war had left hard feelings. Apparently this young man was tough enough to take the heat.

Shelby reached over and patted his hand, leaving her small hand on top of his.

He looked into her deep, green eyes and said, "It's been a long time since I had dinner out with another woman."

She smiled. "I don't bite." Then, after a pause, she added, "Unless you like that kind of thing." She gave him a sly smile.

"After all I've been through the last couple of weeks I needed something like this." He wasn't going to tell her about his research on Tiget Nadovich. He didn't want her to think he was crazy enough to consider Steve Besslia's theories on alien invasions. He still had work to do. He had friends in the State Department stationed in Serbia who might be able to uncover some more information when the time was right.

"You and Steve have done a good job. Whoever is after the circuit board is obviously determined and the UPF doesn't have the resources to help you. Anyone else might have given up."

Wilner smiled, proud of Besslia for some of his good ideas in the case; not necessarily for his theories. "Let's hope we can hang on to the last board."

Shelby nodded. "Where do you have it stored?"

"I knew that they could get to my house easily and the UPF doesn't have a new evidence room yet."

"So?"

"So I hid it in the door panel of my Hive-van."

She nodded. "That's pretty smart. It's usually close to you and no one would think to rip the interior of the doors off."

"My thinking exactly."

They chatted some more about their backgrounds as they waited for the real cow steaks to come. Wilner loved the idea that this beautiful girl operated a field artillery piece and had fought in the second Iranian war.

Finally he asked over dinner, "Your family ever worried about you getting called up if Germany attacks any of its neighbors?"

She shook her head. "My dad had experience with them. He hates them."

"I thought your dad was from Tennessee. You said he wasn't in the military."

She hesitated and said, "He dealt with them in his engineering firm. He'd love to see them put in their place."

"I would too, but I don't want to be one of the marines doing it."

"I'm with you on that one."

They finished their meal, laughing about life in a changing America. He hadn't dwelled on growing up in New Jersey or on how his father had raised him and his two brothers because sometimes he felt like his life started when he had joined the marines.

Shelby said, "I saw the photo at your house of you being decorated. What'd you get?"

He shrugged, not so much embarrassed by the awards, but not wanting to talk about his court-martial. Finally he said, "Silver Star, Distinguished Service Cross and two Bronze Stars."

"Wow."

"Just the way it shook out. You know how everyone does something that could get noticed. I just did it at the right time."

"Ever get in any trouble?" She gave him an impish smile.

"Some." He couldn't look her in the eyes with that answer.

"What happened?"

"Not much."

She took the hint and drank some coffee as they talked about simple subjects like politics and religion.

Tiget Nadovich enjoyed seeing the look of wonder on Alec's face as they entered the meeting hall the family had secured for their reunion. The city itself had fascinated Alec although the new structures built on top of virtually every other building to accommodate the fleeing New Yorkers had robbed the city of much of its charm.

The historically significant buildings, at least significant to the Americans, had all been converted to house people. The population of the city had more than doubled in the course of a few weeks then had declined slightly as many of the original residents of Philadelphia had fled to quieter towns in western Pennsylvania. The state had retained much of its charm from the twentieth century because the new residents offset those killed by the pandemics or lost to the wars. The state's tax base had remained intact, so it had separate police departments and public services in the major cities.

Alec had asked why they had built such nice new condos on top of the old, decrepit-looking buildings. Nadovich just looked at his younger cousin, not bothering to explain the concept of fine old-world architecture. The time had come when the United States was starting to have fine old buildings to match much of Europe. The constant wars and resettlement had taken a toll on historic structures across the Atlantic. The United States had some historic buildings until things like this happened. The leaders coolly made the decision that housing its citizens was more important than showing off old buildings. Nadovich knew the hard decisions one must make to protect one's people.

The meeting hall where they now gathered was an exception. It had been used by the earliest Americans to plot against the repressive regime of the King George and had since been used by everyone from unionizing laborers to partying policemen. Now the administrators believed it was housing a meeting and party of displaced Eastern Europeans. A Serbian diplomat added credence to the claim.

The three cousins walked into the main door and were stopped by a bulky, burly man who said in Serbian, "You're uglier every time I see you."

Nadovich looked up at the giant man. "Maybe every seventy years is too often."

The big man smiled and reached down and enveloped Nadovich in a bear hug.

Nadovich tried to return the hug, but he was trapped underneath the man's massive arms.

The man released him, smiling.

Nadovich stepped back and said, "My God, I can't believe I used to throw you into the air as a baby."

The big man laughed. "Now that was a long time ago." Even with his size, Nadovich could see his own resemblance to Radko Simolit.

"Radko, these"—he waved an arm toward Alec and Demitri—"are two cousins you have never met. Demitri and Alec Nadin."

Radko laughed out loud. "Nadin, is your father Kanir Simolit?"

Demitri smiled and nodded. "He changed the name to Nadin for many reasons."

Radko rumbled with laughter. "I know some of those reasons. He's a good man." He looked at Alec.

Alec mumbled, "He's my uncle."

"I didn't think he'd ever be able to have children, his balls were so big. How is he?"

Demitri laughed. "Well, he now lives in Belgrade with my mother and youngest brothers."

Radko scooped up both men in another hug as he said, "We are glad you could make it here." He set them down and looked at Nadovich. "Come, Lazlo has been anxious to see you."

They walked together through the crowd in the hall as Nadovich recognized some faces and had to stop several times to deliver hugs or kisses to relatives he had not seen in many years. Finally he stood in front of the oldest of all the Simolits living in the United States. Lazlo Simolit had emigrated in the mid-years of the nineteenth century. He had fought as a Union officer in the last year of the American Civil War, he had served as a naval officer under another name during the Spanish-American War, he had returned to Europe in 1917 as a foot soldier, then stayed in his native Serbia until he joined the American army again to fight the Nazis. In all, he had seen more combat than any other single U.S. military man. He had killed more of the nation's enemies than a squadron of fighter pilots and had given up more years of his life to combat than anyone. But the U.S. immigration office still believed Lazlo Simolit was a semiliterate plumber from the Czech Republic. And he enjoyed them thinking that.

Now Lazlo Simolit smiled as he saw Nadovich approach. Nadovich was a little surprised to see that all the years of conflict and his years of worrying about the Simolit clan had taken a toll on him. Although he was much older than Nadovich, he looked to be in his mid-fifties with graying temples and wrinkles around his eyes. Nadovich had seen some of his scars from the various wars. Wounds so severe that even his genetic ability to heal had been unable to eliminate all evidence of the violence.

Lazlo stood up and held out his arms.

Nadovich embraced him and was surprised that both he and the old man were crying. They parted and Nadovich glanced at his cousins only to be surprised again to see the giant Radko crying at the sight of two of the elders seeing each other for the first time in years.

Lazlo spoke English because it was his custom and he had spent so much time studying it and losing all trace of an accent. "I hear much about your abilities, Tiget. I'm glad to see you have plans."

"I'm only doing what you taught me."

"I've taught many but few have done better for our people. Come and sit with me." He motioned to a chair and flicked his head to dismiss Radko and the others.

"You have made me very proud, Tiget. Everyone knows that you're a leader. There are some who want to move to that wasteland you live in." He smiled, still possessing perfect teeth.

"That wasteland, Laz, is perfect for our needs."

"Please explain it to me because I don't see it."

"First of all, the southern tip is not particularly wanted by anyone. Sure, people might be outraged, but deep down most will say, 'Thank God, it wasn't Orlando.' Secondly, its location makes it isolated. With no planes arriving, one rail line and surrounded by rough, storm-prone water, it's like being on an island."

"What about the Miami Quarantine Zone?"

"We intend to annex the upper half of it and, believe me, we will not be like the U.S. government dealing with border violators. They will get the message quickly that we want no visitors from the south."

Lazlo smiled. "You may end up being more a messiah than a simple leader."

Nadovich couldn't keep from smiling. He had considered that himself.

Lazlo continued. "With a legacy like that you need to finally marry and create heirs."

Nadovich put his hand on the older man's shoulder and said, "I have heirs, Lazlo. Have no fear."

EIGHTEEN

In the parking lot of the restaurant Tom Wilner slowed his quick pace as he approached his Honda Hive-GUV. Shelby had made a call just outside the restaurant and he had told her he'd pick her up. The light mist that was now falling would give her bare shoulders a chill, so he thought he'd be polite.

He reached into the pocket of his slacks, under his sports coat, and dug for the keys as he walked. He found himself whistling and he didn't even realize it until a man's voice said, "Nice song there, canary."

Wilner's head snapped to the sound of the man's voice. Instantly he knew that it was one of the Hispanic men he had seen through the window at dinner and that he and his two visible friends had bad intentions. He let his hand linger in his pocket, knowing that his off-duty weapon, a small conventional pistol that some would consider an antique, but would handle a few street robbers, was in his waistband on his right hip.

All three men continued to move closer, spreading out as they approached.

Wilner backed against the car and said, "I'll give you my cash so you can run your ass back to the quarantine zone."

"What makes you think we're from the zone?"

"Because punks like you would either be on a penal farm or in the military if you lived up here."

The man let out a laugh and lunged at Wilner with surprising speed.

Wilner grabbed the pistol that was tucked inside his pants on his rear, right hip, but the hammer of the old SIG Sauer auto-pistol snagged on his pants.

He tugged hard on the gun, feeling his slacks tear just as the man reached him with his fist. Wilner slipped the punch, pulled his small gun free and whacked the man across the cheek with the barrel of the gun.

The man stumbled back, stunned by the blow, but the other two were on him just as fast. The first one swung a three foot piece of steel that caught the barrel of the small gun and knocked it to the ground.

Wilner grabbed that man by the arms, not wanting to give him a chance to swing his odd weapon at him. The other man threw a body tackle on Wilner, and all three went to the ground.

In the scuffle on the ground, looking between one of the men's legs, Wilner saw a fourth thug help up the one that he had struck with his pistol. He didn't like the odds the way they were now, but as he struggled, he felt one man on top of him simply go limp. He looked past him and saw Shelby Hahn standing above him with a broken bottle and the bloody man on the ground had glass stuck in his hair.

He was able to throw a knee into the groin of the other

thug trying to pin him down. As he worked his way to his feet, still a little dazed from the blows, he saw Shelby turn on one of the remaining attackers. She faked with a punch, then delivered a brutal round kick to the man's head. As he stumbled to one side from the kick, she spun and landed another powerful kick on his ribs, throwing him back and to the ground in a heap. Her decisive and graceful movements were mesmerizing. He didn't even move to help because she obviously needed no help as she turned to the last man left standing. The thug backed away from her as Shelby matched him step for step like a predator stalking a small animal.

Wilner followed along, interested in what was going to become of the attacker from the quarantine zone.

Shelby let out a slight, easy smile as she laid a straight right cross against the man's face. Before he could fall she followed up with a left hook to his body. Her bare shoulders and arms tensed with each blow, showing off her muscles and form.

Then Wilner heard a shot. He turned and realized the original attacker, the leader of this little group, had picked up Wilner's pistol and fired once in the air. Now he was strolling carefully toward Shelby with the gun pointed at both of them.

"We tried to be quick and easy, but now we're out of time."

Wilner said, "Okay, my wallet is in my back pocket." He reached slowly for it.

"No, man, you don't understand. We're not here for money."

Wilner felt his stomach spasm. The thought of these men taking Shelby made him ready to risk a close-up shot from his own pistol. He had seen women after they were raped in Serbia. He had even taken personal action against a rapist in Belgrade. That had resulted in his court-martial, but he'd do it again if he had the chance. No way these guys would get the chance tonight. He readied himself to leap at the man with the pistol.

Then the man said, "We want the board."

Wilner paused, confused. "What board?"

"Don't play games. The circuit board."

Now Wilner looked at the whole situation differently. Whatever that board went to, it was valuable. People had gone to a lot of money and trouble to get it back. He said, "I don't know what you're talking about."

The man didn't hesitate to grab Shelby and place the pistol to her head.

Wilner tried to stick to his story, but that shook him.

He held up his hands and said, "Wait, wait. I know what board you're talking about."

"Where is it?" asked the man.

Wilner was about to say the UPF office, but they'd know it was a lie. He couldn't risk Shelby.

Shelby yelled, "Don't tell them, Tom. It's not worth it. This isn't what you think."

The man screwed the gun tighter into Shelby's light-brown hair. The hammer of the pistol was already back from the shot he'd fired in the air.

Wilner wanted to kill that man right now worse than anything he had ever wanted to do.

Steve Besslia had his service pistol jammed in his waistband as he searched the stacks of magazine and newspapers looking for the clues he needed to prove his theories to Tom Wilner. He had been scared since the day he had found the men in his condo. The thing that really bothered him was that he had shot at them so many times with such little effect. The more he considered the intruders and their abilities, the more convinced he was that he was right. They were not human.

He had spent the evening searching for information on aliens, specifically the aliens from mu Arae who had told everyone they were coming. But what if they had sent agents already? Maybe a long time ago. Sent agents to scout and prepare for something big.

There was no shortage of conspiracy theories about the aliens. The Internet was full of them. Although the Internet had undergone serious changes to adapt to terrorism, child molesters, financial fraud and invasions of privacy, there was still a place for someone interested in aliens, Bigfoot or lost dinosaurs.

That fact that he was scared unsettled him. In the army he was a clerk who never saw action. In fact, the only overseas duty he saw was in England where he helped process marriage and immigration requests for all the soldiers who had met women or found family members that wanted to come to the United States. Just before the total ban on immigration the government allowed family members of people in the military, who were willing to join the U.S. Army, a chance to immigrate to the United States.

With most of the world shattered by disease and monetary crises, people were still willing to fight to come to America.

Most of the world had been in trouble when the United States did what everyone was screaming for: mind its own business. Once the military had pulled back and U.S. aid had dried up, then the problems started in earnest. Without oversight, farming procedures went to hell. E. coli grew into the roots of produce because there wasn't sufficient sanitation. Mad cow disease swept through South America when they continued to feed meal made with cow meat to raise new cattle.

That was what weakened several of the countries enough to allow President Hugo Chavez of Venezuela to offer aid and troops to keep the locals quiet. Before long he had made pacts with insurgents in several countries and had control of 40 percent of the continent in an instant.

That was one time people were happy the jihadists were around. Because of their need to sell their own oil, attacks on Venezuela to cut oil production also caused unrest in the people. When Chavez made a feeble attempt to fight back by detaining all Arabs in the countries he controlled, he was hit with such a savage round of bombings that his government was crippled. In a month he went from the leader of South America to hanging upside-down with his mistress in front of the presidential palace.

Steve Besslia was happy he had never seen combat. He liked that just the sight of his UPF badge had scared away a number of potential problems. He had not known fear until last night. Now his fear was not just personal but more global. What if these guys were the vanguard of an invasion? What if they were already in government and the military? He had no way of knowing how many were on Earth. The worst aspect of it was that no one would believe him if he started telling people. Even his friend Tom Wilner clearly had thought he was just distraught.

And if he did start spreading his theory, how long would it be before the aliens tried to silence him? The UPF didn't give him support to do his job. They certainly wouldn't be worth a shit in something like this.

Then, in one of the news magazines, he found a story that made him straighten up inside the small garage. It had a photo of the Uralian spaceship as it slowly passed monitors in the farthest reaches of the universe. On the bottom of the photo were large red letters. SETI. It almost sounded familiar; an organization that stood for the Search for Extra-Terrestrial Intelligence. He knew the group had worked side by side with NASA before the agency had gone belly-up fifteen years ago. The interest in killing fellow Earthlings had eclipsed the need to explore space and funding had died out. So had the interest in extraterrestrial life. Until about six years ago when the first message from the Uralians came. Now money was flowing into the International Space Organization or ISO. But that agency's mission was more in communication and long-range surveillance than space travel. There was no need to travel when our neighbors were coming to us.

Just like there was no need to search for extraterrestrial intelligence when it was calling you up and saying they were on the way.

As he flipped through the pages he noticed that one of their former leaders, an MIT scientist named Curt Fonger, now ran the "mystery of the universe" planetarium for the only outfit with money for something like that: Walt Disney World. Three hours away in Orlando.

That wasn't too far away. Especially if he talked his friend Tom into coming with him.

NINETEEN

Tom Wilner was in a rare position. He didn't know what to do. He knew what he wanted to do. He wanted to tear into these assholes and leave parts of them all across the street. This empty parking lot offered no cover and no help. There were very few people left in the restaurant and if some of them did bother to call the UPF he doubted anyone would show up in time to be any help whatsoever. Most important, they had Shelby.

The man with the gun to her head yelled to him, "It's simple. Tell us where the board is and I'll release her. No problems."

Wilner stared at him silently, thinking of a tactical alternative.

The man tightened his grip round Shelby's neck, jamming the gun hard enough to tilt her head. "If not, you can say goodbye to your girlfriend here."

Shelby said, in an amazingly calm voice, "Don't do it, Tom. It'll be all right."

But Wilner knew it wouldn't be. He could clearly see that this man was a killer and about to shoot Shelby Hahn in the head. Wilner felt his whole body sag as he said, "It's in the door of the van."

"Tom, no," Shelby cried out, but the man tightened his arm around her neck. Another young, Hispanic man opened the door to Wilner's Hive-van. He paused and looked at Wilner.

The UPF cop was resigned. "Pull on the panel of the driver's side door."

The man leaned down and yanked on the door handle with the door braced against his leg. The interior panel popped off in his hand. When he stood up he was smiling and had the circuit board in his hand.

The man with Shelby relaxed his grip slightly. "Smart, very smart." He released Shelby and stepped back a few paces, still pointing the gun at the federal agent.

Wilner said, "Who sent you for the board?"

"Someone who doesn't need to deal with you."

"You got it, now go on your way."

Then Wilner saw a flurry of movement and heard the gun go off. He felt sick thinking that Shelby had tried something stupid and this creep had just shot her.

Mrs. Honzit sat at the small, antique dinner table with Emma and Tommy across from her as they played one of the new holographic board games. This one was like the old classic, Risk, only it was called Empire and players had to use strategy to block other nations from gaining access to natural resources. She loved seeing the children's faces light up when they made a good defensive move. Mrs. Honzit challenged them so they could learn their potential and prepare for the future.

She had eaten the same dinner with them because there were no synthetics in it. She had found real green beans, an actual Idaho potato and goat meat, which wasn't as tasty as cow or lamb, but it was natural and the hardiness of goats made them more and more popular.

Now, as she relaxed, she wondered how the children's father was doing on his first date in years. He wouldn't call it a date, but she could see it in his eyes. He had a thing for this Department of Homeland Security agent. She was pretty in a mid-American kind of way, but a little pale as far as Mrs. Honzit was concerned and needed bigger bosoms. She was cute and athletic, if you liked that kind.

As she watched Tommy consider his options after moving an army into the Sinai to block the formation of an Islamic state, she froze. From the corner of her eye, using her excellent vision, she saw a movement outside through the main sliding glass door. She was certain the door was locked as was the front door. Since the day the house had been searched she had always been sure to lock up to show Wilner how careful she was. Appearances aside, she took her responsibility to the children very seriously. She would never allow anyone to harm them.

She wasn't sure what to do, keeping her eyes up toward the door without being obvious about looking. She did this until she heard Emma's voice say, "It's your turn, Mrs. Honzit."

She shook her head as if she had been in a daze and said, "What's that, dear?"

The little girl smiled and asked, "Were you asleep?"

"No, dear." She stroked the young girl's beautiful, dark face. She looked just like her mother. "I was just thinking."

"Tommy didn't stop the jihadists, so it's your turn."

The housekeeper smiled as she pushed the electronic, random dice ball and waited as the red lighted number tumbled past, stopping on nine. She examined the board and her options. Her army was small but modern. She liked to make neutral moves so the children had a chance to move more freely.

As soon as she looked up from the board she saw the figure of a person move again. This time they were on the patio just behind the sliding glass door.

She couldn't wait until it was too late. She stood from the chair and said, "I'll be right back, children." She walked slowly into the kitchen, opened the second drawer and pulled out the longest knife she could find. She draped a dishrag over it to hide it from the children.

She walked out the other side of the kitchen, away from Tommy and Emma and moved as casually as she could to the side of the sliding glass door. She didn't want to alarm the children, but she had a surprise for anyone on the other side of the door.

Then she saw the figure again. There was someone outside and they were approaching the sliding glass door.

The sound of a gun going off was enough to make Wilner's knees go weak. Not that the sound bothered him so much, but the sound when the gun was pointed at Shelby Hahn made him sick to his stomach as he froze, then looked at the man with the gun. He was pointing it toward the van, away from Shelby. He had fired at someone else. Shelby appeared unharmed as Wilner started to close the distance on the shooter; she didn't hesitate, she kicked the man with the gun so hard he flew forward and the force knocked the little conventional pistol out of his hand.

Wilner didn't wait for him to recover from the surprise kick and threw his whole body into him as the man tried to stand up. He heard the air rush out and the thug grunt, "Umph," as he struck the ground with Wilner's one hundred and ninety pounds on top of him.

Wilner rolled off the downed man to find his next target, but hesitated as he saw Shelby step up and throw a hard right cross to a man's jaw. He staggered and hit the ground. From the other direction he heard a cry of pain and spun.

Then he realized what the one thug had fired the pistol at: Johann Halleck stood with the largest of the robbers twisted in his hands like a piece of rubber. When Johann released the large man he splayed out onto the parking lot's rough surface like a limp fish fillet.

The fourth man, the one with the circuit board, didn't want any part of this and turned on his heel and started to run at an extraordinary pace out the entrance of the parking lot.

Johann started to gallop toward him, his big body faster than Wilner would've thought.

A car rolled past the running man and slowly made its way toward Wilner and Shelby. A long assault rifle barrel popped out the window and started to fire as Wilner dove onto Shelby and fell behind a parked car.

Taking quick peeks around the end of the car, Wilner saw the three injured men pile into the backseat of the vehicle. A few seconds later it was out of the lot. Then they heard a few more shots and the squeal of tires a few blocks away.

Johann Halleck came walking back through the entrance a minute later. It was clear he had lost the man.

As he approached them, Johann said, "Why did you give him the board?"

Wilner stepped toward the larger man. "Because they were

going to kill her." He pointed at Shelby. "Which you didn't seem to care about by rushing in here when there was a gun pointed at her."

"The board is what matters."

Wilner said, "Maybe to you guys, but there are some things more important. I've known men like you. Someone who doesn't value your own life so you'll risk everyone else's." He had to catch his breath. He stepped back. "Life means something to me. Even your life. I've seen enough killing."

Johann seemed unconcerned, even distracted, as he craned his neck to see if he saw a speeding car on any of the roads running close to the restaurants.

Wilner grabbed him by the arm. "Don't you get it? You could've gotten her killed."

Johann shook his head. "Now you might've gotten everyone killed."

TWENTY

Mrs. Honzit gripped the large butcher knife tightly as she took a second to recognize the person outside the door. At first she was struck by the feminine form of the big breasts and tight stomach, then the dark hair and oval eyes forced her to let out a sigh.

Finally Svala had come to visit her children.

Mrs. Honzit unlocked the sliding door and pressed the automatic open button. With a slight whir the door slid open.

Svala just stood there silently, her eyes cutting between Mrs. Honzit and the children.

Tommy and Emma were still concentrating on the game and hadn't noticed her yet.

Mrs. Honzit finally said, "Are you coming in or not?"

Svala stepped inside and as soon as she did Tommy looked up and screamed, "Mommy!" He was off the floor, darting for her before his sister even turned around. A few seconds later, Emma joined them in a tight, silent hug.

Mrs. Honzit stepped back as Svala crouched to embrace

the children. She didn't much care for a woman who would leave her children. Even if she knew the reasons behind leaving Tom Wilner, but these two beautiful children? She'd never comprehend that.

For whatever reason, God had not seen fit for Mrs. Honzit to have any children. Yet. She was over her mourning for her husband who was incinerated by a Bosnian firebomb that went off in Srebrenica where they were living. Her late husband had brought her back to Serbia even though her family still lived mainly in Turkey. Since she was also an Orthodox Catholic there was little recrimination. Had she been a Muslim, God knows what would have become of her.

Now she watched as the children were all smiles. She felt a tinge of jealousy that she spent the most time with these children and this whore could walk right in and steal them away.

That was life.

It had been more difficult than Nadovich had imagined to cross the quarantine line into New York City. On this border all the attention was focused on keeping people out, not keeping people in the zone. There was no illegal traffic that was secretly condoned by the National Guardsmen like there was at the Miami Quarantine Zone. The government believed Manhattan to be a virtual wasteland now. Their only concern was keeping looters out. Although anyone who went in for longer than a few hours came out with radiation sickness.

Nadovich and Radko Simolit traveled together, leaving Alec and Demitri to enjoy the family whom they had spent little time with. The giant Radko agreed to take Nadovich through the perimeter into the city. The waterway was patrolled both by boat and on foot on the far side of the water.

The bridges were all guarded and the Lincoln and Holland Tunnels blocked except for foot traffic regulated by local military personnel. The army and National Guardsmen had a handle on the situation. The only visitors were either military or scientific personnel.

The soldiers here looked fresher and more alert than those around the Miami Quarantine Zone in Florida. He knew that the troops in Florida were spread thin and many had to commit to longer stays in the army or National Guard. The government didn't send criminals to quarantine zones. They were all sent to combat zones. No one had raised much of an argument about it once the casualty lists from the first Iranian war started rolling in. Americans became nostalgic for the relatively light casualties of the second Iraq war at the start of the new millennium.

Now with the seven quarantine zones set up in the country and borders closed with Mexico and Canada the need for troops domestically was growing as well.

Nadovich had not followed the example of Lazlo Simolit and joined any country's military. He fought causes, not wars. His greatest success was resistance against the Nazis. They were also the greatest threat to his people. With the German fascination on experiments, they had inadvertently picked up one of his family members and realized who was living under their dominion. They had plans for the Simolits. Thank God they were stopped and both the Hallecks and the Simolits had been able to use their influence to destroy the information and silence the two doctors involved in the discovery.

Nadovich had started with a core of his own people and recruited from the Serbian population. They hated the invading Germans. They also hated anyone who helped them, which led to renewed hostilities with the Croatians who were spread out among them. He knew a little about military tactics, but this was the first time he had ever employed them. It was also the most responsibility he had ever taken. He had lived among the humans, not paying a great deal of attention to their minor squabbles or concerns until he saw panzer tanks rolling into Belgrade.

He had fought out of a sense of outrage, but found that he liked leading. He liked the respect it gained him. Both among the humans and his own people. The Nazis taught him how low humans can sink, but the resistance fighters made him care about what happened to them. He learned quickly that his decisions cost lives. Usually the others, but some of his own people as well. The weapons employed by the Nazis were devastating and they didn't do things halfway.

He didn't feel compelled to volunteer for any of the U.S. military services. He definitely wouldn't want to end up guarding a border. Luckily they had people in the government who had managed to get Nadovich out of his required service after he was made a citizen. He would not have done well being told what to do by humans.

Radko spoke with one of the soldiers at the entrance to the Holland Tunnel, then slipped him a wad of U.S suds. The giant turned and motioned for Nadovich to come to him.

Radko nodded to the young soldiers and then started down the tunnel on foot fast enough for Nadovich to have to jog to catch him. The dim emergency lights cast long, faded shadows across the dirty floor of the tunnel. The air was stale and thick.

Nadovich asked, "Are we under a time constraint?"

"Only that we get back across while these two are on

duty. We have until seven this evening or we must wait until at least seven in the morning. We're not going too far from here on foot."

As they crossed the tunnel, Nadovich couldn't help but think of the skyline he had seen many times. In those days New York was the place to be. He had seen a Broadway show, visited the Empire State Building when it was still the tallest building in the world. He had even made it to the top of the World Trade Center before the first 9/11 attack.

Now the quiet city was all but forgotten. No residents for six years; the target of numerous attacks. The Empire State Building still stood, but the Chrysler Building was missing its ornate top from the 9/11 attack two years before the nuclear bomb was detonated. In the attack on the Chrysler Building a cleaning crew made up of mostly jihadists had managed to smuggle in and store high-explosives for months in the top of the building. It was a quiet September morning, because by then all 9/11 attacks were quiet. No one wanted to risk being in public when an attack came. The terrorists detonated the explosives remotely, devastating the top of the building. Then, as the rescue workers arrived, they opened fire with old assault rifles, killing thirty-five firemen and twenty-six cops. The response had been monumental. The countries of origin for each of the attackers were immediately bombed by the U.S. Air Force. The new "citizen responsibility" doctrine had been established and every country knew they could be held responsible for the terrorist acts of their citizens. This had been the pretext for several invasions launched by the United States.

As they exited the tunnel, Nadovich took a deep breath. The city air didn't smell much better than the tunnel. Nadovich looked up at a building with scaffolding that had not been used to finish the project. Once the city was no longer fit for human life no one cared what was finished or repaired.

At a subway entrance, Radko pulled Nadovich to the stairs. As they descended he had the feeling he was dizzy. Then he froze and saw why.

"My God, Radko, is that what I think it is?"

The big man grunted and nodded. "Disgusting, no?"

"Is there anything that can be done about it?"

"Not so far."

Nadovich stood transfixed on the stairs, watching the walls and floor move with waves of cockroaches. Millions of them, all along the subway tunnel.

Nadovich shook his head. "I don't think I want to make this trip after all." He had seen enough of the new "Northern Homeland."

Radko chuckled. "Follow me. It's fine, you'll see." He stepped down onto the subway platform and walked straight ahead. It was a trail free of insects.

"How is that done?"

"They lay a path of insecticide. With free run of everywhere else they avoid this little patch of ground.

Nadovich followed him to the end of the platform and saw two men waiting with an odd vehicle that looked like a very short, low subway train.

Radko smiled and said, "Now the tour really starts."

By the time Wilner had dropped off Shelby at the hotel where she was staying in the Northern Enclave, near the restaurant where they had been assaulted, he was exhausted. He had not even bothered calling it into the UPF. Even he knew they wouldn't do anything about it and his boss would probably just assign him the case.

Johann Halleck had been evasive about how he knew to be there and why the board was so valuable. He had made a quick exit, clearly upset with Wilner for giving up the board to save Shelby's life.

For her part, she was remarkably calm about the whole incident. She wanted to work with him to track the gang and recover the board. He wanted to find the gang again, but the board was only a peripheral reason.

As he entered his front door he was surprised to see both of the kids still awake. There was no school tomorrow so he was not concerned about it, but Mrs. Honzit rarely budged on things like bedtime and eating right.

The children jumped off the couch and ran to him. It was half a ploy to stay up a little longer, but Wilner didn't mind.

Tommy looked up at his father and said, "We had a visitor."

Wilner immediately jerked his head up to Mrs. Honzit. With all the odd occurrences he wanted to know everything was all right. She smiled and nodded.

"Who came by?" He wasn't expecting the answer.

Both kids said in unison, "Mommy."

He hesitated, his guts hurting like he had just seen her again. He smiled as best he could and said, "Did she now. That's nice." He wanted to say, "Did she explain where the hell she'd been the past sixteen months?" But he remained silent.

Emma said, "She says we'll see more of her now that she's settled."

Again he remained silent, thinking she's been settled for a while. He also wondered if Nadovich knew she was coming over.

He knew who was behind all the fuss over the circuit

boards. It may be time to pay Mr. Tiget Nadovich a visit. An unofficial visit where he was not acting under the authority of the UPF and not necessarily following their guidelines.

His V-com beeped and he pulled it off his belt. Steve Besslia's face came into sharp focus.

Wilner said, "What's up?"

"We need to go to Orlando."

"I can't, I'm on a case."

"This is related to our case."

Wilner thought about Besslia's use of the word *our* and said, "Talk to me, pal."

Shelby Hahn waved goodbye as Tom Wilner drove his cute Hive-van away. She had given him a sensuous kiss good night and hoped it wouldn't affect their working relationship because, as much as she liked the handsome detective, she knew she'd need a good cop with her more.

He had acted crazy earlier when he gave up the circuit board. She knew he did it because of her, but he needed to get a glimpse of the big picture and what they had to stop from happening. She didn't know exactly what would happen, but Tiget Nadovich had dangerous ambitions.

She immediately went to her nice room at the chain-run hotel. It was one of the few left in south Florida and she thought she might be the only guest for the night. They'd be in for a shock when they discovered she was a federal agent and not going to pay. The government had enacted an amendment to the constitution that allowed military and federal workers on duty to stay at a hotel for free. They didn't have to identify themselves until after the stay. The reasoning was so that they wouldn't be treated differently than any other guest. No one bitched much about a soldier that spent the night for free, but hotels would often tell men and women in uniform that they were booked for the night so they didn't have to give away a room.

Shelby was harder to identify. No one ever thought she was a cop. Especially a Department of Homeland Security agent. Now she searched some of the databases she had linked to from her computer. In the quiet of the room she used voice commands to zip through all the databases available to her.

She started with known Miami Quarantine Zone smugglers between the ages of thirty and forty. Then found one of her attackers. His name was Jose Quintana. She then started looking through online photos of Quintana's associates. It wasn't too long before she found Fredrico Rea. That was the guy with the bushy mustache who had held the gun to her head. She remembered his smell; a combination of cheap chili and exotic fruit like papaya. He had no noticeable accent. According to the information available to her, he had been expelled after Puerto Rico's independence and had repeatedly crossed the border. Once the quarantine zone had been established he was believed to have been in three different shoot-outs with national guardsmen. He also had an intelligence report on him that said he lived in the old section known as North Miami Beach in an abandoned apartment complex he shared with members of his gang, the Zone Troopers.

The only question was if she would bring Wilner with her. He was awfully handy and probably knew his way around the zone. But she didn't want to argue with him about the board again. He was going to have to realize that she intended to keep it. That way she knew it was safe.

TWENTY-ONE

Tiget Nadovich rode in the small car that the inhabitants of Manhattan had constructed out of an old official subway train. This one had nine seats, one of them for the conductor up front. He and Radko sat with a short, intense man with dark features who had introduced himself as Arnald Simolit. Nadovich was unfamiliar with the man, but his intelligent eyes held Nadovich's attention as the train moved at a slow, but steady, rate.

Arnald had no discernible accent as he explained the transportation used in the city. Many Simolits, including Nadovich himself, still had an edge on their precise English. It was the product of learning a number of languages over a long period of time. When under stress Nadovich's accent became more pronounced.

"We have twenty-two of these cars with more than thirty coming online. The biggest problem is the battery packs, which must be recharged once a day."

Nadovich had many questions, but asked, "Where do you get your power?"

"All solar from the panels we've installed on a number of buildings. Our contacts on the outside and with the U.S. government have diverted thousands of the new, high-capacity solar panels."

As the train moved, a grate in the ceiling cast light down on the walkway alongside the track. Three people stood in the ray of light: a woman, a younger man and a child. The little subway car moved slowly enough that Nadovich could clearly see their features as they watched the passing train. Their hollow faces and lifeless eyes followed the slow train as it passed. All were thin beyond comprehension. The woman instinctively pulled the child closer to her. Nadovich could not even determine if the child was a boy or a girl. It gave him the feel of the ghettos the Nazis set up.

Arnald said, "Pay them no mind. They are everywhere."

"Who are they?"

"Humans who decided to stay."

"And they survive?"

"Some do."

"But what about the radiation?"

"It killed many at first, but we think that these humans are not affected as much. They die a slower death by starvation and other disease."

"Why don't they leave?"

"The quarantine zone for one thing. The soldiers shoot them as they approach the checkpoints. Most have nowhere else to go. Some have even started working for us."

"Are you trying to help any of these people?" He pointed at the three people on the walkway as they faded in the distance.

Arnald looked at him and said, "No. Why? They're not part of us."

"But it just doesn't seem right." Nadovich didn't realize he could be moved to concern for humans.

"You sound like a Halleck. Tiget, my new friend, don't lose sight of what must be done to ensure our survival."

Nadovich nodded as the train slowed, then stopped at another station. There was more light and fewer cockroaches; maybe a hundred thousand.

Nadovich looked around and said, "Can't you use pesticide?"

"That is something we're working on. The main insect population is down here. Up above, we have problems with rats."

"Oh, that's comforting." Nadovich looked at Radko to see if he felt the same way. The big man shrugged and shook his head in a commiseration.

They trotted up the stairs to the surface. The sun was so bright it cast reflections off many of the buildings that were near blinding. Nadovich was not used to such bright sunshine down in Florida. For more than fifteen years, as the climate shifted in directions no one had expected, the temperature had continued to drop and clouds become more constant over the southern half of Florida.

As they started to walk down Forty-ninth Street they approached Broadway and Nadovich realized he was looking at a deserted and dark Times Square. Arnald motioned them down the street and they turned on Forty-eighth. They stopped in front of a hotel with the sign still intact: THE EDISON.

Arnald said, "This is our main administrative building. These older hotels have excellent ventilation, good foundations and thick walls. We like this area of the city." He pushed through a revolving door into a lobby with a number of people inside, all in consultation or working on some project. "Come, we have much to discuss."

Nadovich followed the smaller man, but let his gaze wander all through the nicely refurbished hotel.

Johann Halleck shook his head as he thought about how silly the UPF cop had been. Did he think it was gallant to give up the circuit board? After all the combat that guy had seen was he really worried about one woman's life? He obviously didn't know the importance of the last board and what Johann would do to keep it out of Tiget Nadovich's hands.

Johann had to get to the board before Nadovich. He knew that Nadovich and his two cousins, Demitri and Alec were traveling to Philadelphia for a meeting of all the Simolit family. That was a meeting where Johann would like to plant his own bomb. It would solve many of the world's problems. But the treaty between the Simolits and Hallecks had forbidden direct attacks on gatherings like that. Johann didn't think the Simolits would live up to it and was on edge anytime he met with members of his own clan. But he didn't sign treaties and he didn't intend to break them.

He'd find the board with the men who took it. If not for the cop's sensibilities he would've captured and questioned one of the men that night. But he didn't want to give too much away to the UPF detective.

Johann had not been in the Miami Quarantine Zone in some time and knew that was where this gang would end up living. He could use a change. Living so quietly in south

Florida for so long had grown dull. He had to pace himself as most of his kind did. Theirs was a life spread over vast periods of time, not like a human's life span. He had seen others burn out taking up the causes of nations and not those of their family's. He had seen others perish in firestorms of bombs, hail of heavy weapons fire and even blows with swords. But sometimes, as he sat in his lonely living room at night he wondered what was worse. Horrible, unnecessary death or long, lonely lives spent in search of another.

Tom Wilner had listened to Steve Besslia babble about his theory the entire drive up to Orlando. Once they had cleared the Northern Enclave he was surprised how much traffic had picked up. Still nowhere near the jammed highways of the old Florida but many more than down in the Lawton District. He had agreed to come with Besslia because of the man's near obsession with his theory that they were dealing with aliens of some kind. Wilner knew it was ridiculous because Tiget Nadovich was involved as well. Wilner hoped this so-called expert on extraterrestrial life who ran the Disney planetarium would be able to convince Besslia of the foolishness of his position.

Since they were still technically off duty and were traveling way outside the confines of the UPF district they were both assigned to, Wilner had opted to drive his personal Hive-van.

Besslia said, "I'm tellin' ya, Willie, we may be able to break this wide open."

"You mean this alien conspiracy?"

"Exactly. We'll get the proof we need."

"And if there's no proof, will you give up the idea?"

"You still don't believe me, do you? After all the thought I put into this. There's no other explanation. I'm tellin' ya I shot those guys five or six times each. You saw the guy who was slashed with the knife at the bar. He shouldn't have walked away from that."

Wilner nodded as he agreed with those two points.

"And you still don't believe."

They made the final leg of the trip in silence.

The Disney planetarium was part of the Disney Space Center. The Space Center along with Disney World and Epcot constituted the largest and most visited tourist location in the world. The sprawling complex included a roller-coaster, high-tech video games that fired low energy lasers so if you were playing and were hit by a laser you felt it, and the cavernous planetarium, which was the largest structure in Florida now that NASA had shut down and the main facilities had been demolished.

Disney had bought much of the surplus NASA equipment. The original speculation was that the giant corporation with nearly as many resources as the government would attempt its own space exploration program. Instead, they turned the government's old junk into a money-making machine of an attraction. To his credit, the Disney chairman had used the company's resources to pick up the slack in the country's education system now that the government's main focus was war and terrorism. Disney had become the seal of excellence in education, providing scholarships to virtually any deserving student.

Wilner and Besslia showed their identification at the gate and were directed to the administration building to talk to

Curt Fonger, the curator. Instead of the direct route, they wandered to the line to get in the planetarium. The line started to move just as they approached and Wilner just followed everyone inside. Why not, he had always wanted to see it, and it was, possibly, part of his duty right now.

TWENTY-TWO

Tom Wilner was sorry he had not brought his kids as he sat through the show at the Disney Planetarium. It started off with how the universe was viewed over the past centuries and why, as late as the turn of this century, people still thought the universe consisted of nine planets with Pluto as the farthest. Better optics and broad-thinking physicists had changed things slowly until the message from the Urailians. Then the universe seemed to explode. Soon scientists were talking about a million planets that could be called Earth's neighbors.

The show included the garbled binary message first sent by the approaching aliens, followed by a narration from a deep-voiced actor who also made commercials for the new vision improvement drugs offered by different pharmaceutical companies. In his voice the aliens sounded elegant and graceful. In fact, aside from the pleasant content of the messages, there was no way to tell anything about the aliens except that they were advanced enough to travel farther than man had ever considered.

After the show, as the lights came up, a tall man with thick black hair stepped up onto the stage and introduced himself to the crowd as Curt Fonger, curator of the planetarium. He took a few questions on the approaching aliens. Then went on to discuss the nature of the universe from which the aliens originated.

Wilner doubted he ever got questions about anything but the aliens.

As the show ended and people started to file out, Wilner and Besslia kept their eyes on the curator and fought against the streaming crowd to get down to the stage where the tall astronomer was talking with a young female tour guide.

Wilner got in closer to the man and held up his ID. "Mr. Fonger, could we have a few minutes?"

The curator squinted at the badge then straightened as he realized it wasn't some private security police hired by a ritzy homeowner's association. Most people didn't have to deal with the Unified Police Force.

"Sure, sure," said Fonger, motioning Wilner and Besslia to follow him. They all walked down a narrow hallway then turned into an area where offices lined each side of the hall.

The curator turned into the third office and Wilner followed. They took seats with Fonger behind his small desk.

"What can I do for the UPF?"

Wilner hesitated, but Besslia was less embarrassed. "We have some questions about aliens."

The curator nodded. "You mean the Urailians?"

"Yes."

"You know that's not their real name. Just an easy media fix that the Russians pushed to honor their astronomer." He didn't wait for acknowledgment from the two cops. "What do the police want to know about a race that won't arrive for another four years and eight months?"

"Will it take that long?"

"That's our calculation."

Besslia was silent and the curator looked from one cop to the other.

"Why? Do you know something I don't?" He smiled, but was still unsure of himself.

Besslia said, "You used to be the head of SETI weren't you?"

Fonger hesitated like he was being questioned about his association with a jihadist group. "I was the president of it many years ago."

"Are you involved with them now?"

"No."

"May I ask why?"

"For one thing, they are not particularly relevant anymore and for another"—he paused and looked out the door as if he were checking on spies—"Disney would fire me if I spoke with them anymore."

"Why?"

"Because Disney has a corporate image that doesn't buck conventional wisdom."

"Wisdom such as?"

"The aliens and if this is their first visit?"

Besslia stood up like he'd just seen his team score. "I knew it. I knew it."

Wilner said, "Calm down. Let's hear what Mr. Fonger has to say."

The curator was staring at Besslia. "Have you seen them? Are they here?"

Besslia sat on the edge of the chair and leaned in close to the planetarium curator. "Tell me, Mr. Fonger, could they have been here for years? I mean hypothetically."

Wilner realized immediately that Besslia had found a conspiracy soul mate. This guy wasn't going to talk him out of anything. He was going to reinforce Wilner's goofy friend until he wouldn't be good for anything.

Fonger said, "They could've come here centuries ago."

"And they wouldn't be bound to our concept of a life span."

"They may not even be carbon-based life-forms."

"Would they look like us?"

"If they could adapt, yes."

Besslia took a deep breath and said, "Okay, here's the real question."

The curator looked on like he was watching a revival and very happy to meet a fellow nut.

Besslia said, "Do you think that aliens are here on Earth now?"

"Is this confidential?" asked the curator.

"Absolutely. Just us three."

The curator nodded his head. "I've been getting reports for many years about strange activity."

"Like what?"

"People still living in New York. Men who live to be hundreds of years old."

"So you think aliens are here?"

"Absolutely."

Wilner sank in his seat. But he didn't completely discount the theory. He just didn't want to have to deal with Besslia.

Tiget Nadovich sat at a conference table with ten members of the Simolit family who had moved to New York after most of the human residents had fled.

Arnald spoke for the men and women at the table. Some of whom Nadovich already knew.

"You see, my friends, this was not our plan. We simply took advantage of a situation created by the jihadists. When they found a way to detonate the small nuclear device on the island of Manhattan we saw it as a chance to settle in an area together without interference from any government. The humans that stayed provided us with excellent cover. Now the U.S. government doesn't even want to acknowledge that anyone lives here. It will be several years until we make so much noise and activity that anyone will even notice us."

Nadovich nodded. "You have done a fine job. I like how you all live in this one area."

"Transportation is still an issue."

"What about food?"

"We get some from outside. Much is still in stores throughout the city and we are cultivating vast gardens and livestock pens."

"And the humans still here?"

"As I told you. They work for us. We live together in peace."

"As long as they work for you?"

"That is correct. Is that a problem?"

"No. I just envisioned a homeland with our kind alone. No interference from others."

"Is that what you plan for the southern tip of Florida?"

"Something like that. There is plenty of space for crops and the climate, although a little damp, is very acceptable."

Arnald nodded his head at a man by the door and said to

Nadovich, "We have another possibility for you to keep the humans at bay."

"We're open to all options." He noticed two men walk in with a gurney between them. They wheeled it over to Nadovich.

Arnald said, "Lift the sheet and you'll see what I have in mind."

Nadovich turned in his chair and picked at the dark sheet with two fingers. The smell coming from the gurney was nauseating. He lifted the sheet and realized why. The whole idea was a little sickening, but not without merit. And it had already spread enough fear among the humans that it would bother them.

Shelby Hahn had decided to enter the Miami Quarantine Zone by herself. She just walked up to one of the checkpoints, showed her identification and said she was driving into the zone.

A sergeant with the National Guard said, "I wouldn't do that, ma'am."

"It's okay, I have a gun."

"So does everyone else in there." He looked at her DHS-issued Hive. "They'll also notice the car right away. There are some conventionals that roll around in there, but this will stick out for blocks in every direction."

Shelby smiled and said, "I'll take my chances."

The guardsmen made a show out of moving the blockade and allowing her to drive through. She didn't see anyone as she crossed the bridge over the small canal on a crumbling road that used to be one of the main surface streets from the old Broward County south into the former Dade County. She had seen enough movies to halfway expect hordes of starving people to come flooding out of the brush and empty buildings to envelop her. But that didn't happen. Nothing happened. Other than her driving south until she found an unmarked road that ran east and west. As she approached the intersection she saw several people on the side of the road next to a pile of old, abandoned vehicles.

No one even seemed to look up at her as she turned east. She noticed that two of the corner lots had been completely cleared of building debris and now had wide, colorful vegetable gardens planted in neat rows. As she looked out at the light rain falling, she figured they had no problem with irrigation.

Heading east she saw more and more people, including children, and no one appeared rabid or dangerous. A gas station on another corner was sealed off and had a corral of goats. A sign over the door read GOAT CHEESE FOR SALE. A few cows roamed in a vacant lot as she approached the old Interstate 95 overpass. A car crossed over her, heading south on the interstate. Several old, conventional-gas vehicles crossed side streets as she continued east.

This was a regular community. She could smell exotic food cooking and noticed that the residents were mainly Hispanic and some Caribbean islanders, but they seemed to be getting by fine. It made her wonder why the zone was established in the first place. This was a unique quarantine zone. Unlike the others there were no contaminants here. No nuclear fallout or toxins. These were just people. Aside from the rumors that growlers roamed the streets, spreading their man-made disease, there was no real reason the border couldn't be open.

There were small stores selling produce, old car parts, handmade furniture and even solar-powered generators. With the need for air-conditioning greatly reduced, the houses could be run with much less power. The temperatures had not dropped enough to require heat, so all a house needed was power for a few appliances and lights. The improvements in solar power over the last twenty years had allowed generators to work off relatively small cells. The only problem now was that the Sunshine State had little of it left. The misty clouds covered all of the southern peninsula. Many of the solar-powered cells were, more accurately, light powered. Shelby hoped the ambient light was enough to make life more comfortable for these people.

As she drove south on the old U.S. 1, where someone had marked out and painted a red circle and slash across U.S. in the sign, she noticed the neighborhood getting more crowded and a little rougher. Now she received looks from people on the street. Men, gathered together on the corners, called out to her as she passed a little faster than she should've been driving. She was surprised to see several different schools in operation. One of them had the sounds of children singing.

She looked for street signs that might give her an idea where the apartment complex housing Fredrico Rea might be. Finally she saw the faded remains of an old green sign that had the number 103 on it. The wide street ran east and west and had a few cars on it. Even an old, refurbished army Humvee, like the ones used at the turn of the millennium, rolled down the street with six men in it.

Shelby waited until the Humvee had passed. She had her issued high-powered gas projectile pistol called the Fonda. Unlike the UPF, who liked to carry heavy, conventional rounds, the DHS had armed their agents with a more flexible system. The gas-powered guns fired round projectiles like big BBs, but could also fire darts, tear gas rounds, and other nonlethal weaponry. Since the need for military sentencing, the government had shied away from using deadly force. They viewed it as killing one of its own potential soldiers. But she still carried a little weapon she had picked up in Iran. A small personal Flasher that was good for three shots before recharging. In her line of work, with her family history, she thought it was prudent to have a weapon that would stop anything or anybody.

She drew the handgun and checked the gas tube in the handle. It was fully charged. Good for about fifty shots. She had twenty lethal rounds in the gun, a pack of sleeping darts, and other nonlethal agents in a case inside her all-weather jacket.

She would watch the apartment complex for a while and see who showed up.

TWENTY-THREE

Tom Wilner had been in the Miami Quarantine Zone dozens of times over the past few years. He knew the secret: it wasn't so bad. Sometimes he entered the zone while chasing someone from one of his cases. Once he did it looking for a part to an old car he was trying to restore at the time. The truth was that the zone wasn't as dangerous as everyone was led to believe. It was no tourist spot, but it wasn't the hell on Earth that the media made it out to be.

He always entered by way of the old road near the ruins of a football stadium. The guardsmen at that checkpoint were local district residents and knew him. It was also quiet out west and he could sneak in if he had the right vehicle.

He was just happy to be back from Orlando, but was afraid Steve Besslia had bought into his theory about alien invaders even more after what the curator of the planetarium had said. Wilner wasn't sure his friend would be useful for much else until he regained his perspective and started looking at this whole thing as one related criminal investigation.

Today he had used one of the old spare unmarked cars from the UPF station near the checkpoint. The station was a traffic office, so they didn't have much use for an unmarked spare car. Wilner knew they wouldn't be happy about it going into the zone, but they didn't ask so he didn't tell them.

He had found the man he was looking for, Munroe Phillips, almost immediately. He knew that Munroe lived over a produce market and that he made his living smuggling things into and out of the quarantine zone and providing information to whoever paid the most. He was also wanted on the U.S. side of the border for his smuggling venture and was facing a ten-year military sentence if he was caught. That was the leverage that Wilner needed.

Munroe shook his wide head on his pencil-thin neck. "No. No way will I take you down there."

"So you know who it was and where he stays."

"A dude from the district with dark hair was in here last week looking for some muscle. He hired Freddie Rea and his crew."

"Tiget Nadovich?"

"I don't know his name but he's down here sometimes. Why? What'd Rea do?"

"He's got a circuit board I need back."

"Is it valuable?"

"Valuable enough for me to leave you alone down here and not drag you back up to the district if you help me."

"That'd be illegal to take me back. The zone ain't part of the United States no more."

"So who'd complain? The ambassador?"

Munroe sighed and muttered a couple of obscenities.

Wilner watched as the skinny African man had some in-

depth internal dialogue to figure out the relative value of helping a UPF detective.

Finally Munroe said, "C'mon, I'll take you to him."

They rode in Munroe's steam-converted Ford pickup
truck. The water boiler sat in the bed. The truck only moved
at about fifteen miles an hour, but attracted a lot less attention
than a Hive, or even an unfamiliar conventional car.

As he drove, Munroe felt compelled to tell Wilner all the
problems the United States had that the Miami Quarantine
Zone had avoided. The skinny African man said, "We don't
got no lawsuits, no courts slowing everything down."

"But bullies and the gangs are in charge."

"Nope. No one's in charge. If you got a beef and you're
right, people back you up. The key is to keep everything
simple."

Wilner looked at him and said, "You're a bright guy,
Munroe. Why didn't you just leave the zone when it was established? You were already a citizen."

"I was born in Miami. It's my home. Shit, we been welcom-
ing one group of refugees or another since the city was built. I
didn't care who lived here with me."

Wilner nodded, thinking it made sense even if he wouldn't
have stayed.

"Besides, they was drafting everyone and I was about to
turn eighteen. I wasn't made to tote no rifle. And I don't like
the desert. I woulda been miserable."

They drove on east through old sections that had retained
their traditional names. Opalocka, Miami Gardens and finally North Miami Beach. Munroe knew exactly where he
was heading and it made Wilner think his informant might
know more than he was letting on.

As they turned down 103rd Street, the steam engine belching and popping, Wilner saw a familiar car and had Munroe pull in behind it.

Shelby Hahn was out of the driver's side and walking back to the truck as Wilner climbed out. She smiled, her whole face lighting up. "I'm impressed. It took me using secret government databases to find this place so fast. How'd you do it?"

He nodded back at Munroe in the driver's seat. "Secret State snitch. He knows everything."

Munroe came out and met them. "I'll go in behind you."

Wilner stared at the younger man.

Munroe said, "What? I can't go?"

"Why would you? They might have guns."

"I'm your partner."

Wilner let out a laugh. "Watch the cars like a good partner."

"But I want my piece."

"Of what?"

"The money for the board."

"There is no money for it."

"You mean you ain't getting it for this Nadovich dude?"

"No, this is part of a UPF investigation."

"You're kidding me, right?"

Wilner just stared at him, then said, "Wait here."

Tiget Nadovich was glad to be back in Florida, but now the idiot who took the board from Wilner wanted to be paid twice what they had agreed upon. It wasn't the money so much as the effort to find the man and kill him that annoyed Nadovich.

He had brought Radko Simolit back with Demitri and Alec. He had room and the big man might be a help in the busy days ahead.

Nadovich had been shaken by what he had seen in New York. The dark existence. The insects. The remaining humans. None of it felt natural to him and it made him consider what would happen when he followed through on his own plans. It had given him some ideas. He needed to sound more of a warning to get out as many humans as possible before the blast. But he had to consider different variables.

They still had a lot to do as well. He had to retrieve the board, set up the bomb and find Mr. Hammed again.

One reason he had not killed the Lebanese man and his two flunkies was that Nadovich had not been able to get any radioactive material in New York. He knew that Mr. Hammed could obtain the dangerous isotopes he still needed. Nadovich realized that negotiation was not going to work this time. At least negotiating for money wouldn't. He'd find what he needed to trade to get Mr. Hammed to cooperate.

He told the others he'd be gone for a while and started out in his nice Hive utility truck with a good bicycle in the back. He had his own ways into the Miami Quarantine Zone. He preferred to travel quietly without attracting any attention and didn't want anyone from the UPF or the U.S. government to know that he crossed the border occasionally. He had to maintain an air of respectability. At least for as long as he could.

Now he intended to find his retainer, Fredrico Rea, and explain to him the correct relationship with his employer. Nadovich felt certain he could convey the lesson properly.

TWENTY-FOUR

Tom Wilner had no problem entering a gang clubhouse with just Shelby Hahn. She had proven herself and had more guts than any other cop he knew, she could fight like a hellion and her service in the army reflected her tough-minded nature and courage.

They climbed the outside staircase closest to the apartment that seemed to have the most activity. Wilner took one last glance behind him to make sure Munroe was still standing by the cars. He felt responsible for the informant since he had brought him this far east from his own apartment above the produce stand.

He looked over at Shelby with her gas-powered Fonda gun in her right hand.

Wilner said, "Wait a second. You got other rounds for that?"

"Yeah, sure." She reached inside her all-weather jacket and pulled out a small case. "Fast-acting intestine irritator, sleep inducer and four pepper irritants."

"Instead of kicking in the door and opening fire, why don't we pick away at them for a few minutes?"

She shrugged, the bulky jacket making her look like a kid. Without a word she moved the selector switch on her pistol, opened the small case containing other ammo and selected the intestine irritator.

"If someone steps out of the apartment I'll send him to his own bathroom." She smiled like it was a prank.

Wilner was worried they'd be seen out in the open, so he pushed on the first apartment's door and slide inside. He did a quick walk through the place to make sure no one was home. It looked like a single younger male lived in the apartment, with a few fitness magazines, some men's workout clothes and not much else.

Shelby said, "I can see anyone coming or going through the window. I can even get a shot at anyone headed this way."

Then, before she could look back out the window, someone walked past and the door handle to the apartment turned.

Wilner said, "Shit," and jumped toward the door as it opened. A tall, well-built dark man stood there, shocked to see anyone inside his apartment.

"*Quién es?*" he said, as Wilner swung hard for his head with the barrel of his heavy-duty weapon.

The blow sent teeth and blood onto the open door as the man staggered back a step.

Wilner reached over with his left hand and grabbed the man's waistband of his workout pants and tugged him back toward the apartment. As he stumbled into the small living room with a kitchen attached to it, Wilner struck him again across the back of his head, knocking him onto the mattress on the floor.

Shelby looked down at the motionless man as blood poured from two split lips and several missing teeth, staining the dirty white sheets on the mattress. "Not as neat as a sleep agent but probably more satisfying."

Wilner frowned. "Find another target."

Before he could look up from the unconscious man he heard the puff of her pistol. She crouched back from the slightly open door.

He leaned and looked out the window. A man was inspecting his leg where the tiny dart had broken off in his thigh. They were designed to feel like mosquitoes; even though Florida had none left since the weather had turned permanently cool.

After about ten seconds of picking at his pants and twenty seconds of considering how he got bitten by a mosquito when there hadn't been one in south Florida for ten years, the man bent as if a cramp hit him and then darted three doors away from the target door and inside an apartment.

Wilner said, "That's two."

Shelby loaded a blue dart, which indicated a nonlethal sleep agent.

Another man, older and rougher-looking than the others, stepped out of the apartment and leaned on the railing. He reached in his front pocket and pulled out a small box.

Wilner realized he was taking Baht, a narcotic weed from Africa, and stuffing it in his cheek like the old chewing tobacco. Baht use in the United States had dropped off in recent years because selling it was an automatic death sentence. But in all the quarantine zones the rumor was the addictive drug was widely used.

Shelby lined up her shot and fired.

The man slapped at his neck without paying any more attention. He stuck his finger in his mouth to move the Baht around. Then, after less than a minute, he started to stagger and stumble. He turned, flopped against the rail and then fell over and out of sight.

Wilner said quietly, "Not as clean as striking him with my pistol but he won't be back."

Shelby reloaded as five men came out of the apartment to see what had happened to their friend. She fired, reloaded quickly, then fired again.

One man dropped in the hallway as another leaned over the rail to see his friend, then he fell as well. Now the other men knew something was up.

The remaining three men darted inside the apartment and Wilner said, "Let's go."

They were out on the breezeway and next to the target apartment with their pistols out in a few seconds.

Wilner looked at Shelby who nodded. He kicked the door hard and let his momentum carry him inside. Shelby was right next to him.

Then he saw the man step out of the bedroom with a shotgun. The man had its barrel down and coming to bear on them before Wilner could fire. The flash and sound of the blast stunned Wilner as he thought of his next move.

Johann Halleck didn't like feeling as if he were out of the loop, but that was exactly how he felt at the moment. He knew the board was in the quarantine zone and that the cop Wilner had gone to retrieve it.

Now, at the zone bar where smugglers met, and most information about things going on in the zone was exchanged, Johann leaned on the bar. It was still early in the day but the place had patrons. Named the Chaos Pit, it was known for lewd sex shows, home-brewed beer and violence. Although the bouncers or bartender wouldn't hesitate to beat someone who acted out, there were still deadly knifings, back room murders and the occasional massacre. With no laws or law enforcement in the Miami Quarantine Zone nothing was ever done about the activity in the bar. People could come or choose not to.

Johann had contacts that would tell him the progress of Tom Wilner. This trip was to develop a backup plan and learn if Tiget Nadovich had been in the area. Before he could ask any questions on that matter it became clear. Johann looked down the bar and saw Nadovich at the same time he had noticed Johann.

Johann had his combat knife in his belt, but knew that Nadovich could have an E-weapon. He raised his glass of weak beer and slid down the bar closer to his rival.

Nadovich said, "I didn't expect to see you down here."

"I will also confess surprise." He was conscious that his accent was thicker than Nadovich's.

Nadovich nodded, not giving away anything. Then he said, "I don't understand your concern. This doesn't involve you or your family."

Johann looked at the smaller man. "You know the pledge we took. I will not abandon it."

"Your pledge to humans? Please. They would wage a war on us if they knew we were here."

"Secrecy has worked for many years. Aggression does nothing."

"I may need to use aggression on you if you interfere."

Johann chuckled. "Don't get carried away, Tiget. I am not a human to be bullied."

"And I have business here in the zone."

"So do I." He let his hand creep down toward the combat knife on his belt.

Before he could make a move he heard a shout from the stage. Johann saw the big bartender draw a gun from under the bar.

Johann turned for a moment to see what was happening. A tall, skinny man stood with a pistol pointed at a beautiful dancer with small breasts and long legs. He shouted something and the bartender fired.

The dancer fell off the stage as the bartender's round went wide, striking her in the upper abdomen.

The tall man returned fire, jerking the trigger of his old auto-pistol.

Johann felt a sharp pain in his back, then his head slammed against the bar.

That was all he could remember.

Wilner tried to push Shelby out of the way as the shotgun fired. He saw the gang member in front of him jerk wildly as the bulk of the shotgun's buckshot projectiles struck him instead of the intended targets. But Shelby jerked and stumbled off her feet as well.

He wanted to jump to her aid, but his combat training had taught him to keep his pistol up for action and start firing at the target. The man with the shotgun crumpled against the wall as the big, plutonium-tipped pistol rounds smashed through his body. Wilner was glad they had thinned out the number of people in the apartment before they attempted the assault.

Now Shelby was up on her knees, gas-powered gun up and firing at a fast rate, the smaller rounds punching through the wall for good covering fire. She gave Wilner one look and he knew it was time to charge the bedroom. He sprang up and fired twice as he entered. The rear window was wide open with no screen. As he raced to the window, Shelby joined him. They looked out and saw two men running from where they had jumped to the ground.

One man, Wilner thought it was Fredrico Rea, had the circuit board in his hand.

Shelby raised her pistol and fired. The second man stumbled and fell to the ground, clutching the back of his leg.

Shelby looked at Wilner. "You get Rea and I'll question that guy."

Wilner was out the window after the man without answering.

Munroe Phillips had only been at the cars for a few minutes when he heard the gunfire from the direction of the apartment building. His first thought was to run, but then realized no one would link him to the two cops. He had some leeway to see how it turned out. If the cops won the fight and he stayed he would earn some points with them. If they were both dead, he'd take the nice-looking DHS agent's car and sell it farther south in the zone. Either way he saw a potential profit.

Although he talked a good game about being born in Miami and wanting to stay in the zone for that reason, if he had enough money he might try living up in the district. He had heard there was a lot of legitimate work because they had so few people available for employment. The concept of waiting tables or working behind a cash register appealed to him. At least in theory. He had always been a hustler, but mainly because that was the only thing he could be down here in a place without laws or government.

He kept looking down the street toward the apartment complex, anxious to see who came around the corner. Then he saw a single person running wildly around the corner. When the man looked up, Munroe realized it was the man the cops were looking for, Freddie Rea. He had something in his right hand as his arms flailed and legs pumped. He slowed as he recognized Munroe.

"Hey, man, hey," gasped Rea as he tried to catch his breath. "You gotta help me."

"What's up, Freddie?"

"I'm being chased. I need a ride." His eyes cut to the two cars. He leaned over, panting for breath.

Munroe said, "Whatchu got in you hand, my brother?"

Rea held up the circuit board. "Nothing. It's nothing. Can you get me outta here?"

Munroe smiled and said, "Let me see what I can do."

TWENTY-FIVE

At a small, family-run café still within the Miami Quarantine Zone, Wilner sat with his pistol out on the table and ate a goat sandwich. From the table he and Shelby could see her nice, shiny Hive. But despite what they heard and had seen about the quarantine zone no one bothered them or the car.

The waiter, a small Hispanic man, had smiled and said, "All we gots is goat."

Wilner said, "Any beer?"

"All you want."

Wilner smiled and held up two fingers for two more of the small sandwiches. He let out a breath and looked over at Shelby. "You sure you're all right?"

"I told you it just grazed my shoulder."

"But the blood on your shirt?"

"Wasn't mine. Here, look." She unbuttoned the top three buttons of her shirt and pulled it down around her left shoulder. "See?"

Wilner leaned in and saw a red mark on her shoulder that

he never would've paid attention to on himself or another marine during the war. But here, in Florida, on her smooth, blemish-free skin, the red line looked like a crime against humanity. But if it didn't bother her, he couldn't raise too much fuss.

He sat back in his chair and said, "I can't believe we lost Rea and the board."

"I can't believe your stand-up snitch left us too."

"Probably got scared. At least we had your car to get back in."

Shelby looked around. "This is the first time I've been in any quarantine zone. It's not what I expected."

"You mean no wild zombies running around or women being raped in the streets?"

"Yeah, I guess. It doesn't seem that much different than the district. Quiet, uncrowded and a little gloomy."

"I suppose so."

A video broadcaster had a station from the Northern Enclave on behind the counter. The signal was a little weak but the sound was perfect. It did seem to give the whole idea of a separate quarantine zone a little kick in the head. He took in a deep breath of the fresh air and picked up the smell of roasting meat. That wasn't common anymore up in the district. The synthetic meats, while tasting okay, didn't give off a smell when cooked and people were spread out enough now that it was difficult to smell anything coming from a neighbor's house.

Shelby said, "What's bothering you?"

"You mean aside from losing the circuit board and just getting in a shoot-out?"

"Does it bother you after being in combat?"

He had to shake his head. "Not really. Not down here

where no one'll care. They were bullies and punks and if they hadn't used the shotgun we wouldn't have fired."

"Except for the guy I hit with the sleeping dart that fell over the railing."

"He was moving when we left. He'll be okay."

She reached across and held his hand. "You're a funny guy whether you mean to be or not."

He smiled, knowing that he rarely meant to be funny, but he'd take it.

Then he heard the newscaster on the video broadcaster say the phrase they had all dreaded: "Breaking news from Germany."

Both Wilner and Shelby snapped their heads and attention to the newscast. Even the man at the counter turned and looked up at the screen.

The newscaster said, "We have reports that elements of the German Defense Force have crossed the border into Poland. A statement from the National Assembly in the capital of New Berlin says that it is a defensive measure to liberate the starving Poles along the German-Polish border."

He went on to talk about the emerging response from the industrialized nations but Wilner didn't listen. He knew what it meant. One more thing for the world to focus on and one more reason for him to be called back into the marines.

Fredrico Rea liked the old city of North Miami Beach in what the United States called the Miami Quarantine Zone where he and his buddies, who called themselves the Zone Troopers, lived. They had a good protection racket and ran a few whores down in the southern part of the zone. Their biggest problem had been transportation. They had cars stashed up in the district for use inside the United States, but down here they shared an old, ratty Ford conventional gas car. And gas was getting hard to come by down here.

If he'd had gas and a car, he certainly wouldn't be sitting in the empty hotel room near his old apartment. He had told a few of the Troopers, the ones that were left, where he'd be but that he needed to lay low.

The shock of the cop and his girlfriend barging into their clubhouse and shooting the place up had been compounded by that African guy, Munroe Phillips, taking the circuit board and leaving him to crawl into the bushes near his apartment. Now he had to avoid Tiget Nadovich for as long as it took to get the board back. First of all he owed that stealing creep, Munroe. Second, he knew where the asshole lived. And third, he needed to get the board. You didn't cross a man like Nadovich. He had raised his price a couple of times, but if the man insisted he would've been happy just to give him the circuit board.

He was getting restless in the small, bleak room that had no power or water of any kind and smelled of old rain and soggy blankets. But he was tired and a little sore from jumping from his own bedroom window. Now he was ready to get some of the Troopers and go find Munroe to get the board back. If he showed up in the district with it and gave it Nadovich he figured all would be forgiven.

He stood, and wiped his face with an old towel that was in the bathroom, stretched his back and decided to walk back to the apartments, get a gun and some help, then start looking for the treacherous Munroe. He turned and slid the chain off the door and opened it, surprised by a man standing casually outside.

"Hello, Freddie," said the man.

Fredrico Rea stared in shock as he realized someone had talked. "Hello, Mr. Nadovich," was all he could get out.

Wilner had seen Shelby safely back into the district past the National Guard checkpoint. Then got back in the old car he had left at Munroe's and starting looking for his wayward snitch. He thought that the man had just left the area, but then he wondered if he hadn't met up with Fredrico Rea first. Either way it was enough incentive to look hard for Munroe and find out what he knew.

He had used his V-com to call his house and make sure Mrs. Honzit and the children were okay. Something didn't feel right.

Wilner said, "I can come home if you need me, Mrs. Honzit."

"No, we're fine."

"You don't sound fine."

"I've been watching the news. I'm afraid that you will have to fight the Germans. The children, they need you."

"I haven't been called up. There's nothing to worry about."

He hesitated and then asked, "Has Svala been back?"

"No, sir. I think you and the kids are better off if she doesn't come back."

He smiled at the housekeeper's loyalty. "Thank you, Mrs. Honzit."

He then went back to his search for Munroe with renewed vigor. He treated it like any other police job he had completed as part of the UPF, except down here he knew better than to show his police ID. Instead he left his jacket in the front seat and let everyone see his exposed pistol when he started to ask questions. By spreading out a few suds here and there, he narrowed the search for Munroe to a bar in Opalocka he was known to visit whenever he wanted to celebrate, or had a little extra cash. Wilner had heard of the club all the way up in the district. Known for no-holds-barred sex shows, since there were no rules, the club was one of the main attractions for the people stuck below the new U.S. border.

He parked his old car a few blocks away and paid an elderly Hispanic man ten suds to keep an eye on it. Wilner thought that the older man was sincere when he swore an oath to protect it. Wilner slipped his pistol inside his waistband and pulled his shirt over it for concealment.

As he approached the club he saw the sign above the door: THE CHAOS PIT. Then a warning printed in Spanish, French and English: TROUBLEMAKERS WILL BE KILLED. That probably kept things quiet.

A large, muscular man at the door held out his hand. "Ten U.S. suds, fifty Latin dollars or one hundred zone credits."

Wilner looked at him and had to ask, "What are zone credits?"

"The new notes put out by the Independence Council of Miami."

Wilner didn't even know there was an independence council, but he shrugged and handed the man a ten-sud note.

As he walked in the dark, cool bar that was filled with smoke, Wilner realized he could've just paid the doorman for information about Munroe. But he had to admit that he wanted to see what went on inside the famous club.

He stepped past a group of laughing Hispanic men. No one even looked up at the taller Wilner. There were three stages inside the wide, low-ceilinged room. Wilner made his way to the center bar where he could see the entire room.

The big bartender just looked at him.

"Beer."

As the big man placed the beer in front of him he said, "You look like trouble. We don't need no trouble. Already had three killed this morning."

"Who was killed?"

"Dancer, shooter and some poor sap sitting right where you are now."

Wilner nodded his understanding. Before he scanned too hard for Munroe he glanced up on the stages. The place had earned its reputation fairly. On the first smaller stage, a naked woman with an athlete's body and a missing right arm swayed to Latin music, missing all the beat and melody.

On the far small stage, a well-built woman with all her appendages leaned over a small table while a naked midget with a disproportionately large penis prepared to mount her.

The center stage had a woman who was rubbing a large mongrel dog's belly then leaned in to perform something he didn't really want to think about.

Despite the unusual vistas, at least two of which Wilner had never seen before, he lost interest in the club very quickly. He started a careful visual search of the entire club beginning with the people at the bar. No one seemed to pay too much attention as Wilner checked the wide bar, but there were definitely individuals who knew he was at the bar and didn't exactly fit in.

He looked past the midget and woman who were now fully engaged. On the rear wall he saw several African men but none even close to Munroe's slender build.

He felt a nudge from next to him at the bar and turned. The large Hispanic man nodded an apology. Wilner noticed the room was getting more and more crowded.

After ten more minutes, Wilner had determined that Munroe was not inside the bar. He had bought a home-brewed beer and was about to finish it when the crowd cheered for the woman completing her task with the dog.

Out of the corner of his eye, Wilner saw a man enter from the main door and walk straight to the bar. He turned slightly and saw it was Munroe, bopping to the bar without the least concern of who was standing there.

Wilner intended to make him care in just a minute.

TWENTY-SIX

Tom Wilner watched Munroe wander through the front section of the bar, greeting several of his friends as he walked. Wilner leaned back from the bar, using the man next to him to block Munroe's line of sight. He stepped around him and directly behind Munroe as the snitch ordered a beer from the bartender.

Wilner got a good stance to block Munroe if he tried to leave. He watched as the bartender set down a long, thin bottle of the beer brewed in the house behind the bar. The loud, throbbing music kept him from just calling out. Instead, he timed his first comment for Munroe as he turned around to look out on the three stages.

Wilner said, "Hello, Munroe," as the man turned.

Munroe froze and said, "Oh, I missed you back at the apartment."

"Am I the only one you missed?"

"And the DHS lady."

Wilner placed a hand on Munroe's left arm and squeezed,

giving him a taste of what he could expect. "Did you run across Freddie Rea with my circuit board?"

Munroe hesitated and his eyes flicked from the stage to Wilner. "No."

"You're lying to me, Munroe, and it'll cost you. This is the zone, not the United States. I could leave your bloody body right here and no one would care."

"Look, Wilner. What would a board like that be worth? I mean hypothetically."

"Your life."

Without warning, Munroe swung his right hand with the beer bottle in it at Wilner's head.

The UPF detective ducked and jerked his head back, making Munroe miss by a fraction of an inch.

The snitch's arm kept traveling and his follow-through struck the man standing next to him at the bar with the bottle. Blood and beer spilled onto the ground as the man dropped to the filthy floor.

Two of his buddies reacted immediately, both reaching for Munroe.

Wilner tried to block one of the men, but took a punch in the face instead. As the man reached for a knife in his belt, Wilner threw a hard elbow into him, knocking him backward into another group.

Munroe had struggled free of the thug who had grabbed him and now was pushing toward the rear exit of the big bar.

Wilner straightened up to see five separate fistfights right in the area of the bar and the melee seemed to be spreading out onto the bar's main floor as a table was overturned and then shots fired from the rear of the bar.

Wilner was knocked around as he reached for the butt of his pistol to make sure he didn't lose it in the scuffle. He saw the one-armed dancer knocked from her perch and several men rush to protect her from the crushing crowd. The midget and woman on the far stage never lost a beat, consumed by the public personal activity. Wilner craned his neck and could see Munroe darting out the rear door.

Wilner pushed, shoved and punched his way to the front door, which was jammed with fleeing patrons. He raced out of the lot and around the back to see if he could see Munroe. Instead he saw the snitch's awkward, steam-powered Ford truck chugging away down the street. Wilner turned to run back to his own car a few blocks away only to hear gunfire and feel two rounds ricochet off a barrel of waste he was standing next to.

He ducked down behind the foul-smelling barrel and pulled his own pistol, trying to determine if he was a target or just unlucky. Another round hit the barrel and a sour, rancid swill poured out of the hole and onto the sleeve of Wilner's light jacket.

He returned blind fire toward the bar and then heard shots directed toward him. He was pinned down by the gunfire. He hoped Munroe was headed to his apartment to gather his things because that was where Wilner was going as soon as he could move again.

Tiget Nadovich knew how lucky he was. If Johann Halleck hadn't been hit by a stray bullet or two, he might be nursing his own wounds right now. As soon as he saw the big Halleck go down, Nadovich had jumped up and left the Chaos Pit. Now he sat in a wobbly chair across from Fredrico Rea, who was trembling so badly that the old, smelly bed where he sat was shaking.

Nadovich said, "It's very simple, Freddie. I paid you for a job. You completed the task and now I need the circuit board."

"I know, Mr. Nadovich. But I don't got it."

"So when you called me to jack up the price you were just trying to trick me."

"No, no, sir. I had it then."

"And where is it now?"

"Well, the cops came to the clubhouse."

"Wait, wait, wait. The clubhouse over on 103rd where your friends told me you were here?"

"Yes."

"How did cops go there? There are no cops in the zone."

"Not just any cop. The one we took the board from."

"Wilner?"

"Yeah."

"How did he find you?"

"A snitch from down here named Munroe."

"So Wilner has the board again?"

"No. Munroe does."

"How do I find this Munroe?"

"I'll take you to him. I'll make this all up to you, Mr. Nadovich. I'll do whatever it takes."

Nadovich stood and said, "I know, Freddie. I know."

Nadovich made the frightened gang leader drive him in the car shared by all the members of the Zone Troopers. He needed a good drive through the area to scout out possible locations to lay low if it became necessary. It bothered him that Detective Wilner didn't feel restricted by the rules of the UPF about entering the Miami Quarantine Zone.

As they drove, Rea tried to make conversation. "That's some

shit about the Germans and the Polacks. You think they're really trying to help the starving Poles?"

Nadovich looked at his companion and wondered if people were really so gullible. Was history forgotten so quickly? "Freddie, have you ever heard of a country invading another to save its people?"

"Well, the United States has done it a few times."

Nadovich nodded. "Perhaps you have a point but I can assure you that Germany is not feeding anyone in Poland except its own troops." Nadovich did like that the dim-witted gang member even knew about the burgeoning conflict. That meant the rest of the world was paying attention to the same thing and as the time grew closer for Nadovich to act, fewer people would be watching. Except he had the feeling that Svala's husband, Tom Wilner, wasn't going to give up that easily.

They had been driving west in the old, gas-powered car. Without traffic lights or even traffic, the trip was quick. They were now west of the main population and the ruins of the old football stadium where the Miami Dolphins once played was visible to his right. Nadovich remembered watching a game from the stadium but never could understand the rules of American football. It was just as well now that the sport was hardly even played anymore. Ten professional teams. Resources and manpower were too short to allow the frivolous use of young men on a field of sport. The United States needed them in wars across the globe.

Fredrico Rea slowed and pointed at a produce store with a second floor. "That's his place. Above the store."

Nadovich nodded and said, "Wait in the car. I'll be back shortly."

———

Tom Wilner had weathered sporadic gunfire for more than a half an hour before he realized it wasn't as random as he thought. He decided he needed to act so he pulled back. Quietly, using obstacles to block the view of the gunmen who occasionally threw a round in his direction, he disappeared into the rough brush.

The only casualty so far was his jacket, which smelled so bad from the wastewater that poured on it that Wilner had to throw it away. Now, in a simple fiber shirt, he was starting to get soaked from the light rain and cold from the cloudy day. He dropped back, then cut through some more bushes and through a yard that hadn't been mowed in the past few months.

He slipped out of the brush on the next block and completely bypassed the Chaos Pit property. When he cut back he could have easily turned right to his car, but instead couldn't help but turn left. He owed the idiots who had pinned him down for so long.

He kept to the side of the street where wild hedges and trees provided cover and shadows in which to move. He had his pistol out and every few minutes someone ran past him away from the bar where the fight had broken out. It wasn't like a big bar fight in the district or the Northern Enclave where cops or even soldiers might have rolled in to settle things. Anyone arrested with a gun in a bar in what was left of Florida got an automatic five years in the military and ten if there was any reason to believe the defendant was gong to use it. And the way things were it was always assumed, because it was better to have a soldier for ten years than it was to have him for only five.

Now Wilner could see two men down behind an old, rusty

Dumpster. One had a pistol and the other an old, conventional hunting rifle. That explained the different sounds of the shots.

Wilner moved up to within fifteen feet of the two Hispanic men as the one with the rifle stood up and aimed the long rifle toward where Wilner had been hiding. He fired a round and it pinged off a metal rail near Wilner's old hiding place.

Wilner had an abandoned, wrecked car in front of him. The vehicle was old, but provided excellent cover. He leaned against it and aimed his pistol at the Dumpster that silhouetted the two gunmen.

Wilner fired five rounds. Each one struck just above the gunmen as they crouched lower and lower to avoid being hit.

Then Wilner called out, "Drop the guns and walk toward me."

When the men hesitated, Wilner threw three more rounds into the Dumpster.

Now the men tossed the firearms away and scrambled to their feet to walk quickly back to Wilner.

Wilner stepped out from behind the wrecked car, his pistol trained on the two men. "You mind telling me why you were trying to keep me pinned down back there?"

Neither man spoke.

Wilner shot the larger of the two men in the foot.

He screamed, lifting his foot to hop around, then tumbled onto the ground, whimpering.

"I'll ask again, but this time my aim will be better."

The man who was still standing looked at his bloody companion and said, "Munroe paid us to keep you busy."

"Now that makes sense. Where was Munroe going?"

"I swear, mister, I don't know."

Wilner had his own idea. He said, "Should you shoot at people?"

"Well, mister, we are in the zone and there ain't no laws against it."

Wilner snickered at the good answer. "Okay, so I can do this as payback." He pulled the trigger and hit the man in his upper arm.

The man went to his knees, joining his friend.

Wilner turned and was back at his car in a few minutes.

Johann Halleck woke up from the attack in the bar in a Dumpster a few blocks from the Chaos Pit. He had been tossed in the Dumpster when someone at the bar had assumed he was dead from a gunshot to his upper back.

Next to him in the rusty, unused Dumpster was the body of the tall, skinny gunman and the pretty dancer. She was still naked, with a hole almost in the center of her chest. Her eyes were still open and staring directly at Johann. He closed them gently before slowly standing up and crawling up and out of the Dumpster.

He didn't know what time it was, his nice digital watch had been taken. Shaking off the cobwebs, he started his long walk back to the district. He would rearm back at his house, then consider his next move.

Back home he had a handheld flasher that was a little large but still concealable in his waistband. He also had several reliable combat knives. He was good with them and had used them several times, but the effect was generally short-term on any of the Simolit family. A flasher was a different story. Just like burning them at the stake had worked centuries earlier, a good flash of heat from an E-weapon generally neutralized them as well.

TWENTY-SEVEN

Tom Wilner pulled his car to a stop a block from Munroe's apartment. He saw the funky steam truck parked just behind the old building that served as a produce market as well as apartments on the second story. He had his pistol showing since he had lost his jacket but wasn't worried. This was the zone. Not only was it not a crime to possess a weapon, everyone seemed to have one.

As he entered the stairwell at the first floor he heard a loud crash and running footsteps. He started up the stairs when a young Hispanic boy appeared at the top of the long staircase. As he started to fly down the cement steps, taking two at a time, Wilner saw something in his hand and realized it was the circuit board.

Wilner blocked his progress and said, "Wait a second."

The boy looked up like it was the first time he had even noticed him there. "Move, move."

Wilner grabbed him by his small shoulders. The boy was not much older than Emma, maybe ten or eleven. He grabbed the board with two fingers and pulled it from the boy's grasp. Where'd you get this?" He looked at the boy and said, *"Habla inglés?"*

The boy nodded.

"Then where did you get this?"

"Munroe gave it to me through the window to my mom's apartment and said to run. The other man was hurting him."

Wilner heard another crash and looked up the stairs. He let the boy go, saying, "Run. Now."

He continued up the stairs as he tucked the board inside his shirt and pulled his big service pistol. As he entered the upstairs hallway and looked down toward Munroe's apartment, the door to the apartment burst open and Munroe's bony body fell into the hallway. Wilner hurried along without saying a word. He had the gun up as he approached Munroe, then twisted to point it into the apartment.

He froze as he aimed the gun and said, "You."

Tiget Nadovich looked up from a dresser he was searching and saw Wilner. "Do you ever give up?"

Wilner stepped into the apartment, his mind racing at what he wanted to do to this guy who had ruined his life. He knew this wasn't about the case right now. This was about Svala. And that was fine with him.

On one hand Shelby Hahn didn't enjoy being treated like a junior partner and sent out of the quarantine zone while Tom Wilner did whatever he had to do to recover the circuit board. On the other hand she was touched that he was concerned for her safety as well as her job.

She had other worries. First and foremost was figuring out what Tiget Nadovich needed a big bomb for. She and her associates knew the board was intended for some kind of explosive device that could deliver anything from chemical weapons to dirty, radioactive material. She had not fully disclosed her suspicions to the Department of Homeland Security. They would send in too many useless agents and destroy the other plans she had.

She had all the help she needed in a few confederates and the reliable, handy and handsome Tom Wilner.

Everything inside Wilner's, heart, brain and even guts told him to shoot Nadovich right where he stood. He was in the lawless, wild Miami Quarantine Zone. There wasn't even a law against murder here. You could just do it.

He had the surprised man in the sights of his service pistol. His finger tightened on the trigger. Nadovich made no move to evade his apparent fate and made no plea for his life. It was a little like Wilner had reacted when the creep slithered into his life and ruined it. This was the man that Svala had left him for. The man she shared a bed with at night. He was a few pounds of trigger pressure away from being out of Wilner's hair forever.

Then, for no reason other than his conscience, Wilner lowered the pistol. Nadovich was unarmed and not threatening him.

Nadovich seemed to relax slightly at the sight of the gun being lowered. He leaned against the dresser he'd been searching. Perhaps as much to let Wilner know he did not intend to attack as to steady himself after seeing a gun pointed at him by the man whose wife he stole.

"You have a code I admire, Detective. I thought you'd shoot me," said Nadovich.

"I'm still here. Don't count on it as a sure thing yet."

Nadovich chuckled. "It was nothing against you. Svala is a special woman. A remarkable woman. She had to follow destiny."

"And what part of your destiny needs a circuit board like the one you've made such a fuss over?"

"Do you have it?"

"I'm asking the questions." He leaned out to look down the hallway to make sure Munroe was still on the ground. The injured informant had moved to a sitting position, but still looked like he wasn't leaving.

Nadovich stood and stepped away from the dresser. "Detective, it is not my wish to hurt you. But I need the board."

"What for?"

"To protect my own family."

"I'd love to hear how you can do that with circuit boards."

"Please, Detective Wilner. Give me the board and allow me to go on my way. Svala would not be happy if I had to hurt you."

"I tell you what; we can leave together." He held up the pistol from his waist. "I gotta take you back for the bar fight and as a suspect in the UPF attack."

"So I can spend twenty years in a military unit? I don't think I can allow that."

Now Wilner changed his stance and raised the gun. "You have no choice."

Nadovich feinted to his left, then dove directly at Wilner to his right, his hand slapping at the pistol as Wilner instinctively pulled the trigger. The pistol kicked in his hand, inches from Nadovich's stomach.

The man shifted in midair and flew back onto the ground.

He immediately stood up and turned toward Wilner, who was trying to regain his grip on the pistol.

Nadovich threw his whole body into Wilner this time. For a guy smaller than Wilner, he carried a big impact. Both men bounced of the inside wall of the apartment and then tumbled over a table and onto the ground.

Wilner lost the pistol somewhere after the body block.

He felt Nadovich's hands around his arm like a vise and then the smaller man threw him across the room. He somersaulted in the air and landed hard enough against the wall to jar it loose, exposing construction debris that had been sealed inside the wall.

Wilner reached down, his hand shaking and vision blurry, grabbed a rebar rod about three feet long from inside the wall and felt its weight in his grip. The solid iron bar weighed at least ten pounds and felt like a sword as it slid out of the wall easily. He struggled to his feet as Nadovich crossed the room to meet him. Wilner could see a patch of blood where he had shot him in the stomach.

He swung at Nadovich's head with the metal rebar, then, as the man ducked, swung back and struck him solidly in the arm, knocking him into another wall. Wilner could feel the circuit board tucked inside his shirt shift. He swung again, striking Nadovich in the leg this time.

Nadovich recovered quickly and threw an open backhand across Wilner's face that sent him tumbling off his feet.

Wilner shook his head, surprised at the force of the slap. He had managed to keep the rebar in his hand and first used it to get to his feet and then started to swing it.

Nadovich stopped and leaned back to avoid the strike.

Wilner did not swing through all the way and instead pulled it back to his own body, then thrust it out like a pointed sword.

He drove hard into Nadovich's midsection, feeling the rough ridges of the bar as it entered into Nadovich's stomach and guts.

Wilner experienced a stab of horror. He'd never killed someone he knew. Never gotten a chance to speak to a guy he had shot or blown up in the war.

Nadovich held the bar with his hands, looking up at Wilner the whole time. He stumbled back a few feet and collapsed in a heap on the bed. The rod was still sticking perpendicular to his body.

Wilner squirmed at the groan of pain from Nadovich.

Then Nadovich sat up, keeping his eyes on Wilner. He methodically wrapped his hands around the metal bar and slowly started to yank the bar back out.

Wilner stood and stared as the bar came out of the massive wound and Nadovich tossed it onto the ground in disdain. Nadovich sat back on the bed, catching his breath.

Wilner leaned down and scooped up his pistol, then stumbled out the door. He wasn't sure of what he had seen, but knew it wasn't the right time to discuss it with Tiget Nadovich.

He jerked the groggy Munroe up off the ground and dragged him down the hall away from the obviously dangerous and wounded Nadovich.

Wilner didn't know what he was going to do, but he now knew that he had to stop the crazy Serbian. And apparently it was going to take more than impaling him on an iron rod.

TWENTY-EIGHT

Tiget Nadovich had scrambled down to the produce market on the first floor, trying not to show the pain the metal rod through his stomach had caused. It didn't matter because the commotion and gunshots that had come from upstairs had scattered any customers. He stood erect and slowed his pace as he looked for some kind of transportation that would get him back into the district and his house. There was no pretext now. The UPF detective knew he was involved in the efforts to regain the board. He would be a wanted fugitive and, although the police resources were thin, he would bet that Wilner would be able to muster enough forces to raid his house and maybe even enough to capture them.

He found a conventional-gas car that was missing all four doors and had a canvas roof to replace the missing metal one. Nadovich didn't even look around. There was no time to be discreet. He jumped in and found the common type of switch, which was used instead of keys to start most of the older, conventional-gas vehicles. No one stopped him as the old car puttered away from the curb. He saw no sign of Wilner or the informant. He took the car north to the blockade line of the quarantine zone. There were a thousand places to cross through the mucky water of the canal that was lined with razor wire on the far side. There were also bridges that acted as checkpoints. The U.S. citizens were allowed into the zone under certain circumstances, but the easiest way was to simply bribe the younger guardsmen.

He realized that during the trip and turmoil he had no money left in any pockets and no identification. He cursed as he slipped into the chilly water of the canal and started to swim across to the steep shoreline topped with razor wire and electronic sensors. Today he'd do it the hard way.

Tom Wilner wasted no time getting his own car and racing right to the UPF lab off the old interstate. He still had mud and blood on his pants as he mashed the buzzer to the reception area. He laid on the buzzer until the same man as before appeared in the reception area.

Now that the man understood what not to say to a UPF detective, he said, "Wait, I'll buzz you in. We just got the lock fixed since your last visit."

Wilner came through the door and followed the man back into the lab offices. He had to admit the large, empty building was a little creepy without another human in sight.

Wilner said, "You really are alone in here."

"Just me and at night they have an evidence custodian who does some filing and simple forensic tasks." The man looked over his shoulder at Wilner and said, "You look like you've had a hard day so far."

"You have no idea." Wilner paused then added, "We've had

a few things happen on the case that may make this bloodwork very important. That's why I came here instead of calling."

"You coulda stopped for a shower. I wouldn't have minded that."

Wilner sniffed at the stain on his shirt where the wastewater had leaked onto him. It seemed like days ago when he was pinned down by the gunmen at the bar in the zone. In fact, it had only been a few hours. After his encounter with Nadovich, which had rattled him more than any combat he had seen during the war, he'd taken Munroe across the border to the district hospital. He had some questions for his informant, but Munroe was broken up. He had four cracked ribs, a concussion, a broken arm and several serious lacerations. The doctor had assured him that Munroe would be unconscious for at least a day and in no danger of fleeing.

Wilner knew he had to confirm a lot of information before he could jump onboard Steve Besslia's theory that aliens were preparing for an invasion, but he had no other explanation for his fight with Nadovich. The guy was unbelievably strong, and he had suffered a catastrophic, fatal wound, yet had not seemed too concerned with it. Wilner couldn't get the image out of his mind of the Serbian pulling the rusty, rough metal pole out of his abdomen.

The lab attendant said, "I was going to call you, but the results of the blood samples were screwed up so I hadn't got around to letting you know yet."

"Screwed up how?"

"I've seen it before. Not often, but before the database went belly-up we even entered them. It wasn't human blood."

"How is that possible?"

The man shrugged. "You're the detective, not me. I just assumed you screwed up and collected specimens from a wounded animal."

"Can you tell what kind of animal?"

"Not here. I just know that it isn't human DNA. Similar, but not human." He looked at Wilner as if he had more to say.

"What else?"

The lab technician remained silent.

Wilner softened his tone. "Look, this is important. What else do you want to say?"

The lab tech sighed then said, "This is beyond me but something tells me you should follow up on this. If you're certain that it wasn't an animal blood spatter you should have the samples analyzed more thoroughly."

"Where would I get them analyzed?"

"I guess one of the good wildlife labs in Orlando. Probably the Disney lab from Animal Kingdom."

"They have a DNA lab?"

"Best in the world."

"How would I get them the samples?"

"I know a guy up there. I could get him the samples and see what he thinks."

Wilner leaned back against a wall, exhausted. "You'd do that for me?"

"Yeah, sure."

"Thanks, you're all right."

"And you're kinda scary. That's why I'm doing it."

Nadovich tried not to express his concern when he entered his house in the Eastern District. But the bloodstain on his shirt, the soaked clothes and the mud caked on his face indicated that he had spent a day on the run.

Alec leaped off the couch. "Tiget, what happened?"

"It doesn't matter. We need to gather what's important and vacate the house right now."

Demitri wandered in from the bedroom with Radko next to him.

Nadovich wasted no time. "Alec, you and Demitri pack the components and anything we might need to complete our mission. Radko, you'll have to handle that cop."

Demitri cut in, "Alec and I can get the board."

Nadovich had lost his patience and with it his diplomacy. "You and Alec missed your chance. Wilner is tough. He's much more dangerous than the small cop, Besslia."

Demitri looked down at the floor.

Nadovich stepped closer and put his hand on his cousin's shoulder. "Besides, Wilner won't recognize Radko. Maybe he can talk to him first and get the board." He looked to the larger man. "Make no mistake, the cop is a threat to us and is dangerous."

The giant man just nodded.

Nadovich stepped to the kitchen sink and rinsed the dirt and grime from his face.

Svala came through the back door from her favorite spot on the covered patio. She raised her hand to her face and said, "Oh, my God. What happened to you?"

Nadovich looked up at her. "Your husband happened to me."

She froze, then said in a forced calm voice, "Did you hurt him?"

"Hurt him?" he shouted. "Look at me. I was lucky he was too shocked to finish me off."

"Where were you?"

"In the zone." He lifted his shirt, exposing the stomach wound and a bullet hole, then said, "How did you ever live with that maniac?"

TWENTY-NINE

Tom Wilner took comfort in his routine of fixing breakfast for his children. Neither Emma nor Tommy were alert enough to even notice the fresh bruise on his face or the cuts around his knuckles and on his chin. All souvenirs of his encounters in the zone the day before.

Wilner had spent a quiet evening watching the news and old movies the night before. One movie, an antique from the mid-twentieth century, was called *The Invasion of the Body Snatchers*. It had none of the horrible special effects or hokey action associated with the films of that time. The movie concerned a subtle alien invasion of Earth and it was the last thing Tom Wilner had needed to watch. It had taken him nearly ten minutes to find the old film in the online archive connected to his video broadcaster. Virtually every piece of footage ever shot was stored in the massive archive.

Once he did manage to fall asleep, he had tossed and turned in bed all night, considering the ramifications of all that had happened. When he took the computer research he had done on Tiget Nadovich, which had media listings of the Serbian going back almost one hundred years, the lab report on the blood he had taken from Steve Besslia's apartment and his own experience seeing the critically wounded Nadovich shrug off the injury, Wilner could not dismiss the idea that Nadovich was something other than human. Could his wife's boyfriend be an alien? Right now he could think it, but he still couldn't say it out loud. He was expecting Steve Besslia any minute. Wilner wanted to be careful not to feed into any of Besslia's paranoid delusions if that's what they were.

Emma looked up from her premade pancakes and said, "You look tired, Daddy."

He smiled. "Only a little."

Tommy said, "Is Mommy coming by today?"

"Did she say she was?"

"No."

"Then I don't know, buddy." Wilner actually thought he might see his estranged wife later when he and as many of the UPF cops as he could muster went by the house where she lived with Nadovich. There was no more investigation. Nadovich had to be found, arrested and questioned. Not only about what the circuit boards were for, but about the attack on the UPF station and the dead Arab at the sports bar that started the whole case. With the antiterror laws they could hold Nadovich for up to two years without comment, and another three with a brief affidavit. The good cops hated to resort to that tactic. It was a matter of personal pride to try and make a case through investigation before ever making an arrest. At least on the bigger cases.

There was a knock on the side door to the kitchen and Steve Besslia stuck his head inside. He was in his dark, weatherproof UPF uniform with his full duty belt on.

"Hello, boys and girls," he said, stepping into the kitchen.

Before he could sit at the table with the kids, Wilner had a plate of premade pancakes and reptile eggs ready for him.

Besslia smiled and started to dig in just as the children finished.

Tommy said, "Why do you have a uniform and my dad doesn't?"

"Because he doesn't know how to ride a Hive-cycle."

"Really?"

Besslia smiled. "No, he's actually not good-looking enough to be associated with the UPF. Luckily you and your sister look like your mother."

Emma giggled at that.

Wilner did too, then said, "Okay you two. Go get dressed for school." He watched them scamper off down the hallway, then turned to his friend. "You ready to head back to work?"

"What else am I gonna do? Hanging around my condo is getting real old." He looked Wilner over and said, "I can see you've been busy."

Wilner touched his sore right jaw. "I ran into Tiget Nadovich in the zone."

"Man, you shouldn't be bothering that guy unless it's official."

"It was."

"In the zone? C'mon, Willie."

"Well, I was trying to get the circuit board back and ran into him."

"Did you get the board?"

He smiled. "Yep. I've got it stashed in my toolbox in the garage. No one will think to look there."

"What happened to Nadovich?"

"He got away."

"Did you at least get to kick his ass?"

"Sort of." Wilner didn't want to get into the details of his encounter. "But I hope to see him again today."

"You do? Where?"

"At his house, when you and me and a few guys the chief is giving us hit his house."

"Will Svala be there?"

"Probably."

"What about Shelby?"

Wilner winced. His friend had a way of getting into the real heart of a situation.

Wilner said, "No, this is a UPF matter."

"Smart move."

Wilner said, "You been thinking through your theory on aliens and the scout party?"

"I have."

"You still believe it?"

"I do." Then the motorcycle cop said, "What about you? You believe it yet?"

"Maybe."

Nadovich had no trouble finding a decent house in which to settle everyone. This one was larger than his Eastern District home and located farther west, close to the Northern Enclave, in an area that used to be known as Coral Springs. They were the only people residing on the street. A few families lived on the next block. It had not taken long for them to unpack the few bags they had and move all the bomb material into the spare bedroom that was located next to the garage. Having someone as large and strong as Radko helped in moving heavy objects without a dolly. Now Radko had gone out to learn his way around the area and to find Wilner before he could cause any more trouble.

Svala was making the bed as he walked into the upstairs master bedroom that they would share.

She turned to him and stood without saying a word.

Nadovich said, "What is it, my dear?"

"You're not going to hurt Tom, are you?"

"I will do all I can to not hurt him, but I must consider the long-term needs of my people."

Her dark eyes cut up to the taller Nadovich. "I understand, but he does mean a lot to me."

He used English, although he was conscious of his accent. "This I don't understand, but I will respect it. Believe me, it is my sincere hope not to ever meet your husband again."

She smiled and wrapped her arms around his neck.

As he kissed her soft lips he thought that it was good he was technically telling the truth. If Radko did his job he'd never have to lay his eyes on the UPF detective again.

It was only noon and Tom Wilner was already tired as he sat across from Shelby Hahn at a diner on the edge of the Northern Enclave.

She took a tiny bite of a her sandwich and then swallowed and looked across the table at him. "So there wasn't anyone home?"

"Nope."

"And it looked like they moved?"

"Yeah. There was a lot stuff missing from the house. We hit it about nine and it was empty."

"I'm impressed you could get enough UPF officers together to conduct a raid. Why didn't you call me?"

He hesitated, then said, "I, er, it was a UPF matter and I thought I'd give you a break."

"Sounds like the old days when cops tried to steal cases from each other."

"No, it was nothing like that."

"Was it something like you didn't want me to meet your wife?"

His head dropped. This was one smart girl. "Yeah, I guess it was."

She smiled and said, "No big deal. But I want you to be able to tell me what's going on with the case."

"I will. It's just that the whole Svala issue is a little awkward." There was a lot that he wanted to tell her but couldn't. He desperately wanted to tell her about all that had happened to make him at least consider that Nadovich and his group were aliens. Seeing the man severely injured and then survive, the lab results, the old news stories about Nadovich. It added up to something weird and he didn't want to sound like a nut. Not to this beautiful federal agent.

Shelby reached across the table and put her small hand on his, then she rubbed the cuts on his knuckles. "Looks like you did have a rough day yesterday after we split up."

"Yeah, but it was successful."

"You got the board?"

He grinned. "Hidden at the house."

"Is that safe with the kids?"

"No one will ever find it."

"Where'd you hide it?"

He paused and then said, "My toolbox in the garage."

"Smooth."

They went back to their lunches and after a few minutes Wilner said, "You okay? You seem a little down."

"I wasn't going to say anything."

"What? What is it?"

"I got a notice today over the computer. I'm on standby to be called up."

He just stared at her delicate face. "To where?"

"France, for defense against Germany."

"But they're headed the other way into Poland."

"I guess someone has some intel that they have other plans."

"What are you gonna do?"

"What do you mean? I'll report if I'm called. What else can I do?"

"Use your position at DHS. That has to be vital to national security."

"C'mon, what would you think of someone who wormed their way out of their duty? I have to go if I'm called."

He hated the idea of Shelby shipped off for another defense of France. If they had let the United States build the space platforms it had wanted to before the bottom fell out of NASA there would be defensive posts above the conflict.

He was about to say something else that wouldn't help the situation when he heard a commotion in the corner of the room. Two customers and a waitress huddled around a small, handheld video broadcaster. He heard the older male customer say, "Oh, God no."

Wilner stood and approached them. "What is it? What happened?"

The older man turned and looked at him. The color was out of his face.

He said, "A nuclear blast."

Wilner felt his legs go weak. In all the conflicts, no government had used a nuclear weapon. Wilner regained some of his composure and said, "Where? Poland?"

The man shook his head. "No, Israel just nuked Tehran."

The world was spinning out of control quickly.

THIRTY

Once again Nadovich found himself inside the Miami Quarantine Zone. This time he had Alec as a backup and had paid a national guardsman for transit across a bridge and for the return, if he and Alec made it back before the guardsman's 7:00 P.M. shift change. Nadovich also had an old but reliable conventional-gas car that he had bought cheaply and would leave in the zone if he had to.

He knew Mr. Hammed had asked for the meeting in the zone so he could have armed associates who wouldn't hesitate to shoot. Nadovich knew he had scared the man when he had walked away from the attack the last time they had met. It had taken much of the ride in the train to Philadelphia to heal the wound in his head and he still had a light scar that disappeared under his hairline.

But he had let Mr. Hammed live because he knew he'd have a use for the slippery older Lebanese man. Older in human terms but not too old for one of his people.

Nadovich sat at the rear table in the Chaos Pit. He watched

a one-armed woman have sex with a man who had no arms. He smiled at the humans' sense of irony.

He had strategically placed Alec at the bar. Mr. Hammed didn't know Alec and would not expect a confederate on a meeting like this.

After more than an hour of watching various dancers and shows on all three stages, Nadovich saw Mr. Hammed and a large younger man in a long coat stroll into the club.

Mr. Hammed took his time to cross the wide floor, careful not to look up at any of the stages, then sat across from Nadovich with his back to the stages.

His bodyguard lingered at a table closer to the stage where a woman with giant breasts danced offbeat to an old song.

Mr. Hammed said, "I cannot believe you would have me meet you in a place like this."

Nadovich noticed the Lebanese arms dealer straining to get a look at the wound his man had inflicted at their last meeting. "I cannot believe your man hit me with a knife like he did. I'm lucky to be alive."

"This place still offends the teachings of Islam."

"Spare me, Mr. Hammed. If you were as devoted to Islam as you pretend, you would not profit so from someone trying to give the United States a black eye."

Mr. Hammed looked away for a moment, but his eyes fell on a naked woman walking to the stage. "Why would you think I would deal with you after the way you stole our money?"

Nadovich leaned in, grasping Mr. Hammed's forearm as he did. "Do not play games with me. I explained about the money and the boards. We are not to blame."

"Then who is?"

"The UPF."

Mr. Hammed looked away as if he were disgusted.

Nadovich said, "But I'll give you an opportunity for you to earn back the cash. All of it."

Mr. Hammed looked at him now.

"All I need is some nuclear material like we talked about. Enough for a large bomb to irradiate all of the Lawton District."

Mr. Hammed's eyes widened. "You would detonate a bomb in the Lawton District? Why? There are so few people."

"I have my reasons."

Mr. Hammed shrugged. "I have reasons too, but a bomb in Orlando would be more effective." He considered this and added, "You have all the components to a bomb of this nature?"

"Almost."

Mr. Hammed nodded. "I will not get you the material until we are paid your past debt. Despite our mutual goals, now is not the right time anyway."

"Why not?"

"Right now the world is focused on Israel and its actions against Iran. I do not wish to divert attention from the Zionists. This might be the catalyst to get them to leave Lebanon."

For a moment Nadovich realized he and Mr. Hammed wanted the same things for their people. But Mr. Hammed wanted to make a profit doing it; Nadovich just wanted to be left alone.

Nadovich said, "I have a schedule. I want to be able to do it in about two weeks. I don't give a damn how the press carries the news or what the U.S. government decides to do. I want that material and *I'll* decide what to do with it. You'd be wise to cooperate." Before Mr. Hammed could answer, Nadovich looked over at Alec and nodded hard at the man by the stage. Alec straightened and walked up to the man. With a few quick twists and punches he had the man doubled over and headed for the door and the young man's two pistols tucked in his own pants.

Mr. Hammed looked at Nadovich. "Are you crazy? That's my sister's son, Walid."

"It's very simple, Mr. Hammed. Get me the material and you'll get your nephew back."

Mr. Hammed looked at him and said, "You're mad."

Nadovich nodded and said quietly, "It would seem so."

Radko Simolit watched Tom Wilner go into the UPF headquarters in the district. He had followed the fit-looking detective since he had left his house that morning. He had seen him when he and other policemen raided Tiget Nadovich's empty house. Radko had even managed to follow him to lunch with a very pretty young woman. Now he watched as the detective walked into the Unified Police Force's main office.

Radko thought that with all the military news between Germany and now reports that Tehran was a twisted, burned-out shell with more than three million humans dead, the UPF might not be focused on their job. He had seen the news reports of riots and the outcry for immediate attacks on Israel. The world was outraged, or at least the loudmouths were.

The prime minster of Israel had claimed that not only had the small country not fired a missile at Tehran, they had no current reason to attack a country still crippled from an extended war with the United States. Great Britain and the U.S. military confirmed that no satellite evidence of an attack existed. But the Arabs wanted blood and could not be quieted.

It was avoiding that kind of bluster that had made Radko

enjoy riding around the area. There was no stress in this task his distant cousin had given him. One reason he could stay so far behind Wilner and stay out of sight was that there was very little traffic and he had a pretty good idea where the policeman was going each time he got in his Hive. Radko had visited Fort Lauderdale just before the turn of the century. He had enjoyed the sun, but was not crazy about the crowds. Now there were no crowds, but not much sun either. Right now it wasn't raining, but the roads were damp as they had been since Radko had arrived with Nadovich and his two cousins.

Coming from the Philadelphia area he was not used to the concept of a Unified Police Force. Back home, as he now thought of Philadelphia, each town still had a police department. They had not had the drastic decrease in population that cut the tax revenue. He didn't like all the extra humans around Philly—loud, pushy New York humans at that. But he liked that many of the services were not cut.

Radko wanted to help Nadovich with his plans, but he also realized he missed his home. He missed his kids too. Even though the youngest was sixty-seven years old, he liked seeing them everyday.

Nadovich had told him to follow the cop Wilner, retrieve the circuit board and then eliminate the cop if he could do it quietly. Radko was no cold-blooded killer. Even of humans. He had no real use for them and had seen and experienced their cruelty, but he did not kill them for sport like some of his kind. But he had to think of the future of the Simolit family and knew there were things that must be done, no matter how distasteful, to help Nadovich with his plan to provide a sanctuary in Florida.

Radko was a patient man. He had plenty of practice. He

was once imprisoned in Austria for fourteen years and never felt anxious about his incarceration because, like many of his kind, he took the long view on time. He could outwait any dumb cop at any time.

He settled back into the car's seat, which was far too small for his frame, ready to move as soon as Wilner came out. Radko figured he'd approach him near his house because that's where it was likely he had stored the circuit board.

Johann Halleck did not like the fact that Tom Wilner thought he'd be able to keep the circuit board out of Tiget Nadovich's hands. He clearly had underestimated Nadovich and, Halleck realized, didn't know exactly whom or what he was dealing with. But one human's ignorance should not cost lives or help the plans of Nadovich.

Johann had taken a pledge he intended to keep. He had no wish whatsoever to harm Wilner or any other human, but the time had come to take action. He knew Wilner would appreciate it if he ever found out the whole truth. But he thought it unlikely the UPF detective would ever see the big picture. It was too bad. The detective was sharp, honest and brave. He could've helped Johann and the entire Halleck family. But Johann knew the type. He had an oath to a job or a country that would keep him blind to higher purposes.

THIRTY-ONE

Tom Wilner sat in a chair directly in front of the district commander of the UPF. The older, balding man shook his head for what felt like the twentieth time to Wilner.

"Like I told you, Willie, we're stretched too thin. You already got all the help you're gonna get. I'm sorry the house was empty, but you're on your own on this."

Wilner just stared silently at him.

The commander continued. "You're lucky I'm letting you run with this whole thing. Frankly the agent from the Department of Homeland Security is interested enough, so I could let you off the case. But if you ran this guy Nadovich off, that's fine."

Wilner nodded. He considered spilling Besslia's theory about the aliens, but the boss already considered the traffic cop an idiot. And if Wilner told him what his research had found, would the commander consider him an idiot too? Probably, and he might not be wrong.

The commander softened his tone and said, "I know things

are crazy around here. You get notice that you might be called back up yet?"

Wilner shook his head. "Not yet."

"Pete and Jerry both got called back to the army. They must be saving the marines for something else. Maybe they'll send you in to Tehran to mop up and help transfer control to Israel."

"I thought Israel didn't nuke them."

"That's what they claim, but who else could've done it? They have the capability and Iran is always threatening them. I think they just had enough."

Wilner shrugged. "I haven't been called up yet."

"I hope you're not. You got the kids and you're too valuable around here."

Wilner nodded, still pissed off that he wouldn't get any more help.

"Willie, with everyone looking at the Germans and now this Tehran fiasco, who knows what's gonna happen. You're a good detective. Do your job, get home to your kids and don't sweat the ones that got away." He looked at Wilner hard. "Not the crooks or the women."

Svala Wilner sat in the quiet house and dreamed of her children. Although she knew that her destiny lay with Tiget Nadovich and for reasons deeper than she could understand they were tied to each other, Svala missed her husband and the calm little life they had together. It was times like this that she wondered if she'd made a monumental mistake.

It was easy to fall in love with Tiget. He was fearless and a leader. Their people respected him and now spoke his name with a sense of awe.

Her feelings for Tom Wilner started in a similar fashion. During the days of the Balkan Religious War, as many Americans referred to it, the marines stepped in for no other reason than to restore peace. The Serbians loved the occupiers in this situation. The United States had shown no intention of staying, took no natural resources and stopped the Bosnian Muslims from creating any more terror. Svala was among the cheering crowds when the first U.S. Marines, fresh from victory in Iran, rolled into Belgrade.

Not long after that she saw the tall marine sergeant standing in a square chatting with several elderly men. His smile caught her attention first. She shed her heavy coat and strutted by him, knowing what would catch his attention.

It took only a few days before he was telling her about growing up in New Jersey and how his travels in the marines had taught him how wonderful America was. She'd only visited New York once for a short time and his stories of quiet, safe streets and few food shortages intrigued her as much as his passionate way of talking about his homeland. Over the next few weeks she found that the sincere U.S. Marine was a decent, intelligent man who was really interested in her and what she thought about things. She was unused to the Serbian men, especially ones like Tiget, showing much interest in her mind. At least Tiget had seen her taking action and her passion about issues. He often proclaimed what a special woman she was, but he was still too in love with himself.

Svala had never gotten so close to someone who was not one of her countrymen. She was enthralled by the tenderness this combat veteran could show to her and swept up in the passion when he blurted out a proposal on that rainy October afternoon. Everything moved so quickly as she found herself married to an outsider and moving to America in just a matter of weeks.

Tom had proven that his feelings weren't fleeting and that he was dedicated to her and the children. She sometimes cursed Tiget for coming back into her life. He could have waited. He knew that the marriage would have resolved itself in time. But instead he had showed up without warning, knowing that she couldn't resist his connection to her.

Now she worried for Tom's safety. He couldn't know how dangerous Tiget was.

She started to cry softly as she thought about all the pain she had caused.

Tom Wilner let his boss' words run through his head over and over on his way back to his house in the Eastern District. He understood why he was in this case alone. He wasn't even sure what kind of case it was. He didn't know for sure that the defendants were human. That was just crazy. Too crazy to say out loud. Not to Shelby and not to his boss. But that didn't mean it wasn't a possibility.

The fact that aliens now existed was not in dispute. The whole world had seen their spaceship and heard their messages. The only question was the timing of their arrival. Perhaps his wacky friend Steve Besslia was on just the right wavelength to figure it out. If he was and it was true that normal police procedures did not apply, he may not be crazy. The next question was, how to stop them? After what Wilner had done to Nadovich and then had seen him walk away from, normal weapons would not stop them either. And his Svala was right in the middle of it. He knew she wasn't being held as a prisoner. She came and went freely from the house. He just hoped she wasn't part of the scheme that Tiget Nadovich was involved in.

Wilner turned off the main road onto a smaller street that had several of the businesses that Wilner used on a regular basis. There was a family hardware store, a shoe and leather repair shop and a small electronics repair shop that he stopped at all the time. As he turned, he noticed that a dark blue Hive made the turn as well. He didn't recognize the vehicle, but realized he had seen it when he left the UPF headquarters. He wasn't particularly paranoid, but with all that had happened the idea that someone was following him didn't seem so wild.

He took another turn, slowed down and a few seconds later the dark blue Hive took the corner and had to hit the brakes to avoid rear-ending Wilner. Now he was only two blocks from his home and didn't want to lead this guy back to the kids. He formulated a plan and felt for his pistol on his hip in preparation. He knew there was an old park up ahead. No one used it and it was horribly maintained, but it had a parking lot and if this guy followed him in there then Wilner would have no reservations about drawing on him and shooting if he had to.

He watched his mirror as the car dropped back, but still stayed on the same course. Wilner sped up a little, then took the sharp turn into the empty parking lot. The park and its single basketball hoop were also vacant. He had his pistol in his hand already as he brought his Hive to a stop and jumped out of the vehicle as the other car entered the lot.

He kneeled down behind the trunk of his Hive with his pistol sighted in on the head of the very large man driving. He waited and let the big man come out of the car, hardly believing how big and thick he was. He had no problem acquiring a target with all that meat available behind the sights of his pistol.

Radko Simolit squeezed out of the American Hive and immediately saw that the policeman, Wilner, had a pistol pointed at him. He was able to suppress a smile as he started to walk toward the hidden cop.

"Police, don't move," shouted the UPF detective.

Radko ignored him and continued to walk normally, not showing any aggression and no weapons. He knew the cop's pistol wouldn't put him down, but who liked being shot? If he was unarmed he knew the police training would keep the cop from shooting. Until it was too late. He needed this cop alive long enough to tell him where he had hidden the board. Radko hoped he had it on him or in the car. If not, he'd make the cop talk.

He continued to walk and the cop's voice seemed more panicked. "I said stop," he yelled from behind the car. He had not given up his position and still had the pistol pointed at Radko. This was a brave man.

Radko acted as if he had not even seen anyone or heard any commands.

"Don't take another step or I'll shoot," yelled the cop.

To Radko's surprise he did shoot and Radko felt the bullet rip into his right arm. He brushed off the injury as he reached the rear of the car and turned toward the cop. The human stepped back and fired again, this time into Radko's massive chest. Then he fired twice more until Radko was right in front of him and was able to grab the pistol, rip it from his hand and toss it behind him as far as he could without even looking where the heavy pistol landed.

Wilner kicked him hard in the leg and then punched him in the face. These were not even bothersome to Radko, who wrapped his big hands into Wilner's jacket and brought him close to him, the jacket twisted all around his hands. "Where is the circuit board?"

For his question all he felt was a knee in his groin. It hurt, but not enough to chase him off or move him back. He tightened his grip and lifted Wilner completely off the ground. "I asked where the board was."

He didn't want to get ugly so quickly, but knew if this cop had a broken arm he'd be more open to questioning. Radko released the jacket to grab his arm, but was surprised how quickly the muscular cop could move. He jumped back to the front of the car and held up his hands, saying, "Let's talk about this."

Tom Wilner understood the term "déjà vu" as he shot, then punched this giant of a man without any effect at all. Now he had broken his unbelievably strong grip and jumped back. He needed to buy time, but he wasn't sure what for. No way he was going to send this guy by his house to get the board. Not with the kids and Mrs. Honzit there. He backed up as the behemoth tried to close the distance on him. He wanted to have as much of the Hive between him and this monster as possible.

The man moved fast, especially for his size, and tried to leap at Wilner. Just as Wilner thought he was about to lay his massive hands on him again he heard a noise, then saw a blinding flash.

Instinctively he jumped back and couldn't even understand what had happened as the ball of light enveloped the giant man. The blast from the flasher instantly turned him into a huge ball of flesh and bone that sizzled as it melted and oozed into the ground.

The smell, while disgusting, was not unfamiliar to Wilner. He'd seen many people killed by flashers during the war in Iran. It was the context that was so different here. He felt sick to his stomach looking at the sizzling wad of meat. Then he looked up to see the tall blond man holding the flasher that had just saved his life.

It took a moment to realize that it was Johann Halleck who had just intervened in the fight.

Now things were getting confusing.

THIRTY-TWO

Tom Wilner had smelled unpleasant odors before. The stench of combat and death don't fade easily, but the stink coming from the lump of flesh at his feet right now was enough to make him gag. He fought hard not to vomit in front of Johann Halleck.

The tall, meaty blond man stood silently, as if he expected something like vomit.

Wilner obliged him and turned to spit up in front of the car. He retched hard enough to go down on one knee and cough up what little food he had left in his stomach.

Halleck stepped closer and said, "Are you all right?"

Wilner nodded as he stood slowly and turned to face the taller man. He had to lean against the car. Then, out of habit, he reached to his hip to check his pistol. It was missing and somewhere, swimming in his head, Wilner knew the big man he had fought had taken his issued duty pistol.

Halleck patted him on the shoulder and said, "Your gun is in the trees over there. Perhaps we need to take a walk anyway to clear your head." He ushered Wilner away from the car over toward the stand of trees inside the small park.

Wilner could still taste the stench and even hear the body sizzle as they walked away. The fresher air and distance from the body made him feel a little better.

As they walked together, both looking down for the pistol, Johann said, "It's lucky that I happened by."

Wilner stopped and looked at him. "How did you just happen by?"

"I was on the way to your house."

"What?"

"Don't worry, I mean you or your family no harm. Surely you must realize that now. I merely wished to speak with you."

"About what?"

"The circuit board. I want to take custody of it."

"How do you know I even have it?"

Johann smiled. "I'm not stupid. If Nadovich is so frantic for it, my guess is that you recovered it. I know more than you might suspect."

"I bet you do."

Johann pointed and then stepped into the trees. He turned, holding Wilner's pistol by the barrel, then walked back to him casually and handed the pistol, butt first, to Wilner.

Wilner took it, but kept his eyes on Johann. He couldn't figure what the hell was going on or who this guy was.

"Thanks," muttered Wilner as he holstered the pistol. "I have plenty of room on my belt since you demolished my stun baton."

Johann shrugged. "It hurt. What was I supposed to do, let you hit me again?"

Wilner considered this and nodded. "You've got a point."

Johann smiled again, leaning against a picnic table next to them. "I'd like you to give me the board. I don't want to take it from you. All I wish to do is keep it safe and away from Tiget Nadovich or any of his associates."

"Who are you? A concerned citizen? Some kind of government agent? What?"

Johann just stared at him.

"What about Nadovich? I've seen the kind of damage he can take. I saw how useless my pistol and punches were on that guy over there." He pointed to the place where Johann had melted the assailant. "What are they? I've figured out they're not human."

"These are all good questions, but I'm afraid, irrelevant. What's important is control of the board. You've shown how hard it is to keep the other boards safe. Now I'd like a chance to keep it."

"What if Nadovich pays you a visit?"

Johann smiled. "Then I'd have a very fine day."

Wilner looked at him and had the feeling that the history between him and Nadovich was longer and even more serious than his own history with the Serbian immigrant.

Wilner finally said, "I appreciate your help and I believe you're sincere, but I'm going to keep the board." He looked past the big man sitting on the table and saw Steve Besslia rumble into the lot on his Hive-bike. This was becoming a popular attraction.

Johann turned his head, but showed no emotion about the arrival of the UPF traffic cop in uniform.

They both watched as Besslia dismounted and walked toward them as he unstrapped his helmet but kept it on his head. As he got close he said, "Can anyone join this party?"

Wilner said, "What're you doing here?"

"I was headed to your house to see you, or if you weren't around, I'd have chatted up Mrs. Honzit." He looked at each man. Then turned to Wilner and said, "You gonna give him another lesson in fighting?"

"Hope not. But he doesn't take no for an answer."

Johann emphasized the comment by saying, "I *must* have the board."

Wilner said, "See what I mean." He looked at Johann Halleck. "I already told you no. But now we want some answers."

Johann stood up and said, "Then we are at an impasse."

Wilner saw Besslia reach for his stun baton. Wilner reached for his pistol. He didn't want to hurt the big man, but he couldn't have him come to his house when he didn't know what was going on. Both cops took a step back as they unholstered their weapons.

Tiget Nadovich heard the pounding from the second-floor bedroom of the house he had moved to in the Western District. He also noticed Svala's concerned look. Why did things need to be so complicated? He knew Alec and Demitri would ignore the noise because they were not trying to concentrate like him. His head pounded with one of his fake headaches as he considered all that had gone wrong and wondered if his plan would really work. He had found many Arab men to be very stubborn in their approach to negotiation. He hoped he had not gone to all this effort for nothing.

He stood from the couch where he sat with Svala, absently rubbing her soft hair and stroking her cheek, marched up the carpeted stairs and directly to the rear bedroom, then placed his thumb on the secure padlock that bolted the door and stepped inside the room.

He said, "Stop that." Like he was speaking to a small child. He looked at the bound man on the floor and stepped closer. "If you continue to kick the floor I will do something drastic like send you back to your uncle minus a foot. Would you like that?"

The man on the floor shook his head, the tape across his mouth hiding any facial expression. His hands were still secured behind his back and his feet taped together. Nadovich was impressed Mr. Hammed's nephew, Walid, could make so much noise while trussed up like he was.

Nadovich said to him, "I don't like holding you. It is merely a business consideration with your uncle. We live here. I do not want to hear such foolishness again. Do you understand?"

The muscle-bound man nodded slowly and looked down at the ground.

Nadovich said, "Alec will be up shortly to take you to the bathroom and feed you. Remain silent. Okay?"

The man nodded again.

As he returned to the downstairs couch, Svala's dark eyes followed him all the way.

She said, "What are your plans?"

"To keep us safe."

"That includes kidnapping?"

"It does. At least for now."

Nadovich looked up at a clock on the wall. "Has anyone heard from Radko?"

No one could say yes.

Johann Halleck was not concerned about an assault by either or both of the policemen. His main concern was not hurting them if they did something stupid. That would be counter to everything he had stood for. He did realize he had to disarm them. In a calm, but quick motion, he reached out and grabbed the stun baton before the traffic cop even had it completely out of its holster. He saw the pistol clear Wilner's holster and simply redirected the end of the baton into Wilner's exposed side.

The snap of the jolt and involuntary flinching by Wilner caused the detective to squeeze his hand and his pistol discharged, the bullet flying into the picnic table.

Johann twisted the baton out of the traffic cop's hands and at the same time, kicked the pistol, which Wilner had just dropped. The traffic cop stepped back, surprised he had lost his baton, then he lowered his head and started to thrust his body forward to use the helmet like a battering ram on the taller Johann.

Johann struck the helmet hard with the palm of his hand and split the UPF emblem on the front down the middle.

The traffic cop fell backward to the ground, heavily stunned by the blow.

Johann reached down and picked up Wilner's gun, then stepped across the dazed detective and took the pistol from the traffic cop's holster. He tossed both pistols on the picnic table, then leaned each groggy man against small saplings in front of the table.

Johann said, "I'm sorry. I respect men like you. Men who take oaths to protect others. I really do. But I'm getting sick of being struck with batons or shot at with pistols." He looked as each man seemed to recover his wits and his eyes focused more sharply on Johann. "I need the board and I'm not alone. I know others who will recover the board if necessary, but as I said I'd rather work with you and get the board with your approval."

Wilner stared at him.

"Very well," said Johann. "I will do what I must do."

Wilner cleared his throat and said, "Wait, can we talk for a few minutes?"

"Of course."

The detective struggled to his feet, shaking off the effects of the stun baton. He looked over at his friend who looked like he wanted to remain seated for a while. Wilner faced Johann and said, "You're one of them too."

Johann said nothing.

"Are you invincible? Can you die?"

Johann nodded as he considered the question. "No, sadly we are not invincible as my flasher blast on that man proved. Many have died. Some protecting humans from harm."

"But you're not humans."

Johann shook his head. "You will see, Detective Wilner, that we are more similar than you might think. We need each other."

"I could sign a warrant out on you for the E-weapon. Your lawyer wouldn't get you off that."

"The E-weapon, that saved your life?"

Wilner looked down.

Johann said, "I'm sorry I cannot tell you more. But there will be another time. If you're still alive."

He turned and took long strides back toward the parked cars. His Hive was on the street past the park entrance. He paused at Wilner's Hive and the traffic cop's Hive-bike, pulled his Saudi combat knife and took a second to cut a tire on each vehicle. He needed a few minutes to accomplish his mission and didn't want to fight these two again.

THIRTY-THREE

Tom Wilner had Steve Besslia in the front seat of his UPF-issued Hive when he screeched to a stop in front of his house. He'd thought that Johann Halleck's efforts to flatten his tires meant he was coming to the house and it spooked him. The supposedly self-sealing tires not closing the hole as large as the combat knife left in them, so the rubber and polymer tires having just enough tread to screech when the car stopped.

The outside looked fine with the front door shut and a few lights coming from the kitchen as dusk fell and the gray clouds kept the light outside low.

He turned to Besslia and said, "Go around back in case there's a problem. I'll walk through like we don't expect anything."

Besslia nodded, drew his pistol and started to trot around the corner of the house.

Wilner kept his pistol in its holster, but unlike most nights he didn't lock it in his car. He listened at the front door for a moment to anticipate anything unusual. All sounded normal.

There was some muffled TV noise and maybe voices. He placed his hand on the doorknob when he heard a scream. Not just any scream. It was Emma. He knew his daughter's voice and the tenor of her varied screams. This was not the playful one.

His stomach tightened as he imagined what had set off the scream. He yanked his pistol and twisted the knob of the door then rushed inside with the gun out, scanning for anything unusual.

In the kitchen, Mrs. Honzit held Emma and Tommy against her legs as they looked out through the living room toward the sliding glass door.

Wilner leveled his gun toward where they were looking and said, "What is it?"

Mrs. Honzit pointed out the sliding glass door and said, "There's a man out back."

Emma added, "And he had a gun."

Wilner relaxed and stepped toward the door and leaned out to make sure it was Steve Besslia.

He saw the smaller traffic cop standing by the door and holstered his pistol.

It took a few minutes to restore calm and then he led Besslia out to the garage. As soon as they walked into the one-car garage Wilner froze.

"What is it?" asked Besslia.

Wilner pointed at a toolbox on the ground with the lid open and said, "Someone got the board."

It was getting late when Wilner had both the kids in bed and sat on the couch with Mrs. Honzit and Steve Besslia. The housekeeper had not seen or heard anyone enter the garage and the side door had been forced open. The only person she saw was Besslia out the sliding glass door.

The idea that someone unwelcome, whether it was Tiget

Nadovich or Johann Halleck, was so close to his family made Wilner furious. He looked at Besslia and said, "Would you mind staying here for a few days?"

Besslia looked over at Mrs. Honzit and said, "It would be my pleasure."

Shelby Hahn had considered what she was doing from several positions: professionally, personally and then from her desire to do it for fun. She knew that her actions could complicate matters for many people and she didn't want to cloud her judgment, but right now she didn't care. It was late, but she knocked on the door anyway, hoping the right person would answer. If not, she had several cover stories.

After a long delay, which she understood, the door opened a crack. She smiled at Tom Wilner's handsome face.

He pulled the door all the way open and she noticed the big auto-pistol in his hand. A man defending his castle and family. It made him even more attractive, if that was possible.

She didn't wait, stepping up into the house next to him, wrapping her hands around the back of his neck and planting a deep, sincere kiss on his lips.

He responded just as she had hoped.

Tiget Nadovich and his cousins, Alec and Demitri Nadin had tried to contact Radko Simolit for more than two hours before they decided to split up and look for him. Nadovich was a little uneasy about making Svala stay at home alone with their prisoner, Walid, but he was now too concerned for Radko to have a choice. He needed both his cousins to help search for Radko. He knew Svala could handle the bound man and he had not seemed to be terribly bright, so Nadovich wasn't worried about Svala falling for a trick. He didn't like involving her in the whole plan. Her affection for Wilner had been clear and her desire to stay with Nadovich, but not be part of his shadowy world was also clear. For a woman like Svala he tried to make anything possible. But this was an emergency.

Alec, riding his old Harley-Davidson motorcycle, had gone to see if Radko was watching Wilner at the UPF station and then planned to stop at the few bars in the area to see if the big man just got bored and stopped for a drink.

Nadovich and Demitri followed a route from the UPF station toward Wilner's home in the Eastern District. Now that Nadovich knew he was wanted he had to be more careful traveling. There were fewer cops to potentially catch him, but also many fewer people to keep an eye on.

He drove east on the old State Road 84, which had been abandoned in favor of a large interstate built next to it. One of the bigger terror attacks on September eleventh about eight years ago had included explosives packed on the overpasses of the interstate. Three of the overpasses collapsed and the others were weakened enough that they just closed it and traffic returned to the old state road.

Once he had crossed over the old Interstate 95 that ran from the zone north, he slowed in the residential area.

Demitri said, "You think Radko got the board and is celebrating?"

"Perhaps, but he should be on his V-com."

"What could happen to him? He's a giant that can heal almost instantly."

"It's just a feeling I have. I told his father I'd be responsible for him."

"Responsible for him. He's like two hundred and thirty years old."

"Two hundred and fifty-one. I was there when he was born." Nadovich turned the wheel of the big general utility vehicle. "Keep your eyes open for the blue Hive he's driving. The one we usually keep down near the zone."

Demitri nodded and concentrated on each vehicle he saw.

They turned on one of the streets leading to Wilner's house and slowed.

Nadovich said, "There, by the park. Is that the car?"

Demitri's voice raised with excitement. "I don't see Radko."

They pulled in at the entrance to the small park. Nadovich was unarmed but he knew Demitri liked to carry an old Smith & Wesson 9 millimeter. Before the arms company had turned to flashers it had been known for its fine conventional automatic pistols.

He slipped out of the high Hive utility vehicle and heard Alec crunch around the gravel toward him. They approached the car slowly.

"Radko," called out Nadovich.

Then Demitri froze as he approached the driver's side of the car. He stepped back speechless.

"What is it?" Nadovich rushed over to him.

He looked down at where Demitri's attention was focused. On the ground, nearly unrecognizable as a living or dead being, lay Radko Simolit. His clothes melted into his flesh as jagged bones popped out of the mass in different directions and at odd angles.

He could still smell the burnt flesh and noticed the blue paint on that side of the car was burned. The outline of Radko's body left a dark blue and untouched patch. Someone had used a flasher on his cousin from Philadelphia. Someone who was going to die.

Demitri continued to retreat, then stopped and retched into the damp grass.

Nadovich was not sure he had seen one of his people throw up since World War II when the Nazis surprised them all with their brutality.

Finally, after gasping for some air, Alec said, "Do cops even carry flashers?"

Nadovich didn't answer, his attention still on Radko's remains.

"Maybe it was someone else. There are some Hallecks down here."

Nadovich nodded. "But this was on the way to Wilner's house. He was involved."

Nadovich felt a tear in his eye for his dead kinsman. "We'll deal with Wilner once and for all. After we trade that idiot Walid for the radioactive material then we'll get the board and be done with Svala's policeman forever."

He felt the hitch in his voice as he looked back down at Radko.

THIRTY-FOUR

After a sleepless night, Tom Wilner awoke to his V-com beeping. Turning his head he paused as he looked at Shelby Hahn's peaceful, sleeping face. They had been as quiet as possible because he didn't want to risk waking the kids or hearing any comments from Besslia. He looked at the V-com and saw the call was from a UPF office, but he didn't recognize the location right away. He rolled out of bed and slipped into his bathroom to keep from waking Shelby.

Once in the large bathroom, he positioned a wall behind him. He patted down his short brown hair and hit the receive button.

It took another second to recognize the man contacting him. Then, more from the scientific equipment behind the man, Wilner realized it was the UPF lab tech.

The man said, "Can you come up here for a video conference?"

"With who?"

"Whom?"

"What?" asked Wilner.

"The correct usage is 'whom.' With whom are we having the video conference."

Wilner used the full capabilities of the small video screen to get across his annoyance without saying a word.

The lab tech got the point. "Dan Foster, the director of the Disney lab on DNA research, wants to talk about the blood samples you collected."

"Why? What'd they find?"

The lab tech shook his head. "He was evasive and wanted to talk to you. He said he'd even prefer to see you in person if possible."

Wilner thought about a quick trip up the deserted road to Orlando. If he wasn't concerned about everyone knowing where he lived and the spooky things that had been going on he might have tried it. Instead he looked into the video screen of his V-com and said, "I'll be at your office in under an hour. Can you set it up?"

"You got it, Detective."

Wilner cut him off before he said anything else.

Wilner was dressed and had finished a protein shake five minutes after the V-com call from the lab. Steve Besslia had spent the night on his couch, wearing ill-fitting workout clothes that Wilner no longer used. He kneeled down and tapped the traffic cop between snores.

Besslia awoke and then it took a moment for his eyes to focus. Wilner thought about how you could tell that was the sign of someone who had never been in combat.

Wilner said, "I need to run up to the Northern Enclave. Can you stay here for a few hours?"

Besslia nodded.

"No one comes in the house. And the kids have to stay inside. We need to be careful."

Besslia sat up and said, "You can count on me."

Wilner knew better than to count on his friend so he quietly returned to his bedroom only to find Shelby dressed.

She looked up and said, "I was afraid you'd snuck out on me."

Wilner said, "I bet that never happens."

She walked to him and wrapped her arms around his waist and squeezed.

"I've gotta run up to the Northern Enclave for a few hours. Would it be a problem if you kept an eye on things for me?"

"Yeah, sure. What's going on in the Enclave?"

"Just some lab issues with the blood samples I recovered from the guys that ambushed Steve at his condo."

She stepped back. "What kind of issues?"

"I'll know more after I talk to the lab guys."

"Can I come too? Steve can watch the house."

He looked at her and said, "I'd feel better if you were here."

She nodded, but he had an odd feeling about it. He hoped he hadn't made her self-conscious watching his kids, but it was for security not to babysit.

Wilner took advantage of the empty highways and found himself in front of the UPF lab in the heart of the Northern Enclave less than forty minutes later. This time the lab tech was waiting for him and buzzed him directly into the lab.

Wilner said, "You look excited. What'd you find out?"

"Nothing new, it's just that the last few years have been

pretty routine. I went to school for this. It's nice to use my skills on something other than answering the phone or picking up a fingerprint or two."

Wilner said, "Did we have a specific time we were supposed to call?"

The lab tech shook his head. "Dr. Foster said to call as soon as we could. He seemed extremely interested in the samples."

They moved to a small room with a video broadcaster on the wall and a camera that took in the whole room. In a matter of seconds a younger man with gray hair was on the screen introducing himself as Dan Foster.

After several minutes of explaining where Wilner had retrieved the blood samples and how the blood got on the walls, Foster had a few questions.

"And this cop, Besslia, is certain he hit them and the blood is from the wounds."

Wilner said, "Yes, and my investigation backs that up. Now can you tell me what this is all about?"

The scientist hesitated, then said, "The samples are not human."

"That's what I was told, but how can that be? What animal are they?"

"That's the issue."

"I'm afraid I don't understand." But in reality he was starting to understand. This all fit into Besslia's theory about the origin of the attackers.

The scientist said, "The samples have genetic markers very similar to humans. But not completely. Also the samples are from two different sources, but the sources are related."

"How close to human are they?"

"Have you ever heard that a chimpanzee is 98 percent the same, genetically, as a human?"

Wilner nodded enough that the video picked it up.

"That's not exactly correct but close. These samples are about 99 percent the same as a human. They are remarkable samples."

"And you've never seen them before?"

The scientist hesitated. The square gray head dipping as he considered his answer. "I have seen reference to it in some of the old medical journals. So now I've been checking the ones that are archived on the computer."

"And what did you find?"

"A Romanian journal lists several instances of the samples. Some in Romania and some in other Eastern European countries."

"Like Serbia?"

"Yes, Serbia and Croatia were both prominently mentioned. The Romanian journal theorized that these samples and the being that they belonged to could be the source of the vampire legends. Of course other articles refute that. Have you ever been to Europe, Detective?"

Wilner nodded. "I was in Serbia during the Balkan conflict."

"Have you ever heard about anything like this or did you just stumble into it here?"

"I have; actually I saw a man with fatal injuries who recovered."

"Isn't that a product of misdiagnosis?"

"No." Wilner shook his head emphatically. "Not if you had seen them. You can't misdiagnose a bullet to the head."

That brought the scientist up short. He cleared his throat and said, "There are other journals that have noted similar blood samples to what you found."

"And what was their conclusion?"

"There were a number of theories from contaminated samples to . . ."

Wilner said, "To what? Dr. Foster?"

"To alien beings here on Earth."

THIRTY-FIVE

Shelby Hahn set the kids' breakfast dishes in the sink and placed the washer muffle over them. She waited ten seconds, then as she pulled off the cover that cleaned the dishes and dried them almost instantly she saw Mrs. Honzit standing at the edge of the kitchen.

"Where is the mister?" the older woman asked.

Shelby got a very odd vibe from the housekeeper and her woman's intuition told her that Mrs. Honzit was jealous of Shelby's presence.

"He had to go to work. I'm going to hang around until he gets back."

"And the lazy one on the couch?"

Shelby smiled as the housekeeper threw a glance over to the still sleeping Steve Besslia. The kids were watching the video broadcaster and playing a game right next to him and he had not stirred yet.

"I guess he's staying too."

Mrs. Honzit sighed and shook her head. "Then I have errands to run. You will stay with children?"

"Yes." Shelby noticed how it almost sounded like Mrs. Honzit wanted to say "my children." She looked at the housekeeper and wondered if she had a crush on the boss or was in love with the kids? Or maybe both.

After Mrs. Honzit had left, making a point to hug and kiss Emma and Tommy, Shelby played a few games with them and generally nosed around the nice, clean house. She liked being domestic. Firing an artillery piece at Iranian soldiers, she doubted she would ever get the chance to experience something like this and she was surprised how much she liked it.

She knew many of Tom Wilner's secrets from watching him and seeing how he hid things in the house. He was naïve about what people would do to find things they needed like circuit boards. He was blind to much of what was going on right in front of him. She hoped he didn't get hurt by being caught in the middle. He was a good man and he had already had his heart broken. She didn't want anything else on his handsome body broken.

When Besslia was dressed and sitting at the kitchen counter with Shelby, she asked him if he knew where Wilner had gone.

"To the UPF lab."

"I know, but why?"

"Something about the blood samples he recovered from my place."

"But what about them?" She thought she knew the answer and was hoping it wasn't becoming common knowledge. She didn't want to see a panic, or worse an effort to silence anyone who knew the truth.

"I think—" He bent closer and dropped his voice.

Shelby leaned into him.

Besslia said, "I think I know what's up."

"Then tell me."

"I think the blood samples are from aliens."

She sat back up, looking at the traffic cop to determine if he was pulling her leg.

"Really?" was all she could say.

In the giant Chaos Pit, located inside the Miami Quarantine Zone, Tiget Nadovich sat silently at the bar with a beer, still fuming over the fate of Radko Simolit. He had wanted to go to the cop's house right then and kill him, but Demitri had convinced him that he should wait. First to make sure he was able to recover the board and secondly so it wouldn't upset Svala. Demitri pointed out that they weren't even certain it was Wilner who had used a flasher on their cousin and reduced him to a ball of waste.

Nadovich and Demitri had gathered up the remains and buried them in a field near the house where they were currently living. They had made Walid dig the grave so he could get some exercise. Nadovich was too upset last night to dig or consider what his next move was. Now he saw things a little more clearly and knew he had to move forward with his plan.

But that was the problem; there were holes in his plan. He had seen New York with the ghostly humans and the insects and the gloomy, depressing atmosphere. He wasn't sure that a safe haven for him and his family was worth that. His other concern was that a dirty bomb detonated in the wide-open spaces of south Florida would not contaminate a very large area. It may chase away the humans initially, but would it keep them away? He had his doubts.

Out in the car, Alec held big, stupid Walid. The simple trade for radioactive material could be made here. But he knew the other part of the deal with Mr. Hammed involved paying him the one point five million suds he had lost in the bar. That was going to be an issue. Nadovich didn't have all the money. And he wasn't sure Mr. Hammed would accept his credit. That was an issue he'd deal with when the Lebanese man showed up.

The large Hispanic bartender had spoken English to Nadovich as soon as he had sat at the empty bar. He may have recognized him from the day he sat next to the unlucky Johann Halleck. Now he said, "You're not here to cause problems, are you?"

"Why would you say that?"

"Because the other day a guy from the district came in and it was a mess."

Nadovich shook his head. "No, no problems." He looked past the bartender to an open rear door behind the bar. He caught a glimpse of someone fishing through the garbage in the back; a small, thin ghostly figure with wispy hair and a permanently dirty face.

The bartender turned around, saw the scavenger and yelled as he stepped toward the open door. Then the big bartender froze.

Nadovich looked closer and was also shocked. He didn't know what to say, but he realized the big bartender knew why this little man was so dirty and rummaging through the bar's trash.

The scared man, who had been digging in the garbage, looked into the bar and his eyes settled on a woman dancing on the closest stage. He looked hypnotized by the chubby young Hispanic woman with large breasts as she moved to the beat of Latin music.

Nadovich was not sure if he had seen anyone in this condition alive before except on a video broadcaster and then usually in some distant country. Here, in the United States, the few people like this shadow of a man had been relegated to a growing community near Rapid City, South Dakota, in what was called the Western Quarantine Zone. The community had grown to include the towns of Lead and Sturgis. Few military men wanted to risk contracting the bioplague so the slow sprawl west of the reservation met little resistance.

The big bartender said, "Get out of here. Go." He raised his voice but made no effort to touch the small, dirty man.

The growler scampered away silently.

Nadovich said, "I never saw one up close. Do others live nearby?"

The bartender looked at him and said, "Downtown. The old downtown near the bay there's supposed to be a few hundred growlers wandering around. No one has the balls to go check it out and since this isn't part of the United States no more they can't send them to the Western Quarantine Zone. No one wants to hear the growls."

Nadovich considered this and what he had seen in New York when the council had shown him his other options. At the time the sight of the dead bioplague victim had not interested him, but seeing a living, breathing growler gave him some ideas.

As Tom Wilner walked through the door of his home he was greeted first by his kids with big hugs then by Shelby Hahn who also embraced him. He could feel her pistol on her hip under a long shirt. He liked the feel of a woman greeting him. Even a heavily armed one.

Mrs. Honzit was in the kitchen and merely looked up at

him instead of her normal friendly greeting. She had several unknown meat patties cooking on the stove as Steve Besslia chatted with her from the counter.

Shelby gave him another squeeze and asked, "What did the lab say?"

He looked at her.

"Steve told me where you went. What's the big secret?"

"No secret. I'm just not sure how relevant to the case it is." He controlled how he said it. Still wondering what the implications of everything he'd learned were.

"The case?" She looked shocked. "I thought we had more than just a case in common. I'm just interested in what you're doing. That's all." She released him and turned toward the bedroom.

He caught up as she entered the room, looking for her purse and the few belongings she had brought.

He said, "I'm sorry, Shelby. It's just—"

"What? It's just what? You think I'd try to steal your case?"

"No. It's not that at all. It's just sort of weird what's going on and I didn't want you to think I'm crazy."

"You know what would make you crazy?" Her face had relaxed a little.

"What?"

"Not telling me the truth and letting me walk out of here pissed."

He smiled and realized she wouldn't judge him and maybe he needed another opinion than Besslia's. "Okay, I'll tell you everything." And he did.

THIRTY-SIX

At the Chaos Pit in the Miami Quarantine Zone, Tiget Nadovich still thought about the growler he had seen. The hysteria and concern over the victims of the bioplague was still rampant through most of the world. The disease was a man-made, weaponized bacteria but could spread with contact. No one seemed sure how much contact but it was documented by scientists studying the deadly plague. The two best-known experts on the disease, Robert Gleason and Eric Raab, had been killed in a terror attack aimed at stealing vials of the disease. The Centers for Disease Control's main lab in Atlanta was the scene of a massive firefight as more than thirty jihadists had tried to storm the building.

The younger of the two scientists, Eric Raab, had become a national hero after a photo of him using a fallen soldier's rifle appeared in the media across the country. He defended the lab until he was forced to lock himself inside a lab and start a fire to destroy all the bacteria before the jihadists could use it as a weapon.

One of the reasons the quarantine zone had been established in Miami was that bioplague victims had streamed into the area along with Caribbean Islanders and South Americans. A few days after exposure they were too weak to move around much, and the disease usually incapacitated and killed the victim within two weeks. But some people, perhaps as much as 30 percent of the population, were effected by the bioplague but not killed. They suffered the horrible cysts on their neck and face, their lips often swelled and split, they lost weight from the constant vomiting, but they somehow survived. In some cases, where food was abundant, they started to recover slowly. Poor nutrition had helped spread the disease in several countries.

That was why the government had seen fit to annex much of South Dakota and create a "reservation," which they provided with food by airdrop. The sick people inside the quarantine zone were subject to death if they ventured from their designated area and the National Guard had not hesitated to use deadly force. But they were not dying off as originally predicted.

The whole situation and the human's fear of the unknown and unusual was what played in Nadovich's mind now. Then he saw Mr. Hammed walk in the front door and his mind dropped the subject of bioplague. Mr. Hammed was alone.

The Lebanese man spotted Nadovich and turned directly toward him and took the seat at the bar next to him.

"Is Walid all right?"

Nadovich nodded.

"He is my sister's son, but I have raised him here in the United States for the last eleven years. This is not good business, what you have done."

"I regret it was necessary to take Walid. But I assure you he was well-treated and is close by now." He looked at Mr. Hammed. "Did you bring the material?"

"No, I could not transport it. I have the location of the warehouse where you can find it."

Nadovich turned to look at him more closely.

"Do you have the money?"

Nadovich reached under his loose jacket and pulled out an envelope with all the cash he could scrounge up or scare out of others. He slid it across the table. "One hundred thousand suds for the location of the warehouse."

Mr. Hammed scribbled down a map on the back of a napkin.

Nadovich looked at the directions, familiar with the area. He cut his eyes up to his business partner. "No tricks."

Mr. Hammed said, "I swear there are no tricks. I have several pounds in a safe box, but the entire container weighs three hundred pounds and I cannot move it alone. If you had left me Walid then I might have been able to bring it." He gave Nadovich a harsh look then said, "You said you'd have all my money."

"You may have Walid back as a show of good faith and by the fact that I cannot afford to feed him any longer, but the rest of the money will not be delivered until after I have constructed the device."

Mr. Hammed stood and slammed his hand on the bar. "That is outrageous. We had a deal."

"Yes. The deal was for me to return your nephew. The money is good faith for our future business transactions."

He looked up and saw Alec and Walid at the front door. Nadovich had told him to bring in the hulking prisoner after Mr. Hammed had been inside for five minutes.

"Go ahead and take him," said Nadovich. "I'll go to this warehouse for the material in a few hours and then we'll talk about money."

Mr. Hammed stormed out silently, grabbing Walid by the arm and yanking him out the door.

Nadovich didn't hesitate to turn to the bartender who had seemed completely uninterested in what they had been talking about. Nadovich asked him, "Where did you say that man and the other bioplague victims lived?"

At the district hospital, Tom Wilner spoke with the same doctor who had treated the victim of Johann Halleck's knife attack, and Wilner himself, after he had been caught in the attack on the UPF station. The young dark man smiled as he saw the detective walk toward him in the empty hospital hallway.

"What's happened now that the UPF has to upset things around here?" The doctor's teeth seemed to glow from his dark face.

Wilner nodded back. "Just visiting a fella I brought in the other day. Munroe Phillips."

"He doesn't heal as quickly as some of the ones you were associated with, but he'll live."

He led Wilner to a private room where Munroe was recovering. Now, when the UPF was paying, people were treated right. After the doctor had left, Wilner sat down beside Munroe. He leaned on the high bed slightly. "So how'r you feeling?"

Munroe frowned at him. "About as good as I could expect after that guy Nadovich threw me around like a piece of fruit. What the hell is going on? I ain't never seen the UPF scared of no one."

"It's kinda hard to explain and it's getting harder. But I gotta find Nadovich and have a hunch he might be in the quarantine zone a lot. If I granted you full amnesty, would you go over and look for him?"

"You gonna stop him if I find him?"

"I'll do my best."

"Then I'll go. I owe that son of a bitch."

Wilner smiled. "And what do you expect to do to him?"

"Turn him in to you. If you can't get me some payback, no one can."

Wilner spent much of the afternoon showing Nadovich's official state identification photo that he'd downloaded from the office computer. He hit the popular bars and some of the informants he had used over the past few years.

One female bartender at the southern edge of the district said, "I know him. Good-looker with long, brown hair. I think he had a couple of other guys with him."

Wilner nodded. "That's right."

"He was in earlier. I heard him borrow an old beat-up car from one of our regulars."

"Which one? You know his name?"

"Yeah, an old drunk named Todd. I think his last name is Schupper. That's him over in the corner." The tall young woman with long, shapely arms pointed toward a lone man with shoulder-length hair and thick, black-framed glasses.

Wilner nodded absently as he approached the man at the other end of the room. He looked up but had no concern on his face.

Wilner sat in the chair across from him, waiting to see his

reaction. That was half of police work: reading people's re-actions.

The man just gazed up as if an old friend had joined him for a beer. He didn't look drunk. In fact, his glasses seemed to hide an intelligence that someone like the bartender would mistake for something else.

Todd said, "What can I do for you?" He waited a second and added, "Officer."

Wilner smiled. "The lovely bartender over there said you loaned a car to someone today."

"Maybe, why?"

"I need to find him."

"Again I'll ask, why?"

Wilner leaned in closer and whispered, "Because I need to talk to him."

Todd let out a laugh and said, "Sorry, I didn't realize there were any UPF officers with a sense of humor."

"We don't keep it long when someone is wasting our time."

That straightened Todd's face. "Well, I did sort've make a financial agreement with a man today."

Wilner waited then said, "Look, Todd, you're not in trouble. I don't care what you did, or where he was going. I just need to find him."

Todd considered this and said, "Okay. I did rent him a car today."

"How about some details."

"I rented him a beat-up old conventional Dodge to go into the quarantine zone for a few hours."

"Where in the zone?"

"I have no idea. But there aren't that many places for tourists to go in the zone."

"How were you gonna get the car back?"

"I wasn't."

"You didn't care if you ever saw your car again?"

"Wasn't my car." Todd kept his straight face.

Wilner liked this quiet man who fooled people.

Tiget Nadovich carefully and slowly entered a compound of small shelters and tents that all seemed to focus on the ornate federal postal building in what was once the dead center of the old city of Miami. Later, he and Alec would recover the radioactive material that Mr. Hammed had provided, but for now he had a strong urge to speak with the people of this secluded village in the heart of what was once a southern metropolis.

Nadovich's clear complexion and upright walk set him out from the residents here, who all seemed to stoop over and had boils and cysts around their faces. Several of the locals gave him a curious, if not outright hostile, look. Some pretended he was not there and the rest didn't seem to really know there was a stranger among them.

He walked with a slow, steady pace, waiting to see if anyone would confront him. That would be the person he needed to speak with. A leader of some kind.

The very presence of these people confirmed his worst view of humans. The fact that one of them spent the intelligence that God gave him to create a weapon with such horrible effects proved that they were a wasteful race. The additional horror was that the officials of a country would use it and expose civilians to such a plague. It was ignorance that no one realized the live victims would move from place to place spreading the disease. Ignorance like that made the humans more danger-ous. Perhaps one day they would mature or evolve into a more responsible species. But from what Nadovich saw, now they were a violent, thoughtless race that could very well destroy the planet for all species.

After he passed what he felt was the center of the camp, where the old entrance to the post office spilled out into the main walkway, Nadovich saw a contingent of four people walking toward him. These people walked more upright and had a purpose in their step. As they came closer, he saw that the one in front was a woman whose age he could not guess under the veil of pus and cysts. Two men and another woman were behind her. The men were both tall and the other woman looked young, her long blond hair flapping in the wind be-hind her.

The sun peeked out of the constant clouds and bathed the group as it approached Nadovich.

The woman in front said, "You are in the wrong place, sir."

Nadovich gave her a slight nod and smile. "I assure you, I am exactly where I mean to be."

"You understand that we are all bioplague carriers?"

"I do."

"And you are not afraid of infection?"

Nadovich chuckled.

"Then why are you here?"

"I have a proposal for you. A relocation plan to a place where no one will bother you and you would be welcome."

Now the woman chuckled. "And where would this fanta-syland be?" Her teeth were bright and healthy behind her cracked, blistered lips.

"In the Lawton District, not thirty miles from here."

"That district is in the United States. They would ship us

off to South Dakota, if not kill us outright for violating the quarantine zone."

Now Nadovich smiled, appreciating this woman's grasp of reality. "What if all that changed?"

THIRTY-SEVEN

Tom Wilner took the old car at the UPF station he had used the last time he entered the Miami Quarantine Zone. He had listened for any discussion of a body melted by a flasher found in the Eastern District but heard none. Earlier when he drove past the park the car was gone, with no sign of the violence that had gone on. Wilner knew he was in this alone.

His V-com beeped and he looked down, then mashed the receive button.

Shelby Hahn's pretty face filled the screen.

"Where are you?"

Wilner hesitated then said, "About to enter the zone."

"What for?"

"I have info Nadovich is there."

Shelby's face turned as she adjusted her unit in her hands. "I have a few things to do. Are you okay with me leaving Steve here with the kids?"

"Yeah, I'm probably being overdramatic anyway."

She smiled. "No, I think you're being smart. At least with the kids."

"What's that mean?"

"I wish you'd wait for me before you went in the zone."

He smiled. "Not this time. I need to figure out what he's up to. I don't intend to confront him if I can help it."

As soon as he finished his call with Shelby, Munroe beeped him.

Munroe was using an old communication unit with no video. But Wilner knew his voice.

Wilner asked, "What do you got?"

"I just got offered a job to help jump some fellas when they try to pick up a crate."

"In the zone?"

"Yeah."

"What's that got to do with Nadovich?"

"I heard the man who hired me, Mr. Hammed, tell another man that he expected Nadovich later that day."

"You're sure?"

"Oh, I'm sure, and they've hired plenty of men like they expect real trouble from this cat. We both know he can cause real trouble and it would take a lot of men to stop him."

"How many men?"

"Eight including me."

"Where exactly?"

"Warehouse off the old I-95 just south of Seventy-ninth Street."

"The other men they hired look tough?"

"Haven't seen them yet."

"When are you gonna be there?"

"Anytime now."

"On my way." He signed off and headed to the bridge into the zone.

Tom Wilner arrived at Seventy-ninth Street just west of the interstate less than an hour after speaking to Munroe. His crossing into the zone was slowed by an officious sergeant who was going to deny Wilner entry until Wilner explained that it was worth thirty suds for him to get in. The sergeant dropped his act and Wilner drove the old UPF car he'd picked up from the station into the Miami Quarantine Zone. The conventional-gas car was so beat-up it looked ratty even for the zone.

Wilner had also picked up a few extra high-capacity clips of ammo for his pistol. He wasn't taking any chances this time when he met up with Tiget Nadovich or any of his cronies. The problem with Munroe's instruction was that there were a number of warehouses on the block. He parked off the street that ran west of the block where all the street signs had long since faded or been knocked down. He slowly walked along the side of the two-story building, peeking in through the open or broken windows as he went. He avoided his instinct to crouch. That would draw more attention than just walking around a building in the old town of Miami.

He walked into an alley between two buildings and found Munroe sitting on a short stairway.

Wilner's eyes swept the area, looking for a trap out of habit. He had survived both Iran and the Balkans by being alert. He didn't want to be ambushed this close to the U.S. border.

Munroe stood up and met him.

The lean African man said, "The man who hired me, Mr. Hammed, is inside with a big guy who's his nephew, I think. If we go up these stairs to the second floor he won't even notice you."

"Where are the other men?"

"They ain't come yet. He expects them any minute."

"You know what Nadovich is picking up?"

"No. I seen a metal box in there, but I don't know what's in it."

"How big is the box?"

"Two feet by maybe three feet. Like a footlocker."

Wilner tried to think of what would be in a box that small that was worth the effort everyone was putting into it.

They climbed the stairs and slipped in an unlocked door. The second floor was like a loft or a balcony with a few ancient desks with dust and grime accumulated on them. Over a metal handrail, Wilner could see two men talking near the far wall of the first floor. There were two wide doors for vehicles to come inside. There were other crates and a couple of conventional cars in pretty good condition on the first floor.

Munroe said, "That's the man who hired me. Mr. Hammed."

Wilner leaned in close. "Here's the plan. You go on down to show you're ready to do what he says. If anything starts, or I have to shoot from up here, just split. I don't need help. You're a distraction. If I don't have to worry about you I'll be better off."

"You sayin' for me to turn my back and run like a coward?"

"Yes."

"Good." Munroe bopped out the outside door and a minute later appeared downstairs and approached the two men by the box. Wilner could see the men didn't care who they had hired and they treated Munroe dismissively.

Wilner was surprised how smoothly everything had gone up until now. He was in a good position and prepared. He also had surprise on his side. Now if he only had a better idea of exactly what kind of being Nadovich was he'd feel better about his situation.

The wide bay door opened and a group of seven men stood outside, then entered the warehouse. The leader walked directly to Mr. Hammed. These were the other hired muscle. Wilner could tell Nadovich was not in the group and assumed the others had been hired to confront the Serbian.

Then he saw the leader turn on Munroe and shove him hard, knocking the thinner man off his feet as the other men started to circle him.

Wilner leaned up to the handrail and realized these were the men he had taken the circuit board from: the Zone Troopers. And they had a big issue with Munroe.

Maybe things weren't going as smoothly as Wilner had hoped.

The bumpy ride from the center of old Miami up to the warehouse seemed to exacerbate Nadovich's headache, or at least what he thought of as a headache. He looked over at his cousin Alec, who bounced silently in the passenger seat.

"What is it, Alec?"

"I don't know what you want with those people."

"You mean the plague victims?"

"Yes, who else would I mean?"

"Alec, they can't help what became of them. You can't catch it. What do you care who I talk to?"

"They give me the creeps. They're disgusting."

Nadovich nodded. "That's exactly why I was talking to

them. If they scare you, imagine what they'll do to the humans."

"I don't understand."

Nadovich took a moment to explain it clearly. "If our plans for a safe haven are long-term, we must not only scare the humans away, we must find a way to keep them away."

Alec nodded understanding, then asked, "We'll still be able to do it on September eleventh?"

"We will and that's important."

"So the United States will blame jihadists."

"That, and it will be easier to convince them to leave before the bomb detonates."

"Why do you care if there are a lot of casualties? They're humans."

"The fewer dead gives us a cleaner environment, reduces the outrage from the rest of the United States, and they won't feel the need to retake the district. The United States will exclude us like they did the Miami Quarantine Zone."

Alec said, "Okay. Now I get it. But what about the circuit board? We still need it."

"And we'll get it."

"How?"

"Think about it, Alec, what is the detective's weakness?"

"Wilner? Maybe his bones or his inability to heal."

"No, Alec, his weakness is his children. He would do anything to protect his children."

Johann Halleck felt like he was in this by himself since Sig had gone up to Minneapolis to visit his father, Dag Halleck. Now Johann was talking to that same Dag Halleck on his V-com. Even for one of them, Dag Halleck looked remarkably good for his age. The ancient man claimed that his insistence on living in cold climates had kept him well preserved. That may have been a factor, but the fact that he had migrated to the United States ninety years ago and missed much of the stress that others in the family had experienced had to help.

Dag listened to Johann's assessment of what had happened in the past few weeks in southern Florida.

Johann said, "Aside from knowing Nadovich plans to build a large bomb, based on the circuit boards he had purchased, I don't know exactly when and where or even why he'd make such a bomb."

"You must remember, Johann, that the Simolits do not think like us. They have never taken the pledge, in fact, they are the reason all of our family felt it was necessary to take it."

"But they've never killed humans for no reason. Except the Nazis. They went after anyone who ever even spoke to an occupier."

"That was based on an emotion. Revenge is a powerful motivator. They have no apparent argument with the government here. I believe their patriarch here, Lazlo Simolit, is quite the American patriot."

"Yes, I know. How do you think he will react to me killing his son Radko?"

"He may seek retribution if they are sure who did it. We will deal with that when the time comes. Right now you must keep the circuit board you have from Nadovich."

"I don't think the policeman, Wilner, realizes I have it yet, but he'll figure it out soon. He's very intelligent."

"He sounds like he could be an ally in the future."

"He could be."

"Where is the board now?"

"I have it and if necessary I can always destroy it."

Old Dag shook his head in the small video screen of the V-com. "We may need the board to negotiate later, or, perhaps the day will come when we need our own bomb. Keep it intact."

Johann nodded.

Dag added, "We didn't last this long without taking in all considerations and planning for all contingencies."

"I'll keep you informed of any developments." Johann knew he would because he might need help. In a way he sometimes felt closer to the Simolits. They were outsiders in a world dominated by humans. The two groups just took different paths.

THIRTY-EIGHT

Wilner knew that decisiveness won battles and that at this distance he had to have the advantage over a bunch of untrained gang members. He drew his duty pistol and steadied it on the handrail, taking sight on the back of the gang leader, Freddie Rea.

That was the combat veteran in him. The cop in him shouted out, "Police, let him go. Do it now."

He watched as all the heads snapped up at his position. The crowd started to back away from Munroe, who was pushing himself up from the floor.

One man on the far side of the group reached for an old pistol in his waistband.

Wilner made a minor adjustment in his sight picture and squeezed off one round. The depleted uranium-tipped bullet passed through the man's chest so quickly that he didn't move and no one reacted.

Then the man dropped straight to the ground, motionless.

Freddie Rea screamed in Spanish and the group scattered.

The two men who hired the thugs hesitated by the box. They were no immediate threat so Wilner didn't worry about them.

He heard a gunshot from his right, but the bullet didn't hit near him. He swung the barrel of his pistol in that direction and dropped a small, wiry man with a round to his head. He repeated the maneuver on the other side after someone fired two more shots.

The older man, who Wilner figured was this Mr. Hammed, crouched behind the thick box and raised a weapon. It only took a fraction of a second to recognize the crack of a hand-held flasher as he fired it.

Wilner turned and dove away from the railing, sliding against the wall, away from the lower floor. As he covered his head he heard the blast strike the rail and spill over to a desk behind the rail. He smelled the burnt wood and melting metal, the sizzle of decomposing composites gave off more noxious fumes. He knew he had to stop that guy before he got off another shot.

He whipped his arm back over the rail adjacent to the melted and still hot section hit by the energy blast. Wilner sighted in on the man with a fairly large pistol-like flasher. It was a foreign manufacture and Wilner couldn't easily make out what type it was. By its size it might hold as many as five or six shots. He lined up his sights and fired three rounds, one of them striking the older man in the shoulder and throwing him to the ground. The flasher spun out of his hand, twisting across the concrete floor of the big warehouse.

Wilner knew to keep firing at anyone who crossed the floor toward the weapon. He didn't think this could get any worse. Then it did.

———

Tiget Nadovich and his cousin, Alec, knew before they opened the wide bay doors that something was out of the ordinary. The gunfire coming from inside the warehouse tipped them off. So did seeing Mr. Hammed's Hive parked a block away. But Nadovich had no interest in conflict, only in recovering his radioactive material to use in the bomb they were about to construct. His plan was simple: ignore everyone and grab the chest containing the material.

Alec had the old Dodge backed up to the door with the trunk open when Nadovich shoved, first the right door, then the left one, and watched as they slid down the track on their small wheels.

The first person he saw was Mr. Hammed sprawled on the ground with a bullet wound in his shoulder. His nephew, Walid, hovered over him, anxious to protect his meal ticket.

Nadovich walked straight to the box. He had no weapon and no gunfire was directed at him. Then a round pinged off the box as he reached for it. His eyes turned up to see where the bullet had come from and he saw UPF Detective Tom Wilner behind the sights of a large auto-pistol. Didn't this guy ever give up?

Alec rushed in and together they lifted the box, struggling under its deceptive weight.

Walid dragged his uncle to the cover of some crates as Wilner opened up on Nadovich.

The two men struggled across the floor. Nadovich felt like each step was over uneven turf as his feet had a hard time settling under him with the weight of the box on his body. The ancient car's shocks didn't hold the weight well and the whole car shifted to one side and the rear.

Just as they had unloaded the box, Nadovich felt a bullet dig into his side. The gunfire from the lower floor erupted up toward Wilner and the detective faded back from the rail.

Nadovich could see a smoking section of the rail. Now he realized he smelled more than just the gunpowder, he smelled the sulfurlike odor of a discharged flasher. Other men were hidden on the first floor, some with guns. He knew Wilner could take care of himself, but he still needed him alive to retrieve the circuit board. This was an odd circumstance. He had to save the human he wanted to see dead the most.

Nadovich looked over his shoulder to ensure Alec had the box secured and was ready to leave. When he was satisfied that all was in order, he turned and ran toward the nearest man with a weapon firing up at Wilner. As he lowered his head to knock the man off his feet, he realized it was Freddie Rea, the man he had hired to get the board from Wilner in the first place.

Freddie Rea didn't even see the charging figure and took the full blow hard, then fell back into a stack of smaller crates.

Nadovich stood upright and looked down at him. Rea tried to raise a handgun but Nadovich batted it away.

"Stay down and don't move." Nadovich stood above him with a broken wooden dowel in his hand like a long wooden spear.

Freddie Rea nodded and eased back down on the broken boxes. Blood started running from one of his ears.

Then Nadovich heard a shot and felt the sting of a bullet in his leg. He whirled around and saw Mr. Hammed pointing a small pistol at him. At almost the same moment Wilner burst in through the side door with his pistol in hand.

Mr. Hammed turned and aimed at Wilner, forcing Nadovich to dart toward him and draw his fire. He saw the muzzle flash and felt two bullets in quick succession enter his shoulder as he drove the broken dowel into Mr. Hammed's chest. Mr. Hammed dropped the gun on the concrete floor right next to him.

Nadovich backed away as Mr. Hammed started to choke and wheeze as blood flooded into his lungs from the wooden dowel sticking through his chest. Then Nadovich stared down Walid, hoping the big man didn't do anything stupid. He hated to admit it, but he liked the slow nephew to south Florida's leading jihadist.

He nodded his head toward the door and Walid took the opportunity. He looked up at the unmoving Wilner with his gun still pointed down. Then Walid ran out of the warehouse.

Nadovich turned to face Wilner.

The detective still didn't aim his gun. He said, "Why'd you do that?"

Nadovich said, "I need the board."

Wilner shook his head. He was breathing hard, but Nadovich didn't think he was wounded.

Wilner said, "I can't give it to you."

"Then I'll have to convince you." He started to limp toward the car, blood now running from three wounds. He was amazed at how well Wilner was accepting that he could move around with the damage he had suffered.

Wilner stepped closer and raised his gun.

Nadovich said, "Go ahead, shoot. I took your wife. You have the right." He could tell the cop wanted to kill him. He could taste it. But the training drilled into him kept his finger off the trigger.

Wilner hesitated with his gun pointed at Nadovich's head. Instead he said, "What's in the box?"

Nadovich smiled and said, "Our destiny." Then he flinched

as he heard the flasher in time to look in the direction of the African man, Munroe, who had the large weapon in his hand.

Nadovich dove out of the way as the energy charge disintegrated a crate next to where he was standing. He darted for the car.

Wilner had to back away as the smoke provided the perfect cover.

Frustrated, Nadovich knew he had to get back to the district quickly. He grunted at Alec to get behind the wheel of the car. They were headed away from the warehouse in seconds.

At the end of the block he yelled to Alec, "Stop."

Alec mashed the brakes, causing the tires to skid on the damp, decrepit road.

Nadovich said, "That old gas-powered Ford has to be Wilner's car."

"Yeah, I guess."

"We need some time." He saw a long section of metal rebar like the piece Wilner drove into his abdomen a few days ago. "I'm going to buy us some time."

It was dark by the time Wilner got out of the Hive-Humvee the national guardsman drove him home in. He knew when he saw the metal rebar stuck through the engine block of the old UPF car that he'd be stuck in the zone for a while. The only trick was smuggling the flasher from the warehouse back across the border.

One of the national guardsmen knew him from an earlier visit and he helped him out. Now he was as tired and sore as he had ever been.

As soon as he opened the front door he knew there was a problem.

Mrs. Honzit sat on the edge of the couch weeping into a handkerchief and Steve Besslia leaned against the breakfast bar with a bloody towel against his forehead.

Wilner raced to him. "What happened?" He looked around frantically. "Where are the kids?"

Besslia didn't say a word. Instead, he handed him a hand-scrawled note that said it all: "The board for your children."

THIRTY-NINE

Tom Wilner had to sit on the edge of his couch and fight the nausea, which was rising in him. He had faced tanks, Iranians, Bosnian Muslims and even a Serbian rapist but nothing had ever frightened him like this. The image of his daughter, Emma, and son, Tommy, being scared or in danger sapped him of his ability to concentrate.

Besslia hit him with several questions.

"Do we call the UPF? Should we try and find them ourselves? What do we do?"

Wilner looked up at the long gash in Besslia's head, which had been caused by an unknown man who jumped in the family room after forcing open the sliding glass door. The wound looked bad, but Wilner could tell that it wasn't too serious because the bleeding had slowed and Besslia didn't even notice it.

He glanced over to Mrs. Honzit, who sobbed quietly at the dining table. She hadn't said a word.

Wilner looked at her and said, "Did you recognize the men?"

She turned her face and shook her head slowly, her lus-trous curly hair swaying as she did.

"Were they the same men who searched the house before?"

She hesitated, and in that instant, Wilner got the idea that she knew more than she was letting on.

He looked back at Besslia. A comment Johann Halleck had made about not knowing who with the UPF was on the Simolit payroll came back to mind. That was why the big blond man didn't talk after the bar fight. Wilner considered how someone had snuck into the house and taken the last circuit board from his toolbox. The thief knew exactly where to look. Nothing else was disturbed. Wilner had only told two people where the board was hidden. Besslia and Shelby. He glanced back at Mrs. Honzit and realized that she had probably heard of the loca-tion too. She didn't look like herself at the moment. Her face was red and tear-streaked but she had the younger, sexier look to her today. Had she known someone was coming by?

Wilner shook his head, trying to stop the flow of para-noia. But rational thought didn't explain where his children had gone.

He was now convinced that Tiget Nadovich was an alien of some kind. Seeing him in action and finding the metal re-bar shoved through the hood and into the engine of his car in the zone convinced him that he needed to regard the man as a threat to all humans, not just him.

But that made Johann Halleck the same thing. Johann had at least appeared to be helpful.

Wilner knew what he had to do. He had to find his kids and put a stop to Nadovich by any means necessary.

He spent a few more minutes considering where the kids could be held, and if the UPF would help him or hinder him. If he didn't call them now he could call them later. But if he did call them, he wouldn't be able to tell them to leave later if he needed to.

He didn't like taking the law into his own hands. The one time he had snapped, the one time he couldn't take what he had seen and took action in Serbia, he was almost ruined. Was that what was holding him back?

He called Shelby on his V-com.

She answered immediately from her car. "I've been waiting to hear from you. Are you all right?"

Wilner shook his head.

Shelby caught his look even over the tiny video screen. "What is it?"

"Nadovich took my kids. He wants the circuit board."

"But you don't have it."

"That's what I hope to explain. I have to be ready to do whatever is needed to get Emma and Tommy."

"I'm on my way." The screen went blank.

Wilner didn't try to dissuade her. She was good with her weapon and tough. If he could trust her. In which case he wanted her and Besslia close by.

Mrs. Honzit tapped on the door to his bedroom. He looked up and just nodded. She came in and sat next to him on the edge of his bed.

He was surprised at how close she leaned into him and then she placed her arm around his shoulder and squeezed.

"What does this mean, 'the board for the children'?"

He turned his head to her. "They want to exchange Tommy and Emma for the circuit board I had."

"You don't have it now?"

He shook his head.

Mrs. Honzit said, "Where is it?"

"It was in—" He stopped and looked at her. Why did the housekeeper care where the board was? It had to be because of the kids. Didn't it? He scooted away slightly from her. "What do you know about this, Mrs. Honzit?"

"About the kidnapping? I told you all I saw."

"But that's not all you know."

The curvy woman stood up and backed away from the bed. "You are mistaken if you think I would ever put those children at risk. I thought you were smarter than that." She turned and marched out of the room.

Wilner just stared after her, knowing that he had hit a nerve, but also certain he didn't care about anything other than getting his kids back safely.

Then he heard his V-com beep. The number was unknown to him, but he was taking any calls that came in.

Tiget Nadovich sat in the large, empty house with Svala, trying to work up the nerve to tell her that her children were in a car with Alec and Demitri right now visiting any store or restaurant they wanted. Alec had already called to say he told the children that if they were good he'd take them to see their mother. So far they had stopped for ice cream, and were now headed to a wildlife museum so the kids could see stuffed examples of extinct animals like the panther, pelican and armadillo.

Nadovich wanted the whole mess to be cleared up before Svala found out what had happened. Once he had the board he would return the children unharmed. Then, when Detective Wilner was found dead, Svala would raise them in a proper environment.

As he sat next to Svala on the couch, watching the news, his mind raced and his head hurt as usual.

"Look," said Svala, pointing at the video broadcaster.

Nadovich nodded as he watched footage of German tanks rolling through the Polish countryside. It was not the first time he had seen it.

Then on the screen they saw footage of German tanks and infantry that was halted only one hundred miles inside the border.

The on-scene newscaster explained that the Germans had stopped their activity until the circumstances of the Tehran nuclear attack were more clear. It appeared that a nuclear blast had reminded the Germans that other countries might use any possible means to stop them.

To Nadovich it meant that the world might not focus as much attention on Poland but still had the Middle East to worry about.

The next story showed the Israeli prime minister protesting that his country had nothing to do with the attack on Tehran. It seemed that some countries were starting to believe them. Russia had even started to analyze the radiation and preliminary indications showed that the enriched uranium may have come from a former Soviet reactor.

Nadovich sighed.

Svala looked at him and said, "What is it? This is good news."

"It may be for some, but for those of us who wanted people's attention focused elsewhere, these conflicts were fortuitous.

He stood up and said, "I have some calls to make." He

had his V-com out and ready before he was all the way in the garage of the older house. One of his human contacts had given him Wilner's personal number, and now he wanted the surprise of a call from him to hit the detective hard.

Wilner came on the screen and spoke first. "Give me back my kids, asshole."

Nadovich smiled. He had gotten to him. "Aren't you even interested in how I got your number?"

"All I want is the kids."

"All I want is the circuit board."

"But I don't have it."

"You can get it."

"No, I can't. I don't even know for sure who has it."

"Detective, please don't play games with me."

"Look. I know what you can do. I even know what you are."

That caught Nadovich by surprise.

"But I don't have your board."

Nadovich stared into the monitor and realized he believed the cop. But he had other ways to confirm his veracity and he was going to use them.

FORTY

After his short conversation with Nadovich, Tom Wilner knew what he had to do. He had to prepare to break the law here in the United States. It was one thing to act like a maniac in the quarantine zone, but he had taken an oath to uphold the law here in the United States.

He had two conventional pistols, one of them his duty auto-pistol, a good K-Bar marine combat knife and the flasher he had smuggled in from the quarantine zone. Whatever Nadovich's strengths, Wilner felt confident he had enough firepower to overcome them.

His concern now was not only getting his children back, but also letting someone in power know that there were aliens on Earth, and that they were here for a reason.

As he lay everything out on his bed he also thought about Mrs. Honzit. Could she really be in the employ of Nadovich? Or was it something else? The thoughts he was having about his housekeeper were disturbing and not the least because he had never concealed anything from her. She knew basically whatever he knew.

He turned and left his bedroom to find Besslia to explain what he was going to do, and that it was important for Besslia to find someone to tell them what they'd discovered. Wilner felt certain that if he used the DNA evidence and some of the research in the newspaper archives, Besslia would be able to convince their bosses about the threat.

Walking through the quiet house, Wilner was struck again by the absence of the children. He didn't see Besslia in the living room, then wondered if the traffic cop was bothering Mrs. Honzit again. Wilner walked down the hallway to her door and rapped gently.

He heard the Turkish housekeeper say, "Enter."

In the open doorway he stopped and looked at her as she set some clothes in an expandable suitcase sitting open on her bed.

"Where are you going?" he asked.

"It is clear you do not trust me, so I am leaving."

He hesitated. She was right, he didn't trust her. But he didn't want her to leave just yet.

"What if you answered some questions before you left."

She stopped arranging the clothes in the suitcase and straightened. She was wearing a different kind of dress than what Wilner was used to seeing her in, which showed off her full, excellent figure. He realized she looked like an entirely new person.

"What do you wish to know?"

"What do you know about the children's kidnapping?"

She focused her dark eyes on him and said, "I know that they are safe or I wouldn't have allowed them to be taken.

I'm sure if you give Tiget Nadovich the circuit board you will have the children soon."

She said it so calmly that it shocked Wilner. He said, "So you are involved with that creep?"

"You mean the creep who stole your wife?"

He didn't flinch. "And now my children."

"You have no use for the circuit board. Please just give it to him."

"I already told him I don't have it." He kept his eyes on her as she slowly moved from the twin bed. He wished he had brought one of his weapons he had laid out on the bed.

Mrs. Honzit said, "I don't want to hurt you but . . ."

Wilner stepped away from the wall so he could move if he had to. He could tell by the way Mrs. Honzit set herself that she knew how to fight and every cop knew that women were the most dangerous street fighters.

Johann Halleck raced through the light traffic in the Eastern District. He didn't want to confront Wilner while his children were missing, but knew that the detective needed all the facts before he did something stupid. Johann also intended to tell him that he had the board and what he believed the board was going to be used for.

Johann had seen how irrational humans could be about their children. In his long life he had seen many families torn apart by the brutality of other humans. From the Irish under British rule, to the Native Americans in early America, to the Nazis' treatment of most of Europe and Russia he had seen children killed and mothers die from the grief. He did not intend to see that here.

He also wanted to ensure that Wilner realized he had no part in the abduction and that they were on the same side in this fight.

He still had a few miles to go.

FORTY-ONE

Tom Wilner thought about shouting a warning, then remembered there was no one in the house to hear him. It was one of his old habits from the marines. He wished he knew where Besslia was because it looked like he was about to have his hands full.

Mrs. Honzit had maneuvered into the open part of the small room. She never let her eyes leave him.

Then the housekeeper said, "Now you see me as a woman. Not what you expected."

"Are you a woman or one of them?"

She nodded her head. "You're a very bright man. I am a member of the Simolit family, yes."

"Why did you come here?"

"Many reasons. I don't know the big picture, but I know when my family needs me." She sprang at Wilner and wrapped her strong arms around him as she drove him into the wall.

Wilner was stunned at how fast and strong she was. He

felt her powerful legs drive him back into the wall of the small guest bedroom, cracking the drywall.

He shoved her to one side, then was surprised again by a powerful elbow thrown into his ribs.

He responded with a knee into the housekeeper's stomach, then his own elbow to drive her back. After he had a few feet of distance between them he shifted and backed out to the hallway with Mrs. Honzit in close pursuit.

She lunged at him again as he fended her off. Backing into the kitchen he grabbed an antique, heavy glass pitcher, and swung it hard against her head. Her dark hair glistened as it shattered against it. That rocked her, but to Wilner's horror didn't slow her much. These Simolits were a tough bunch.

She picked up one of the sharp carving knives in the wooden block and faced Wilner with it in front of her. She didn't grip it like a scared woman. She held it like she had stabbed men in the heart before. Wilner wondered in what century she might have done something like that.

She said, "I didn't want to hurt you, but if you don't have the board, you're of no use to us. Tiget says you're a danger." She swept in quickly with the knife.

He raised his left arm to fend it to one side and felt the blade cut into his forearm. He caught a glimpse of the wound as he brought his arm back to his side. The blood was already running down his arm.

Mrs. Honzit cornered him next to the refrigerator. He knew he was in a tight situation. But it wasn't the first time. He got ready for his counterattack.

Steve Besslia came back into the house from the backyard where he was watching the clearing sky. He saw the sun for the first time in at least four months. He'd been watching the news, so he was a little encouraged that Germany had stopped, at least temporarily, its march through Poland. Now even some countries hostile to Israel, like France, had started to listen to their denials about nuking Tehran. The search and rescue of civilians was still continuing in the Iranian capital, but the death toll was going to exceed the firebombing of Riyadh, Saudi Arabia. That one the Israelis claimed credit for and the world had backed them up after the Saudis had launched a bioplague-filled warhead at them. The biological weapon had not dispersed like it should have. It killed about a thousand people, mostly citizens of Palestine who worked in the Jewish state. The video of blistered kids dying a week after the attack had allowed the Israelis to take off the gloves and pound the capital of Saudi Arabia with a devastating combination of incendiary and concussion bombs that killed more than a million people, destroying 80 percent of the structures in the once great city. The attack was extreme enough that no one had retaliated from the Middle East. After that terror attacks actually subsided inside of Israel.

Now Besslia, ready to do whatever he could to help Wilner get his children back, walked back into the house. He saw Wilner in the kitchen with Mrs. Honzit. It took a second for him to appreciate the housekeeper in a tighter dress than she normally wore. He saw her move her arm, then it took three full seconds for him to realize she had a knife. This confrontation was more than just employment-related.

Wilner shouted to him, then swung a right fist at Mrs. Honzit. She took the punch, shook it off and tossed Wilner over the counter into the little dining area. He landed on his nice antique wooden table, breaking it in ten pieces as it collapsed under him.

"Shit," yelled Besslia as he raced toward the housekeeper.

She twisted slightly and seemed to throw him off easily as she focused on Wilner, who was retreating now through the dining room.

Wilner shouted, "Watch out, Steve, she's one of them."

Besslia knew exactly what his friend meant. He was face-to-face with one of the aliens. He was going to defend his planet.

As she approached Wilner, with the knife still in her hand, Besslia's eyes darted around the room for a weapon he could use. The dining-room table was shattered on the ground where Wilner had fallen on top of it. One leg of the table lay by itself. A tapered oak stake. He grabbed it on his trek to the frenzied housekeeper and raised it, trying not to think about all the times he had dreamed of seeing Mrs. Honzit naked, then drove it down hard through the center of her back.

Even after she had fallen to the ground, he shoved it through her body, twisting and grinding it into her internal organs. Blood spurted up around the table leg. Besslia didn't loosen his grip or the pressure. He winced at the gruesome sight of the wood ripping the flesh of her back.

After a few seconds he heard a voice and realized it was Wilner yelling at him.

"Steve, Steve, it's okay. She's down."

They both leaned in close.

Besslia said, "But is she dead?"

Wilner shook his head. "I don't know. It looks like it."

Then both men jumped at the sound of another male voice. "She's dead."

They turned and saw Johann Halleck standing in the front doorway.

FORTY-TWO

Tom Wilner turned, ready to fight Johann Halleck, but knew that he didn't want to.

Johann remained calm and still, then said, "That's why people used to drive stakes through the hearts of vampires. It destroyed enough of the central organ that we couldn't even recover."

Besslia said, "You're a vampire?"

Johann chuckled, unconcerned with the carnage that lay before him. "Hardly, but ignorant people once thought we were. That's where the legends came from."

The shock of Mrs. Honzit's attack, the appearance of Johann Halleck, coupled with the disappearance of the children, had caused Wilner to lean back hard against the wall, then drop to a sitting position.

Besslia took the hint, collapsing away from the corpse of Mrs. Honzit with the giant table leg protruding from her back.

Besslia said, "Then she is really dead."

Johann nodded.

"And you guys are aliens."

Johann smiled. "Alien in the sense that we're not human, but we are of terrestrial origin."

Wilner, still trying to catch his breath, looked at him now. "What's that mean?"

"We're a species from the planet Earth, just like you."

"But you're not human."

"Neither is a lion or a monkey, but you don't think they're aliens, do you?"

"But they don't look human."

Johann nodded. "Good point." He sat on a stool at the kitchen counter where he could talk to both resting men. "We are a hominid species just like Cro-Magnon or Neanderthal. The only difference is that we were never documented. Somewhere along the evolutionary chain of events our species separated from yours. Not much, but in a profound manner."

Besslia said, "So you can resist injury better?"

"Among other things. We heal quickly and do not face disease."

Wilner eased up to step to the kitchen counter. "You live longer."

"That's correct, Detective. We live longer because we don't have disease. We can heal from most injuries. That doesn't make us invincible. As you saw, I killed that man with a blast from a flasher. Officer Besslia killed your housekeeper with a rough wooden stake. Many means of death will work on us."

"How long do you live?" asked Wilner.

"Many, many years. I am three hundred and four. My mother just had another child. Some of our elders are more than five hundred. But time does catch up to us, eventually."

Wilner could barely comprehend what this man, or being, was saying. But he didn't doubt it. His manner and delivery, not to mention what Wilner had seen himself, made it clear that this incredible story was true. "How many of you are in the world?"

Johann smiled. "An excellent question, but one I will not answer completely. I have already told you too much. It was just that you had seen so many things and figured out a lot of it yourself. I'm confident no one would believe you if you tried to spread the story anyway."

Wilner nodded, realizing that anonymity would be important. "Are there millions of you?"

Johann shook his head. "No, not nearly. Once we had many families, but we warred among ourselves as well as through human surrogates. Now there are but two great families left. Mine, the Halleck family, and the Simolit family. Tiget Nadovich is one of the Simolits."

"And he has my kids."

Johann held up a hand and said, "The children are not in danger."

"How can you be so sure?" asked Wilner.

"Because Tiget Nadovich is their father."

FORTY-THREE

Shelby Hahn screeched the tires of her Hive as she pulled in next to Wilner's van in his driveway. She burst through the unlocked front door and stopped short when she saw the three men in the kitchen.

Wilner looked past the men to her and said, "Come on in, Shelby."

She took a step inside, then caught her breath as she saw a body facedown on the floor with a wooden table leg stuck in its back.

"Is that Mrs. Honzit?"

Wilner said, "Yes, yes it is. It seems she was a member of the Simolit family you told me about." His voice sounded funny, as if he were intentionally keeping it calm and even. His words and tone were measured.

She eased closer to them.

"She attacked me."

"Did she know where the children were?"

"No. But Mr. Halleck here tells me not to worry."

"Why not?" She looked at all three men and took the stool next to where Wilner now leaned against the kitchen counter.

"He tells me that not only are my children not mine but that my wife, Svala, is a member of a different species or race of"—he looked at the big blond man—"what did you call them?"

"Hominids or bipedal primates."

Wilner just said, "A different species."

Shelby tried to control her breathing.

Wilner said, "You don't look surprised by that."

"Well." She was uncertain how to proceed.

Wilner said, "Go ahead, what were you going to say?"

"I thought she might be a Simolit but then I found some proof."

"What proof?"

She told him to wait as she rushed to her car and retrieved the photo and news story she had taken from the frame in Tiget Nadovich's Eastern District house. She was back at her stool in less than a minute. She looked up into Tom Wilner's anguished eyes and wondered if this would help. She knew that he had to hear the truth.

She said, "I found this the day I was in Nadovich's house." She laid out the photo that showed Nadovich cheering the end of World War II with Svala next to him cheering too.

Wilner took it from her and stared for a long minute at it, holding it up and rereading the accompanying story. After he had finished, he looked at her and said, "I saw this on the Internet but it just had her arm in the photo, not the whole scene. How is this possible?"

Shelby didn't know what to say. She just gave him time to consider all that had been said to him in the last few minutes. This was hard for any man.

Wilner turned and stalked off to his bedroom.

———

Steve Besslia had to hear more from this "near man," Johann Halleck. He took a stool and faced the taller man. That was all he could think of him as, a man.

Besslia said, "So you have no connection to the Urailian ship on its way?"

"Just fascination like the humans."

"And your race hasn't traveled off the Earth?"

"No."

"And you've been living history for three hundred years?"

"I have."

"Do you have any unusual powers, other than healing?"

"We're a little denser than humans. Somewhat stronger and just by the length of lives we learn to move more economically than humans. God saw fit to hide us in this human disguise."

"Have you ever been shot?"

"Oh, yes, many times."

"And it still hurts?"

"Absolutely. The worst was a musket ball at Waterloo."

Now Besslia didn't know if the big man was pulling his leg or not. But he had plenty more questions.

As Wilner sorted his weapons one more time, Shelby entered his bedroom.

Wilner mumbled, "Why didn't you show me that photo?"

"I didn't think you'd believe it for one thing and I didn't want you to think I was trying to come between you and Svala."

"What do you know about these hominids? The Hallecks and the Simolits."

She hesitated, then said, "Everything."

"So it's all true?"

She nodded.

"And how old is my wife?"

Shelby shrugged. "I'd guess at least a hundred and twenty."

"Do you think I could even have fathered a child with her?"

"There's more to being a father than providing sperm."

"You're avoiding the question. Could I be Emma and Tommy's biological father?" He kept his eyes on her.

She slowly shook her head and let out a barely audible, "No."

"I still have to get them back."

"I agree."

"And you can't come with me."

"Why not?"

"Because, unlike the quarantine zone, we can be prosecuted for not following procedure here."

"You intend to break the law?"

"I intend to get my kids back."

She stared at him.

"What is it?"

"I just never saw you prepared to violate the law so flagrantly."

"I've done it before."

"When?"

"In Belgrade. During the war."

"What happened?"

"I executed a rapist without a trial."

She just stared at him as she realized she wasn't the only one who could deliver a surprise.

Tiget Nadovich had tried to call Mrs. Honzit back to see what she had found out, but had been unable to reach her. He had sent her to the Wilner house to watch the children and raise them in a safe "human" atmosphere until they were reunited with Svala. By keeping them in the house it was one less thing he had to worry about. They learned to deal with humans more effectively. And most important, they weren't around his house making noise and causing trouble.

Now they were on the way to his house and he still had not informed Svala of all that had happened.

He found her in the upstairs bathroom next to the room they shared, surprised to see her naked, brushing her dark, luxurious hair. He stood, still awed by her beauty. Her perfect figure, the light ripple of muscle over her stomach, her large, round breasts that bounced with every stroke of the brush, her shapely legs and hips and a face that conveyed innocence and intelligence all at once.

He knew she was intelligent. Many times she had shown she could outsmart Nazi interrogators and checkpoints. But she was not so innocent. Nadovich had seen her slit the throat of a Nazi colonel. She had executed male and female collaborators. She had even planted a bomb that had later killed several children. For that she had anguished for a long time. But ultimately she cheered as loudly as anyone when the Nazis returned to Germany in shame. He had kept a photo taken near the end of the war as Yugoslavia became free again. He had not seen the framed photo and news story in a while and hoped he had remembered to bring it to the new house.

Now he looked at his on-again, off-again lover of more than ninety years. She had not changed one bit in that time.

She caught his look in the mirror and said, "What is it? You have never seen me naked before?"

"I have, but never grow tired of it."

She smiled.

Nadovich said, "I was thinking of allowing the children to come here."

Her face lit up. "When?"

"In a few minutes." He'd explain the details as needed.

FORTY-FOUR

Wilner watched Shelby's face as she sat on the edge of his bed. The story of his court-martial was not one he recounted often. She was an attentive audience. He'd already explained how he had found three women raped by the same man in Serbia. One had died of the beating the rapist had given her. It had troubled Wilner more than the snipers and random terror attacks.

He sat next to her and said, "Then one night, on a patrol in Belgrade, we heard a woman scream. We raced into an old apartment building and followed another scream to an apartment on the second floor.

"I kicked in the door and found this man engaged in sex with the woman who had screamed."

Shelby said, "She must have been overjoyed to see you."

He shook his head. "She was already dead. He had choked her to death before we found them."

Shelby stared at him.

"The woman was eighteen. Just a girl. The man was about

thirty. He gave us a good fight, but five marines in battle gear put him down with a rifle butt to the head.

"As we dragged him from the apartment building, an older woman stopped us. She was a Serb, but spoke excellent English. She said he had already been arrested for rape, but he had connections and would get out.

"I told her that was ridiculous. And as we started to drag him away he started laughing.

"I stopped and we stood him upright. Now he was belly laughing. He said in English, 'I will be free in one hour. This is my country. Not the United States of the great America.'

"I told him he was all done. There would be men to take evidence and convict him for what he had done.

"He just laughed again and said, 'Yes, I know. I been through this before. Why not save me the time and release me now?'

"He continued with his jabbering until I started thinking of the women I had seen and the look on the face of the dead girl back in the apartment. I just snapped and pulled my duty pistol.

"The guy looked at me and laughed again. Even as I placed it to his head.

"Finally I couldn't take his laughter and jerked the trigger, hitting him square in the forehead."

Shelby looked sick. She had her hand on her mouth. Then removed it and asked, "What happened to you?"

"I was arrested and was going to be court-martialed. Probably sentenced back into the military in a criminal unit for the rest of my life."

"Then what happened?"

"He wasn't dead."

"Who? The man you shot?"

"Exactly. He got up from the U.S. military morgue and walked away."

"Oh, my God, he was a—"

"Undocumented hominid subspecies." Wilner looked at her. "And I, just today, figured that out."

"And that's one of the reasons you're hesitant to break procedure?"

"The main reason, but that's nothing compared to Emma and Tommy. I have to get them back."

"Then I'm going to help you."

Svala Wilner cried when she embraced her children. She didn't know yet how they came to be at her house, but for the moment she was just happy to see them. She squeezed Tommy close and felt his tiny body squirm against her hug. Then she kissed Emma five times on her chubby cheeks.

She looked over her shoulder at Tiget.

He shrugged and smiled. "Anything that makes you happy."

"But Tom?"

"He is safe."

She had a lot to understand but for the moment intended to spend time with the children.

Later, after she had sent the kids to clean up and she had prepared a meal of real chicken and real green beans, she had Tiget come into the kitchen.

"How did you get them? Tom would not approve of this."

"No, we took them from Mrs. Honzit."

"And what did Tom have to say? I know you heard from him."

"He wasn't happy, but we can work out his visiting rights later."

She looked at him and knew he wasn't telling her everything. As usual.

Finally he said, "I needed to use the children as leverage."

"Leverage for what?"

"You husband has a circuit board I need."

"For what?"

"You don't wish to know this. You never have."

"Now I do."

He looked at her in a way that had always made her legs weak. Then he said, "Svala, my darling. You know I am nothing without you by my side. You must believe me when I say that you would not approve of how I go about creating our homeland here."

"Does it involving killing?"

"Has any homeland worth having ever been created peacefully?"

Her feeling of joy at having her children with her faded quickly as she started to see what it might cost. "You're going to launch a terror attack, aren't you?"

"Sort of. We will get the humans out of the area, then I have a plan to keep them out."

"What will become of my husband?"

Nadovich didn't speak. She knew that he did not like to lie to her. Finally he said, "Detective Wilner knows too much of our plan. I will have to deal with him."

Now Svala was faced with a choice she never wanted to make.

FORTY-FIVE

Tom Wilner was still trying to understand Svala's real identity and her role in the plot. It was hard to accept that she was something other than what he had always thought: an orphaned college student from Belgrade. But as he reflected, he realized that she had not aged. Not at all. He could not remember her ever being sick. Or hurt. She had fallen and tumbled down a stone riverbed once when they were hiking in Georgia. He raced after her, thinking she was seriously injured. By the time he had reached the bottom of the steep rock face that the river ran through, Svala was already standing, assuring him she was unhurt. Apparently because she really was unhurt.

And the children. Neither had ever been sick. Not even a runny nose. And they favored Svala's looks dramatically. Dark hair and dark eyes, high cheekbones.

He froze as he realized he was also describing Tiget Nadovich.

Shelby Hahn stepped across the room to him. She wrapped

her arm around his shoulder and gave him a squeeze. Almost like Mrs. Honzit had earlier. Before she had tried to kill him.

In all the combat he had seen, all the friends killed, all the mayhem left by both sides in two wars, he had never felt so despondent.

He turned to Shelby. "How could I have fallen for such a monumental lie? I never had a clue about Svala or the kids."

"Sometimes love makes you blind. It's not like you would expect something like this."

"Something like what? Marrying the wrong species?"

Shelby didn't comment.

"It's not that I want her back now. Too much has happened and she's been gone too long. It just hurts somehow."

Shelby nodded.

Wilner stood up and marched out into the living room where Johann and Besslia were in deep discussion.

"Would the kids realize what they are?"

Johann said, "Not instinctively. They probably haven't even noticed that they don't get sick."

Wilner looked at the kitchen counter where the photo of Nadovich and Svala lay at an angle. "And she is definitely one of you?"

Johann nodded.

Wilner said, "I know you have the circuit board. If Mrs. Honzit and Nadovich don't have it, you had to take it the day you saved me in the park."

"I have the board."

"Will you give it to me to trade for the kids?"

Johann hesitated. "I'll explain what I know, then you have to decide if you still want to trade it."

"Of course I want to trade the circuit board for the kids."

Johann held up his hand and started to speak slowly. "Do you know what was in the box that Nadovich took from the zone?"

"No, what?"

"I'm told by reliable sources that the man who supplied it, Mr. Hammed, had been stockpiling radioactive material. That information, coupled with the need for the circuit board means that they intend to detonate a large dirty bomb."

Wilner considered this, then asked, "Where?"

"My guess is here."

"Why would they do that?"

"Only the Simolit family could answer that. But if the only component he is missing is the circuit board, then what would stop him if we turn it over? Thousands would die."

Wilner plopped down hard on an open stool. His eyes wandered around the room, falling on the bloodstains where Mrs. Honzit's body once lay. He knew that Besslia and Johann said they would handle it and had already moved her somewhere. He felt his stomach rumble and a tremor in his hand, then looked back at Johann. "Would your race be affected by radioactivity?"

Johann shook his head, "No, the limited exposure we have had has not produced any illness. Even now a large number of Simolits live in New York City."

"So your interest in stopping this detonation is what?"

Johann rubbed his face and finally said, "We, that is, the Halleck family, tired of seeing the Simolit family prey on humans, took an oath. We call it 'the pledge.' It's a simple pledge to protect humankind from others of our race. We occasionally get involved in human conflict, but not often. You once asked me if I had been in the military."

"I remember."

"I was with the English army against the Nazis and earlier against the Ottoman Empire. The Ottomans were under the direct influence of the Simolit family and the conflict was largely one generated by Simolit pawns. That included the assassination of Archduke Ferdinand." He looked at Besslia and Shelby, then added, "The Halleck family has assimilated into human culture as scientists, artists, even government officials."

Wilner stared at him, convinced of the sincerity, but stunned by the scope of the statement.

Then Johann said, "Do you still wish to hand the board over to Nadovich? Is it worth risking a catastrophe when your children are not in danger themselves?"

He was careful not to move. He didn't want to give off any signal until he had decided what was important and what options he had. Finally, feeling everyone's eyes on him, he said in a weak voice, "No; no we can't give him the circuit board."

Johann didn't gloat. He just patted Wilner on the shoulder.

Wilner looked up and said, "It doesn't matter, I still need to get Tommy and Emma back."

"I'll help," Shelby said.

Johann added, "Me too."

"You know I'm in," Besslia said.

Since Nadovich had devised the second phase to his plan, he realized that things were getting complicated and busy. He had sent Demitri and Alec into the zone through a checkpoint where he had spent a lot of suds to retrieve members of the growler community in Miami. So far in their three trips, each in separate vehicles, his cousins had brought about twenty-five more people to the house.

He hoped this plan would work because just bribing the guardsmen had cost him a fortune. Now he had to worry about feeding them and was even now looking for a house nearby that would hold them. Of course, if all went well, they could live in any of the houses nearby. He intended for them to live near the Northern Enclave because they would scare the most number of humans away there.

He still had to find the board in order to create a bomb that would scare people out of the district. And that's what he intended to focus on while his cousins ferried up more bioplague survivors.

Wilner and the others had spread out to search the Lawton District for Tiget Nadovich, Svala and the kids. Wilner had spoken to every informant, bar owner and busybody he knew. By late in the afternoon he was feeling low, having made no progress.

Besslia had called to say that he had checked in the southern edge of the Northern Enclave and hadn't heard a thing. Johann was investigating anything provided by his intelligence sources, which included his own people. By some of the information, Wilner could tell he had people who were cops in his intelligence network.

Then Shelby called him. A light, cold rain had started the hour before. He pulled the collar of his all-weather jacket up around his neck and huddled in front of the V-com.

"What do you got?" he asked.

Shelby, indoors and looking comfortable, said, "I found some unusual activity at one of the checkpoints into the quarantine zone."

"What kind of activity?"

"Two Hives, driven by younger men with long, dark hair, have been shuttling people up from the zone all day."

"What kind of people?"

"My informant doesn't know."

"But that would be against the law. Why aren't the guardsmen stopping them?"

"My guess would be money. Lots of it."

Wilner said, "I'll meet you at the checkpoint in half an hour. We'll see what we can figure out."

It was the only lead he had.

FORTY-SIX

As dinnertime rolled closer, Nadovich knew with more certainty that he had misjudged how difficult it would be to arrange for all the sick people he was bringing up from the Miami Quarantine Zone. The house was packed with smelly, rotting people. Svala rushed around the kitchen preparing whatever food she could as several of the refugees helped serve it.

The children, Tommy and Emma, played with a young African girl who had caught the plague from an Armenian traveler. Once she was infected, her family had placed her in the care of the little community in the quarantine zone.

Nadovich had arranged sleeping quarters for his wards in the house next door to his. The few neighbors he had were on the next street and probably wouldn't notice the activity. He had planned to only bring up about thirty people, but once the transportation started, everyone insisted that another two or three people come along. Now he figured that Alec and Demitri would be making the trip back and forth for another three days. So far neither of his cousins had complained. Alec had told him that the dripping pus and bloody sores had ruined the interior of one of the cars. Nadovich didn't care. These people would be just what he needed as a shield.

As he sat in the small study with just a desk and two chairs, a light knock on the door drew his attention.

"Enter," he said.

The woman he had come to know as Suzanne, the leader of the group, stepped into the small room. She now wore a veil to hide much of her disfigured face.

Nadovich looked at her but did not stand. "Yes?"

She was tentative, then said, "I wanted to thank you for housing and feeding us."

He just nodded.

"But I have to ask."

"What?" He tried to hide his annoyance.

"Why aren't you afraid of catching the disease? I know you said your family was immune, but how is that possible?"

"God's will, I suppose. Just as you are not supposed to survive at all. Simply good genetics."

She waited, then said, "And why have you brought us here? You don't strike me as an activist."

"There you are wrong, madam. I *am* an activist."

"For what?"

"For a freedom from . . ."

"From what?"

He thought of a close enough true answer. "From the United States."

"And what do we have to do with that? If the government caught us here they would either send us back across the quarantine zone or ship us out to South Dakota to the bioplague reservation."

"And you don't want to be there?"

"I don't want to be treated like cattle and shipped all over. I like it here."

"Then here you shall stay."

She sat in the other chair, her eyes fixed on him. "I'm not stupid. I know we are to be some sort of scarecrows for you. Use us to chase off the local residents."

He nodded. "I never thought you were stupid."

"Then tell us the truth."

"The truth is that our needs and goals intersect. You will have abundant housing up here and I will have you between me and everyone else. It will all work out." He thought he detected a smile underneath her veil.

In a small bar at the southern edge of the Lawton District, Johann Halleck sat for a few moments. He had visited every commercial establishment he could think of to find out if Tiget Nadovich had been seen. He had mentioned the name to the young bartender who had immediately gone to get someone for Johann to speak with.

A heavyset man with long, bushy sideburns and a filthy apron followed the younger bartender back in through a rear door.

"You the man looking for Nadovich?"

Johann nodded.

"Why?"

"I have something he needs." Johann would draw him out any way he could. He intended to act independently from Wilner. He didn't want to put him in harm's way and knew that Nadovich would come if he was alone.

"What do you have?" asked the heavy cook.

"He'll know."

"You're pretty sure I can get ahold of him."

"You look like a man of great resource." Johann looked around the grimy bar and said, "I will return tonight at ten. Tell him my name is Halleck. I'm sure he'll be grateful."

Johann left before the man could say anything else.

Shelby Hahn climbed back into Wilner's Hive and said, "Yeah, they bribed the sergeant and two of the guardsmen." It was the only unusual activity they had heard about in their long day of searching. She had confirmed that two men who fit the description of Nadovich's associates or family had been crossing into the zone all day.

He looked out over the dash at the checkpoint with three uniformed national guardsmen standing on the district side of the bridge.

"They just admitted it?"

"Under duress. I told them it was a national security issue and they'd be reassigned to a criminal unit on a front line somewhere. Next thing you know they're cooperative." She smiled, sounding like a real cop in front of this real cop.

Wilner said, "So what are we looking for?"

"Two cars with five to six people each."

"Who're they bringing over?"

"He has no idea, just they weren't soldiers or anything. Mostly families. Women and kids in each car. He didn't look too closely."

"Does he have any idea when they'll be back?"

"The sergeant says they're over in the zone right now and should be back through anytime."

Wilner smiled. "Excellent. All we do now is follow them back to their base of operations."

"Then what?" She wanted to know how this by-the-book cop intended to act now that his world had crumbled around him.

"Then we either search the house or question these two until we find out where Tommy and Emma are."

"Then what?"

"What do you mean?"

"Are you content to just raise the children with the knowledge that Nadovich or someone else might try and take them again?"

"When I'm done, Tiget Nadovich won't be a threat to anyone or anything."

Shelby felt a chill as she wondered what he would do if he knew the whole truth. Would he be as harsh? She'd know soon. The secret couldn't be kept forever.

FORTY-SEVEN

Tiget Nadovich noticed that the noise in the house had increased since everyone had eaten. They were all shown a comfortable place to sleep too. Some for the first time in years.

Svala helped care for several of the children, cleaning their sores and dressing the open wounds. She seemed happy to be of use. Nadovich realized in the time that she lived with him she lacked the purpose that had made her so remarkable. During the big war he had seen how driven she could be when faced with a challenge. She had helped refugees fleeing from the Nazis, learned to treat serious wounds and discovered the grief of losing a patient as she became closer to the humans. In a way, Nadovich wasn't surprised when she had fallen in love with Wilner. She had never seen the differences with humans as much as the similarities. She was very private about her feelings. Now, with a purpose, her tendency for helping came out.

Nadovich's V-com beeped. He pulled it from his pocket.

He recognized the man immediately. A bartender near the zone he often paid to round up help or fix a problem.

Nadovich said, "Yes, Robert, what is it?"

"A big blond guy named Halleck says he'll be back at ten with something you want to trade."

That surprised Nadovich. He had not considered that Johann Halleck had somehow acquired the board.

"Thank you, Robert. Someone will be there to greet him."

Nadovich saw the man's tiny image stare back at him.

Nadovich added, "I won't forget what a help you were."

Then the man smiled.

Nadovich shut off the connection, then tried to raise Alec on the V-com. He had a new job for his cousins.

Inside the house he heard a child's playful scream as Tommy chased a younger boy down the hallway next to the small office.

Nadovich wanted this whole thing wrapped up as soon as possible.

Tom Wilner and Shelby Hahn had followed the two cars from the checkpoint all the way north into the Western District to an area that was once called Coral Springs. Block after block of vacant houses stood as testament to the once heavy population. Wilner had a hard time imagining thick traffic among crowded neighborhoods. Now it was easy to look down each street and see only a few vehicles scattered among the vacant houses. They were all larger, two-story structures consistent with the turn of the century need for space. Many sociologists theorized that families wanted more space both as a status symbol and to put more distance between each other. Wilner remembered sharing a room with his older brother and bumping into his father if he turned wrong on the pallet of straw. He wouldn't have minded more space between himself and his family.

Shelby said, "There," as they passed one street. He slowed the vehicle, cut the lights and pulled the car back to face down the street. He could see a group of people climb from each car then shuffle up toward the house. The way they walked reminded Wilner of the hokey monsters he'd see in movies when he was a kid, all hunched over and moving with an irregular gait.

He lifted a pair of night vision, range-finding binoculars and made a couple of quick adjustments. He could see two men that were not like the others. He focused on them standing apart at the end of the driveway.

They had long hair like Nadovich and were in their early thirties. At least they looked like they were in their early thirties. He wasn't sure if they were the same men he had seen at the bar the night this all started, but they looked similar. He refocused the binoculars on the shuffling figures. He couldn't get a clear view of their faces until two stopped and looked back at the other men at the end of the driveway.

He zoomed in on their heads, their faces filling the lenses of the binoculars.

"My God," he said out loud as he realized what he was seeing.

"What is it?" asked Shelby as he absently handed the powerful binoculars to her.

He felt his stomach turn as he considered the ramifications of what he had seen.

Then Shelby murmured, "Why on Earth would he have growlers moved up from the quarantine zone?"

"Is that your concern?"

"Isn't it yours?"

"No, my concern is if my children are in that house. What if they're exposed?"

"They're fine."

"What?"

"They're immune, just like Nadovich."

"How do you know that?"

She hesitated, then said, "He wouldn't have growlers around him if he could catch it. It's part of their genetic makeup to not catch disease."

Wilner shook his head. "It doesn't matter. I have to get in there to grab Tommy and Emma."

She looked at him. "You're not immune to bioplague. In such close quarters, around so many infected people, you'll be exposed. Even if you don't develop the full symptoms you'd be subject to being shipped off to the Western Quarantine Zone, the bioplague reservation."

"Is that what the law says?"

She looked serious. "It's considered treason to knowingly travel in the United States after exposure to bioplague."

"Would you arrest me?"

"I will to keep you from going in there and uselessly risking your life."

"You don't get it. Even if Johann is right. Even if I'm not their biological father. You said it yourself—I'm still their father. I have to get them back and keep them safe."

"By killing yourself?"

"I don't have a choice."

She looked at him, then sighed. "There is another way."

"What other way?"

"I can get them."

FORTY-EIGHT

Tom Wilner looked into the beautiful face of Department of Homeland Security Special Agent Shelby Hahn and pictured it with the cysts and lesions of a growler. It made her offer to rescue his kids all the more meaningful.

Her green-tinted eyes met his.

He said, "I can't let you risk the same thing."

"I wouldn't be."

"Why not?" Then he looked at her and asked, "Is there an immunization like the conspiracy nuts say? Do federal agents get the shot?"

She snickered. "No." Then she carefully reached to her face, lifted her right eyelid and removed her contact. She did the same to her left eye. Now she looked at him with deep blue eyes.

Wilner said, "I don't understand. Why does eye color matter?"

"It's not that I have blue eyes. It's my genetics. My whole family has blue eyes."

He stared at her, slowly starting to piece it all together. Then he said, "Your family name is Halleck, right?"

She nodded.

Johann Halleck had returned to the bar well after dark. He'd called the traffic cop, Besslia, to tell him what he had planned in case it didn't work out the way he had hoped. He ached for a face-to-face encounter with Tiget Nadovich. As he thought about the possible terror attack the Serbian could launch he became angry, but he knew that wasn't the start of his feelings. He had first met Nadovich in Germany around 1860.

After an argument with a young man over a woman, Nadovich had engaged in a sword duel and killed the man.

Johann had known the twenty-three-year-old student for most of the young man's life and had, himself, taught the student to use the saber. Had the fight been instigated by the student or even been self-defense, Johann might have allowed forgiveness to enter his heart, but it was neither. Nadovich had baited the young man, then, without fear of being killed, easily beat him.

Johann had not known the circumstances for many years until Nadovich had run into him at a tavern in England. He gave that grin of his that reminded Johann of the depictions he had seen of the devil. Then he said he hoped Johann used a sword better than he taught it.

Immediately Johann knew what he was referring to. The confrontation was cut short by soldiers in the same bar, but over the years Johann had exacted his own revenge. Denying Nadovich one victory or another. The one thing he couldn't bring himself to do was join the Nazis. Even though they were Nadovich's hated foes, they were also humanity's worst enemies.

Now he twitched at the thought of running his combat knife into Nadovich enough times that his heart finally stopped beating. He couldn't help but smile thinking of it. Then he saw the front door to the small, empty bar open.

He was prepared to share a little banter with Nadovich before killing him, but then was stopped short.

He looked at the two men entering and said, "What's the matter, your cousin not confident to meet me by himself?"

The younger of the two, Alec Nadin, said, "He's busy now. But we speak for him."

"I didn't intend to speak."

"We need the board. I understand that you have it."

Johann was inclined to let these two little fish go so he could catch his prize. Until Demitri spoke.

Demitri said, "Tiget hopes you have improved your sword-fighting ability since the last time he got to test himself against one of your students."

Johann knew right then that this would be a long, bloody night.

Wilner looked into the blue eyes of Shelby Hahn and shook his head. "I fell for it again."

"You didn't fall for anything. I didn't want to lie and I certainly didn't want to hurt you."

"Those are human emotions. Are you familiar with them?"

"Oh, yes, and comments like that, from a man I care about, hurts more than you'll know."

He stared at her, sorry for the comment, but still finding it hard to grasp that she was so different from him. They all looked like humans. Nadovich, Svala, Johann Halleck and Shelby. But he knew they were very different from him. He recalled the Disney scientist equating their DNA to being different like a chimpanzee was different from a human. Did these beings look at humans like a lower, simian cousin?

He brought his gaze back to her. "That's why you didn't seem frightened the night the gang member held a gun to your head demanding the circuit board. That's why you told me not to give him the board. He wouldn't have killed you."

"No, probably not. But it would've hurt."

"The raid on the Zone Trooper's clubhouse. The shotgun blast did hit you. The blood on your blouse was yours."

She nodded.

"Let me see your shoulder."

She turned in the seat, pulled down her shirt from her collarbone. There was no mark where the shotgun pellet had struck her.

He shook his head. "I never imagined . . ."

Shelby grasped his arm. "It's hard to imagine something like us. But you have to realize my feelings for you are real. I'm sure Svala's were too."

He looked back down the street and knew he had to focus. He wouldn't be able to work out his judgment of women tonight. Sitting here with Shelby, he wasn't sure his judgment was all that bad. "What's your idea to get the kids?"

"If we could get Nadovich out of the house, then maybe I could slip in. The kids know me. They'll come."

"You won't be at risk for infection?"

She shook her head. "No more than anyone else in that house and they're not worried about it." She looked down the street. "We saw the other two men leave a little while ago in a single car. That should mean that only Nadovich and Svala are there."

"How can we be sure?"

"We can watch a while longer."

Wilner said, "I have another idea." He pulled his V-com off his belt.

FORTY-NINE

Tiget Nadovich rubbed his temples, trying to relieve the pounding in his head. He couldn't even tell anyone he suffered from what appeared to be migraine headaches because no one would believe him. He'd be the first member of his race who had suffered from an illness. Yet here, in what was his quiet home in the Western District, as he watched a mob of strangers enjoy the meal that Svala had made, he couldn't concentrate due to the pain in his head.

He did feel as if all his plans were coming together. Alec and Demitri were on their way now to meet with Johann Halleck, who claimed to have Nadovich's circuit board. No matter the outcome of the meeting he doubted if Johann would cause him problems again. The family rivalry had been the seed of hate the two men shared, but the real animosity had sprung from a simple saber duel in which Nadovich had killed a young German man whom Johann had trained. Nadovich knew he had antagonized Johann over the incident, but the big Halleck had taken it too far, and now had to be dealt with.

Nadovich needed the circuit board, but didn't know who had it. Something told him that Johann Halleck wasn't going to give up the board.

He stepped into the makeshift dining room that had every table in the house shoved together with any possible table-cloth thrown over them. Svala had made a stew that reminded him of goulash. She had managed to feed forty people, including the nine children in the group. Now she hustled around the long table, filling water glasses and chatting with her guests.

She was truly remarkable. She had not spent much time with her children in a year, yet even with the tearful reunion, she was now concentrating on the people that needed her help. Tommy and Emma raced around the house with several of the growler children.

He was startled by the sound of his V-com. He had not expected either Alec or Demitri to call so soon. He hoped there wasn't a problem. Instead he was surprised to see the call coming from Tom Wilner. He pressed the receive button and could see the detective calling from inside a vehicle.

"Yes, Detective, may I help you?" He purposely concealed any smugness or condescension. He wanted to resolve the circuit board issue, then he'd have his fun with Detective Wilner.

"You could send me back my children."

He looked over his shoulder at some squealing in the dining room. "Believe me, Detective, I would love to. Have you somehow found my board?"

"I'll have it."

"When?"

"Meet me in an hour at the Big Cypress Bar."

"How appropriate, the bar where you started your interference in my plans."

"Just show up."

"Alone, I suppose."

"I don't care if you bring an army. I want to get rid of this board and get the children back."

"How very noble of you. I will not disappoint. I will not be able to bring the children now. They are safe with your wife."

"You can tell me where to get them when we meet."

"That's unusually reasonable of you, Detective. I will be there in an hour." He shut off the V-com without hearing a response.

Nadovich stepped out the front door and saw the remaining vehicle in the driveway. He opened the driver's door, the smell of rotting flesh and pus drove him back a step. Alec wasn't kidding when he said the interior of the vehicle had been ruined by transporting the growlers. There was still Alec's old Harley-Davidson antique, gas-powered motorcycle in the garage.

Once back inside, he found Svala sitting with some of the growlers. He pulled her into the kitchen.

"What's wrong?" asked Svala.

"Nothing, my dear. I must leave for a while."

"Now? With all these visitors? Why?"

"Believe me, it is important or I wouldn't be going."

Svala gave him one of her scowls.

He backed away from her, out into the garage. He was on the big motorcycle heading down the street on his way to the bar where everything had started to go bad.

———————

Steve Besslia had paused outside the bar down in the southern edge of the district. He had his gun under a dark, all-weather jacket and the knife his new friend, Johann Halleck, had given him. He was nervous, but was confident Johann wouldn't lie to him. The big man had said it would all work out.

As he approached the front door, Besslia froze as he heard a loud crash from inside. He drew his pistol then rushed to the front door, pushing it in as he entered the bar.

It took him a second to process what he saw inside the old bar.

On the ground was one of the men he had shot at in his apartment. Johann Halleck stood by himself across from him. The man had landed on a table, crushing it on his way to the dirty floor.

The bartender had a shotgun in his hand. Besslia leveled his big duty pistol at him then shouted, "UPF, drop the gun."

The bartender complied, dropping the bulky gun onto the bar.

The man who had been knocked down on the ground slowly got up and brushed himself off. He casually joined another man with dark hair standing a few feet away from Johann.

Besslia kept his pistol up.

The man closest to Johann lifted his shirt, showing a nasty red scar on his side. Then the man said, "That didn't work last time. I doubt it'll work now."

Besslia lowered the gun. "You were the guys at my condo."

They both smiled.

"You're part of the Simolit family."

The men looked at Johann. One of them said, "You have been loose with your mouth, Johann."

Johann said, "He has earned the right to know the truth. You're a threat to his people."

"*We're* a threat to his people! Please, Johann, you know how they have treated us for a millennium. Burned at the stake, hunted like wolves, shot with silver, wooden stakes driven through our hearts."

Johann shook his head. "That was superstition. These are different times. When have you last heard about something like a wooden stake?"

Besslia didn't mention driving a table leg through Mrs. Honzit's heart just a few hours earlier.

The dark man said, "It still happens back in Eastern Europe. Now that the EU has dissolved, Romania and some of the other countries will slip back into ignorance."

Johann turned to Besslia and said, "This is not your fight. If you choose to leave, I will understand."

One of the men said, "That's right, run, human, run."

Besslia smiled. "I was wrong, I admit it. I thought you guys were aliens. You're just a cheap imitation of plain old Earth-bound humans. I owe you."

One man moved with blinding speed as Besslia raised his pistol. He got off one shot into the man's stomach before he was knocked down and the gun sent spiraling across the floor. Besslia scrambled to his feet, snatching up a piece of the broken table leg near him. He swung the table leg like a bat, a blow glancing off the man's shoulder. Out of the corner of his eye he saw Johann and the other man grapple, their arms interlocking, both men grunting in effort and pain.

Besslia squared off with the man across from him, the bloodstain spreading on his shirt. Besslia remembered the knife that Johann had given him. That was his best chance. If he could get to it, tucked in his belt behind him. That was what he focused on now.

Svala heard the big motorcycle crank and looked out the front window to see Tiget roll down the driveway past the Hive-utility vehicle. She was ready, with the keys already in her hands. She had asked Suzanne, the leader of the growlers, to keep an eye on the house and her children while she dealt with a personal matter. She trusted Suzanne, having spoken with her much of the evening. She was an interesting, intelligent woman who once ran a high-powered law firm in Washington, D.C., until people had gotten so fed up with frivolous lawsuits, the stagnation of research and development partly due to legal reasons, that Congress gutted the ability for lawyers to sue. Suzanne had then moved to West Palm Beach to manage an aid firm that concentrated on getting food and medicine to the Caribbean Islands. While visiting one of the relief offices in Haiti she had contracted the bioplague from a local. She was then denied re-entry into the United States. After the ban on immigration and the formation of the Miami Quarantine Zone, she heard about the growler settlement in the heart of the former city. Now she was a leader, and tonight, a babysitter.

Svala hurried out to the Hive-utility vehicle. As soon as she had the driver's door open she stopped. The stench was crippling. She looked inside, seeing stains on the passenger seats. She didn't know what it was but knew she had to follow Tiget. His plan had gone too far and gotten out of hand. She didn't know the details, but when he started using the poor victims of the bioplague it had gone too far. She wanted a place to call her own as much as any member of the massive Simolit family. But not at the expense of human life. Not at the risk of her children losing contact with the people of the United States. She had come to love this country since she came home with Tom Wilner. Despite its flaws it was still considered the greatest country in the world. It was the world's best hope to stop the Germans. It was also one of their few hopes if the approaching Urailians proved to be hostile. The people of the country were capable of incredible kindness and generosity. She wanted Tommy and Emma to understand that and experience it as a citizen not as some fugitive from a new quarantine zone.

For all those reasons as well as her feelings for Tom Wilner, whom she knew Tiget was going to meet, she felt the compulsion to follow him. She didn't know what she could do, but she was tired of sitting on the side and asking people to leave her out of all decisions. Now was the time for her to act, even if it was against one of the men she loved.

She managed to slide into the seat, gasping for fresh air from the open window. She didn't even mind the light, cool rain splashing her from the open window. She pushed the big utility vehicle to its limits to catch up to Tiget and now could just make out the taillight of the motorcycle. With her window open she could also hear the rumble of its engine.

She stayed back as the motorcycle pulled onto the old Sawgrass Expressway. She knew where he was headed. He was going to the Big Cypress Bar. The last time she had been there her husband had tried to stop the fight with the Hallecks that started all this trouble.

Tiget could recover from most any wound, but she knew he would underestimate her husband. She was certain he had never met a human like Tom Wilner before.

———

Shelby Hahn had slipped away from Wilner's car. She then watched him drive off to meet Nadovich. She couldn't convince him to avoid the leader of the Simolits in Florida. He had told her to find a way to take the children somewhere safe. He knew she could do it. She knew she could do it. But she didn't know if Tom Wilner could overcome Nadovich's superior genetics.

She lingered outside the front door to the house, listening for anything unusual. She heard a lot of unusual activity. It sounded like a party with music playing and kids running around. She peeked in a couple of widows to determine if she could slip in the front door undetected. These people didn't expect an intruder. Why would they? Who would try to enter their ranks?

Once inside she hung back, slipping into the kitchen, trying to see into the dining and living rooms. She was startled by an up close view of the bioplague victims. Some wore veils or bandanas across their faces, but the boils and fleshy lumps were clearly visible. Even on the children.

She knew that the government feared a spread of the bioplague more than anything else. The chemical compound that was used in the bioweapon was developed in France or Switzerland years before. Designed to be used as a deterrent, some industrious Frenchmen had sold the formula to several desperate militaries of Eastern Europe and the Middle East. The weapon had been officially deployed three times, killing a million people. What no one had counted on was that there would be survivors who would spread the disease until their deaths. That had taken the disease from Armenia to nearly fifteen other countries, which then spread across the globe.

Had it not been for Robert Gleason and Eric Raab working to find out the dynamics of the disease, the origin might not ever have been discovered.

Shelby shook her head at her first close-up view of these poor people.

She saw Emma, playing with another girl who was heavily veiled. She called out in a harsh whisper, "Emma."

The little girl looked over and smiled at the sight of Shelby, then walked into the kitchen.

"What're you doing here?"

"I'm going to take you and Tommy back to your dad's house."

"Is Mommy coming too?"

"Not tonight, sweetheart."

"She's gone right now. Can I wait to say goodbye?"

Shelby hesitated and said, "Get Tommy quietly and we'll figure it out."

As she stood upright she heard a woman say, "Figure what out?"

A veiled woman stood in the doorway, clearly protective of Emma.

FIFTY

Tom Wilner had spent more than twenty minutes working on his backup plan. He strung wire across the alley behind the bar between the lone remaining power pole and a pipe running on the outside of the building. The Everglades and the wide Zone River, which flowed south, were next to the alley. The river, formed in the last decade from the near constant rain, which started when the climate changed, moved rapidly until it met the old Miami River and faded into the ocean. After Shelby had called him to say that Nadovich was on an vintage Harley-Davidson motorcycle, Wilner had thought of one possible trap. As a combat veteran his mind often thought out these traps based on terrain. In the flat, now empty southern tip of Florida, good terrain was hard to come by. He also looked at terrain with an eye toward tactical advantage. Out here on the treeless edge of the Everglades this was the best idea he could come up with. He used a bale of heavy gauge communication wire that worked with a number of devices. It was strong but thin. Very hard to see. It was also cheap so no one would notice the loss of one bale. He worked quickly, keeping some of the landmarks in mind in case he had to fall back to this plan. He knew he wouldn't have time to pay attention to details if things didn't go well inside. He looked at the flowing water, wondering if it would provide refuge if his plan failed.

Wilner, having finished his booby trap outside, had waited in the quiet bar for the last ten minutes. He had wanted to help with the kids but knew how susceptible he would be to the bioplague, so agreed to leave it all to Shelby. Besides, he intended to settle some debts with Mr. Tiget Nadovich when he finally showed up. He had his duty pistol and the large flasher he had smuggled back from the Miami Quarantine Zone. He felt confident that he could stop Nadovich no matter if he was more than human or not.

He sat at a table facing the door across the wide floor, feeling like one of the old gunfighters from a Western movie.

There was a small crowd in the place, which he hoped to avoid but didn't worry too much about it. Getting back Tommy and Emma, then stopping Nadovich were his concerns today. Nothing else mattered anymore.

He had the flasher hidden under his shirt, tucked in the front of his belt. His service pistol was in a holster on his hip. On the other side of the room the remains of the melted jukebox from the night of the first fight sat in the same place. The sagging, useless machine was now more of a curiosity than an entertainment device. Even now a young woman looked at the melted hulk and touched the glob of glass that had gathered on the front of the machine.

Wilner wondered what would be left as a tourist attraction

after tonight. He hoped it wouldn't be the remains of his body. He had often thought how he didn't want to die in an Iranian desert. Now he realized he didn't want to die in an isolated Florida bar either.

Besslia floated through the air of the bar for what seemed like the fifth time, as his blows had proven ineffective against the man he knew only as Demitri. He had figured out that the man engaged in the struggle with Johann Halleck was named Alec.

Now, as he landed hard on the floor of the empty bar, he managed to reach behind him. He could finally wrap his hand around the handle of the knife he had hidden in his belt.

Demitri stepped across the room, reaching down to grab him by the jacket again. The attacker was distracted by Johann landing a brutal blow on Alec that sent him hurtling across the floor into the wall next to the front door.

Besslia used the opportunity to draw the knife. As Demitri's head was turned he plunged the knife into the man's exposed neck. He felt the blade slice through muscle and cartilage, then saw the look of shock and surprise on his face.

Besslia yanked the sharp blade out of the bloody wound, then shoved it hard into his chest, just under his rib cage. He kept the pressure on the knife, driving it, twisting the whole time, deep into his chest.

Demitri gasped for air, the neck wound robbing him of oxygen and the chest wound sucking air into a punctured lung.

Besslia scurried out of the way and backed into Johann who turned to see what his fighting partner had done.

They watched in silence as the man writhed on the floor,

blood spurting out in every direction like some kind of sprinkler.

Johann said, "We must finish him."

"Finish him? He's done."

"Possibly, but we must be sure. I'll keep Alec at bay."

Besslia slowly scanned the room until his eyes fell on his duty pistol, lying near the bar that the bartender had fled. He leaned down, picking up the pistol, then he turned to fire three times into the man's head.

He looked up at Johann. Besslia thought he might be sick. He had just executed a man, or at least a being that looked like a man.

The other man, Alec, stood and said, "We'll remember this." Then he disappeared out the door.

Besslia started after him but Johann held out a hand. "There has been enough killing."

Besslia looked back at the still body on the floor and felt relief at the sentiment.

Shelby Hahn had settled at the dining table with Tommy and Emma in sight at the far end of the room. Across from her sat Suzanne. The woman had made it clear that Shelby would take Svala's children over her dead body.

The two women recognized some shared quality and came to a quick truce to at least discuss the matter.

Shelby said, "Do you know who your benefactors are?"

Suzanne shook her veiled head. "We don't care. They have offered us a better life, which we have accepted."

"They're immune to the bioplague. Doesn't that interest you?"

"You don't seem too worried about catching it either."

"That's correct. We're the same. We're not considered human."

"Again, that doesn't bother us. I have heard us described as no longer being human either."

"But Tiget Nadovich preys on humans. He considers their lives expendable."

Suzanne kept her calm and said, "Just as the humans prey on us."

Shelby sighed. "I understand you're victims and misunderstood, but the fact remains you're a threat to the humans. You spread a deadly disease. He intends to use you somehow to spread that disease. He also intends to detonate a large bomb. Possibly a radioactive one."

"Although that does concern me, my immediate interest is the safety of those children. You appear to be sincere but I have made a pledge to Svala, which I intend to keep. You can use violence but that is the choice you must make." She leveled cloudy eyes at Shelby, which were more intense staring out from the top of her veil.

Wilner flinched every time the door opened to the front of the bar. He wondered if he should just open up with the flasher as soon as Nadovich walked inside the bar.

When Wilner's V-com beeped, he answered it immediately.

Shelby Hahn's face appeared. She kept it short. "Tom, I have the kids but there's a new development."

"What's that?"

"I also have the bioplague victims. I got a hold of a school bus and I'm moving them to a safe place."

"Back into the zone?"

"Not exactly."

"You could be arrested for treason for that. Or worse, be labeled a terrorist."

"I'll risk it."

"Tommy and Emma are safe?"

"Yeah, they thought they were just visiting with their mom. But, Tom, I have to warn you."

"What?"

"Svala might be coming to you at the bar. You should just leave. The kids are safe. Please don't risk a confrontation with Nadovich."

"Sorry, it's overdue." Then he saw the door open and he looked across the room. Tiget Nadovich glanced around then started to walk straight for him. He looked back into his V-com. "Too late anyway. It's showtime." He shut off the V-com and stiffened as Nadovich drew closer.

FIFTY-ONE

Tiget Nadovich sat across from the human who had caused him the most trouble of anyone in almost a hundred years. He stayed calm, trying not to focus on his headache.

Wilner didn't flinch as he looked back. The man had a pleasant face with a scar that showed he had seen combat in his ridiculously short life. The thought of this human making love to Svala upset him in a way he was not used to. He told himself what he was about to do was all for the family. That it had nothing to do with his personal feelings for this man. He simply knew too much. If not about his plan for a homeland, then he knew too much about them.

Finally Nadovich said, "You have something I need."

Wilner looked at him without emotion. "Really? You should have said something."

"You are not in a position to play games, Detective. I still have your children."

Wilner nodded. "I've heard they're more likely your children."

That caught Nadovich by surprise. He knew that the UPF detective had figured out a lot about them, but he didn't think anyone would provide that information.

"Regardless, I am certain you wish to see them again."

"You're correct. But I can't provide you with a circuit board that will activate a dirty bomb."

That surprised Nadovich even more. "You are very bright." He paused for effect and added, "For a human."

"What I can't figure out is why, exactly, you're so determined to do this."

"Look around you, Detective, tolerance is not exactly the hot commodity in the world today. How do you think we would be treated if anyone found out what we are?"

"You might be surprised."

"I would be, but not in a pleasant way. A Nazi army officer named Otto Skorzeny discovered our identity. Have you heard his name before?"

"Yeah, he rescued Mussolini from the mountaintop prison."

"Yes, his raid on the Campo Imperatore Hotel was flawless. He also led several other commando raids that are legendary. He discovered our secret, then had the idea that if we were so resistant to injury, had no real fear of death, he could create a unit of commandos comprised only of our kind."

Wilner stared at him implacably. "What happened?"

"Even his crazy boss didn't believe we existed. We were able to rescue the two live captives he had and back then DNA had no meaning. But it gave me a glimpse of what humans could conceive for us if we did not act."

Wilner nodded. "Then the attack on New York provided you a chance to see what living apart was like."

Nadovich smiled. "Exactly. Those Hallecks are well-informed. Our people live there without any human contact and cause no problems."

"Did they detonate the bomb?"

"No, they had no part in the plot."

"You want the world to believe the same of an attack down here."

"September eleventh is in two days. There are always attacks on that day. No one will question one more bomb detonated on your sacred day."

"And the growlers are to keep people away, right?"

Now that shocked Nadovich. "How did you know about my new friends?"

"I'm a UPF detective. We know everything that goes on in the district."

Nadovich chuckled. "Then you know I can't let you leave this bar."

He saw Wilner reach in his waistband and realized he had a weapon of some kind. Nadovich flipped up the table between them and drove the detective back hard against the next empty table. Nadovich felt the front of Wilner's shirt and grasped the weapon's handle. He yanked it as Wilner fell back.

Nadovich quickly realized he had grabbed a handheld flasher. Before he could fire the weapon he felt pain in his leg as Wilner pointed a conventional pistol at him, opening fire.

Steve Besslia now saw that Johann Halleck was injured. Blood seeped onto his shirt near his kidneys in the rear, staining it in a widening patch. Johann's legs buckled slightly as Besslia caught him by the arm, then helped him to a chair.

Johann looked up and nodded. "I'll be fine. It's just a shock to sustain an injury sometimes." He looked over toward the dead body. "Not as big a shock as getting killed like Demitri, but still a shock."

Besslia had his gun in his holster because he had not seen any sign of another person. He had heard a vehicle drive off after Alec had fled, but felt safe in the small bar for now.

He raced behind the bar to retrieve a white dish towel. He picked the only one that wasn't green with bacteria. He hurried back to Johann and pushed him forward in the chair. "Let me get a look at the bleeding."

Johann leaned forward, allowing Besslia a look.

He pulled up the blood-soaked shirt gingerly and saw a gash that could've been caused by anything. It was deep, running four inches parallel to his belt. He wiped away some blood, then applied pressure directly on the wound.

He felt Johann go still and quiet and was suddenly scared that the wound might have been serious enough to kill the big man.

He placed two fingers on Johann's neck, feeling a strong pulse. He relaxed slightly while maintaining the pressure on the wound.

Finally Johann groaned. "It should be fine now." He sat back up.

Besslia removed the rag, now soaked in blood, and was shocked to see the wound closed. A thick dark line marked the location but no blood escaped.

Besslia said, "It's that easy?"

"Hardly. I just stopped the bleeding. I'll have to be still to concentrate later to heal the wound completely." He looked at the body. "That's why we're not finished. Although he looks dead we must be certain."

"How?"

Johann looked around the room and said, "Burn him. Right in that spot."

"Are you sure?"

"It must be done."

Besslia stared down at the body, looking for any signs of movement. He was already troubled by shooting the dead man in the head three times.

Johann said, "Then I will do it." His accent making it sound like a sacred task he must complete.

Besslia said, "No, I'll do it." He stood and thought about what propellant would burn him. Then he went back to the bar and looked for a bottle of whiskey. He found the highest proof he could, then doused Demitri's still form. Johann provided him with a small lighter. He pressed the igniter and tossed the lighter onto Demitri. The flame caught on quickly, engulfing the body.

Besslia stepped back to Johann.

Johann said, "You did well. Thank you for the help."

Besslia looked up at the taller man and said, "Help is a two-way street. Sounds like you've been helping us for a long time."

Johann smiled.

FIFTY-TWO

The shots from Wilner's gun had scattered the patrons in the bar. He and Nadovich were in an isolated corner, but it still sent people racing out the door. This bar already had a reputation and the melted jukebox was a testament to that truth.

Wilner backed away from Nadovich, who was hit but not too badly. Wilner hoped Nadovich couldn't figure out how to operate the flasher too quickly. He threw a couple of more rounds down toward the table Nadovich now crouched behind.

Then he heard the snapping sound of a flasher firing and, without looking, dove farther down the bar, away from the corner where he had been firing.

The blast engulfed the end of the bar, igniting the wooden top and melting two metal stools. The plastic covering the pads on the bar stool disintegrated, dripping down the legs as the heat caused them to buckle and twist.

Wilner was about to pop up over the bar while the weapon recharged to fire off a few rounds when he saw someone slip into the bar from the front door. He looked over, catching the fast-moving form and the dark hair of a woman. He yelled, "Get out of here." He peeked over the bar, seeing Nadovich standing with the flasher in his hand. He had apparently gotten used to it quickly.

Nadovich dodged to one side when he saw Wilner, but he kept the weapon in his right hand like a pistol, waiting the ten seconds for the weapon to be ready to fire again.

Wilner stood, ready to flee out the door and fall back to his next plan when he saw the woman stand up near him. It was Svala.

She called out, "Run, Tom. Just run."

He wasn't going to argue.

Nadovich yelled, "No!" He had the flasher pointed at him. "You're not going anywhere."

Wilner heard the crack of the weapon and even saw the flash, but also felt the force of his body being knocked out of the way.

Svala had thrown her body into his like a speeding car. Even her smaller body at that speed was enough to knock him across the floor.

His head snapped and twisted, giving him a quick peek as she stood directly where he had been. He caught a glimpse of the yellow blob of the E-weapon as it enveloped her and heard her short, agonizing scream.

He landed, shaking his head to clear it. He looked over to where Svala had been standing, but saw only her burnt, sizzling form melting onto the table next to her. Several beer bottles popped and cracked as some of them dissolved to what used to be his wife's head. Luckily he couldn't make out her face in the ball of flesh, bone, wood and glass.

From across the room he heard a scream.

Wilner stood and saw that a standing Nadovich had dropped the E-weapon, frozen with horror at what he had done.

Then, slowly, his dark eyes shifted over to Wilner. The only emotions they showed at that moment were pure hate and rage.

FIFTY-THREE

Tom Wilner knew he was in a tight spot. He didn't have time to look for his pistol, but knew he couldn't stand toe-to-toe with Tiget Nadovich. He was still in shock over seeing Svala killed by the flasher, but his combat training taught him to move on for now and grieve later. His experience in Iran reinforced that lesson.

He had a plan and knew to stick to it. He turned, then darted for the door, unsure if Nadovich had recovered sufficiently to follow him. He was in his Hive, cutting through the giant, unpaved dirt parking lot of the bar in a matter of seconds. He slowed the car, waiting for Nadovich to come out the door.

It took only a second for him to see Nadovich's dark hair as he rushed out the door, looked at Wilner in the Hive, then jumped on the large motorcycle he had parked next to the front door.

Wilner peeled out in the dirt along the rear of the long building. Up ahead was his trap. He purposely ran the car up onto the sandy berm along the flowing Zone River that separated the bar from the start of the massive Everglades. He hopped out and saw that the front of the car was off the ground. It looked like an authentic wreck. Or at least he hoped so.

Wilner sprinted down the back alley and ducked slightly under the wire he had strung earlier. He could hear the motorcycle rumble around the corner. Once he was in the alley the noise from the loud motorcycle exhaust was deafening.

Wilner didn't even look back. He could hear Nadovich gun the engine, then pick up speed as he chased down the man he hated most in the world. Wilner looked over his shoulder once and saw Nadovich riding down the center of the alley. Then the man ducked low, like he was trying to reduce wind resistance and he passed under Wilner's well-constructed booby trap.

Wilner didn't panic, but knew his chances for survival had just decreased dramatically. Fleetingly, he wondered if Nadovich would raise Tommy and Emma. Would anyone hunt him down as a cop killer? He thought of Shelby, then shook his head. He wasn't dead yet.

Wilner leaped to one side as the motorcycle passed. He picked up an old piece of aluminum that looked like a support to a screen enclosure. It was light, but had a good, jagged end.

Nadovich slowed the big bike at the other end of the alley, saw Wilner with a new weapon and then gunned the engine of the bike, racing right at him.

Wilner started to run back with the aluminum pole still in his hands. He remembered at the last second to duck slightly at the wire, then stopped about ten feet past the wire. He turned, raising the pole as Nadovich closed the distance with the motorcycle.

This time Nadovich didn't need to chase him. He sat tall and arrogant in the saddle of the motorcycle.

As he was about to reach Wilner the wire caught him in the chest.

Wilner flinched, then dove to one side as the motorcycle wobbled and then spun into the same berm where Wilner had grounded his Hive.

As he hit the ground he saw the wire dig into Nadovich's chest, shooting him into the air like a bag of old laundry.

He froze as he saw Nadovich roll on the ground, then move like he was getting up.

Behind him he heard a vehicle slide to a stop on the gravel alley. He turned to see Steve Besslia and Johann Halleck emerge from a Hive. They rushed forward and Wilner noticed they both had weapons in their hands.

Nadovich was on his feet now, shaking off the effects of the crash.

Besslia raised his pistol and starting popping off rounds.

Nadovich turned and dove toward the building where there were several storage tanks and pipes.

One of Besslia's bullets caught him and spun him as Johann fired a flasher. The flash of light striking Nadovich and the storage tanks at the same time. The main tank held some form of fuel because it erupted in a devastating explosion like the newly active volcano in Oregon.

The force of the blast knocked Wilner back and sent his Hive tipping toward the river.

Smoke drifted across the lot as Wilner tried to clear his head. Besslia helped him upright, but they could only see the cloud of smoke.

Johann joined them as the smoke cleared and they could see the giant hole in the wall where the tank had been. A huge mass of melted, fused metal and brick formed near the building.

Wilner felt weak, his legs shaking as he had to back to the wall of the building and plop onto the ground again.

He had finally seen too much combat.

FIFTY-FOUR

Tom Wilner sat back on the couch in his own home in the Eastern District, picking at some of the dried blood around the bandages on his face and arms. His children were asleep in their rooms. Shelby Hahn, in her official capacity as a Department of Homeland Security agent, and his boss sat across from him in comfortable chairs.

His boss said, "So it was all gang-related?"

Wilner nodded, looking at Shelby.

The federal agent said, "Yeah, that Nadovich gang was tough. But they're all either dead or have fled the state."

Wilner's boss stood up, smiling. "As long as they're out of UPF jurisdiction, we're happy."

Wilner didn't say anything. He wanted to put this whole episode behind him. He definitely didn't want DNA tests or autopsies on any of the bodies found in the district the night before. His story was simple enough and resources scarce enough that no one would question it.

His boss patted him on the shoulder as he headed to the

door. "You did a great job, Willie, take off as long as you need. Get those kids settled, then worry about the UPF."

"Thanks, boss." But his voice cracked, betraying the emotions he was going through. He kept quiet until his boss had left.

Later, after some sleep, Wilner awoke to the smell of a real meat meal. He padded into the kitchen to Shelby who was moving from the food prep machine to the refrigerator. She turned, then smiled. He just stared at her.

She asked, "What is it?"

"You know."

"Because I'm different from you?"

"You lied to me."

"But I got your kids back, so I figured on a little forgiveness."

He kept looking at her. She had her green contacts back in. She stepped over and gave him a hug, then a kiss on the lips. "You have to understand I was raised to keep my life a secret."

"Are you even from Tennessee?"

"Everything I told you was true. I am from Tennessee. My father does hate the Germans. What I lied about was why. Not because he was an engineer. He fought them as a U.S. soldier. You'd like him."

"How old is he?"

She was silent, then said, "Old in your terms."

"How old are you?"

"Not quite as old in your terms."

She took his hand, leading him out to the living room. As

she turned on the video broadcaster she said, "Look at what's happened in the last day since we've been busy."

He heard the newscaster say, "And Germany has agreed to the cease-fire."

Shelby said, "We're off call-up status until something changes."

Wilner said, "And Israel is in the clear?"

She nodded. "It has been conclusively proven that it was an Iranian nuke that went off in a storage unit." She smiled. "The world can go back to focusing on the Urailian starship."

"But what about me?"

"You've got a lot to tell the kids. About Svala and at some time about themselves."

He sagged on the couch. "I know. I didn't think my life could change so much in such a short time."

"Nothing has changed. Just how you look at things."

"I can't learn the truth about the kids. I can't have a DNA test because I don't want anyone to suspect anything unusual."

"Then just enjoy the life you've built and the friends you've made."

"What will you do?"

"I could convince my agency that they need an agent down here full time."

He couldn't help but smile.

"I'm already working on designating the housing development where I left Suzanne and the bioplague victims as a special refuge. If I was assigned down here I could keep a better eye on them. Help if they had a problem."

"Will Johann stay?"

"Probably. He likes it here. He has a new friend in Steve Besslia."

"So your advice is to shut up and enjoy life."

"And see what comes next. You may be needed for combat. You just don't know. But right now those kids need their father. The man who raised them. The man they love." She kissed him, saying, "I need you too."

Wilner kissed her, then leaned back on the couch. So much had happened he felt drained. But he and the kids were safe and that's all that mattered.

He looked up at his wall chronometer and realized it was noon on September eleventh. He'd see how he felt in the next twelve hours.

He had been concentrating for nine days. That was to ease the pain and gain the strength to open his eyes. Now Tiget Nadovich could see a rough ceiling and hear voices speaking in a Caribbean mishmash of languages.

Someone noticed he was awake and the round, pretty face of a middle-aged woman appeared over him.

He tried to speak, but it came out garbled.

The woman leaned closer and said, *"Qué?"*

Finally he summoned the strength to ask, *"Dónde esta?"*

She nodded and said, "Miami."

Instantly he knew that the blast at the Big Cypress Bar had blown him into the Zone River and he had drifted into the Miami Quarantine Zone.

The woman used a damp cloth to dab at his face. He knew how he must look and the care she must have taken to comfort him.

"What is today?" he asked in Spanish.

She looked puzzled and said, "September twentieth. You must rest now."

He knew his life had been destroyed, but this wouldn't be the first time. He would rest now. Maybe for months. Then he could reclaim what was his.

Except for Svala. She was lost forever. He felt a tear in his eye, then it ran down his charred face.

Turn the page for a preview of

THE

DOUBLE

HUMAN

James O'Neal

Available now
from Tom Doherty Associates

TOR®   A TOR·HARDCOVER   ISBN 978-0-7653-2015-5

ONE

Tom Wilner watched in silence as each family walked through the entrance to the housing development on the southern edge of the Lawton District, his waterproof windbreaker beading up with droplets from the constant drizzle. His service pistol felt like an anchor on his hip.

Steve Besslia said, "This is a shitty assignment."

Tom Wilner shrugged. "Watching people move doesn't sound that tough to me."

"I know, I know, you don't have any Iranians shooting at you or Bosnian car bombs but just standing here with our thumbs up our asses is boring."

"Do you really want the alternative to boring?" Wilner had seen it and was perfectly content with boring.

"I don't know, Willie," started his friend, Steve Besslia. "None of 'em look too happy to be down here."

Wilner cast a sideways glance at the uniformed cop and said, "Would you like it?"

"What'd ya mean? I *am* here."

"I mean forced to relocate like this. I don't blame them one bit; especially when there are no jobs down here, no entertainment and it's too cold and rainy to even go to the beach."

"Government is paying for the move, providing free housing and a stipend for two years. You and me moved on our own, work sixty hours a week and pay for our housing."

Wilner shrugged. It didn't matter that Florida was no longer the sunny garden spot it had been when he was a kid. He liked it here. This was where he was raising his kids and they had all lived together as a family. For a while at least.

A young woman with brown, stringy hair stomped up to them and looked at Besslia. "You the Nazi assigned to shoot us if we complain?"

Besslia shook his head. "No, ma'am, I'm here to shoot the gators if they try and grab a kid."

The woman's eyes widened. "What kind of hell have they sent us to?" She hurried away, shouting, "Sara, Kenny, where are you?"

Besslia smiled and said, "Used to be the tourists around here that you could mess with. Never thought new faces would be so rare." He looked at Wilner. "At least you don't get those kinds of comments as a detective. No one even knows who you are unless you badge 'em or draw your weapon."

Wilner shook his head. "You know it's not like the old days. Not enough people to cause too much trouble. They're always happy to see a cop; particularly this close to the Quarantine Zone."

Both cops' V-coms started beeping in unison, so they knew it was a police call. Their newest communication units incorporated police radio, video communicator, mail service and a GPS locator service as well as a host of information services available to the police and public.

Wilner flipped his open first and heard the bland, clear, un-accented voice of a dispatcher.

"Any unit in southern Lawton District. Call of assault on or near the Eastern District boundary just north of Miami Quarantine Zone." The message repeated twice more.

Besslia said, "Let's go."

"One of us should stay here as assigned."

"You kidding? When's the last time we got a call like this?"

Wilner looked up at the dark sky. It was difficult to tell day from night anymore. He had not seen the sun in three weeks. He didn't bother answering the patrolman, instead he started jogging toward his government-made issued hive, which was a hydrogen-powered vehicle.

Besslia trailed him, jiggling and clanking his duty gear, his heavy pistol slung low on his leg for easy access while riding his big Hive-bike.

Wilner knew the only populated streets in the area where the assault was taking place and cut under the decaying remnants of the old Interstate 95. He used his V-com to tell Besslia to cover the approach from another angle, shouting, "Steve, cover the back, I got the front door." He punched the accelerator and felt the newly issued vehicle respond well. Sometimes the production hives were sluggish, which earned them the nickname "Hindenbergs." When the government started competing with the private carmakers, the one thing they eliminated was speed and fuel regulators. His tires screeched as he turned onto the unmarked road where several old but clean apartment buildings stood. Most of the residents either had government subsidies to live in such an unpopulated area or worked at jobs in the southern part of the Lawton District. A few were smugglers who specialized in crossing the border into the Miami Quarantine Zone.

As he approached the front of a four-story building he caught sight of a woman jumping up and down, waving her arms.

Wilner jumped the old crumbling curb and brought the big cruiser to a halt next to the front door. Before he was even out of the vehicle, the woman was shouting, "He's killing her, he's killing her."

"Where?" Wilner drew his big, 11-millimeter, police-issued autopistol.

The woman, panting now, gulped out, "Second floor."

Wilner didn't wait for any more information; he was inside the lobby of the building scanning for stairs. He had not grabbed his backup weapon. He now kept an unlawful energy weapon in the car. In the marines they had called the handheld version of the weapon a "flasher" and now that was the street name for any powered, light-beamed guns. Events of the past few months had taught him the value of the extra firepower and the truth was the streets were full of these surplus military weapons.

He took the stairs two at a time and then slowed by the second-floor door. He raised the gun in front of him and caught his breath.

He felt his pulse slow and then he burst through the door. The long, wide hallway was empty so he started moving forward quickly, scanning the rooms, most of which had no doors. About half of the apartments had someone in them. He heard a noise and froze. It came from in front of him. Instinctively he crouched and edged forward, gun up and following the movement of his eyes.

At one of the last apartments with an open door, he peeked around the old wooden frame. Another sound came from inside.

In the back of his mind, Wilner wondered where the hell Besslia was. He should have pulled up by now.

Wilner couldn't wait. He slipped into the open apartment silently and slid along the wall, the next room in the sights of his duty pistol. He turned and eased down the hallway toward the open bedroom door. Shadows moved inside the room at the end of the narrow hall.

His pulse increased now as he consciously tried to control his breathing. He paused momentarily at the door, then stepped in with his gun pointed at the figure crouching next to the bed.

The scene stunned him for a second. After all he had seen—combat in Iran, ethnic conflict in the Balkans, murders here and over in the Quarantine Zone—this image froze him.

A man with short graying hair looked down at a naked woman, laid out neatly on the bed with a slight trickle of blood leaking out onto the white sheet from her neck. Wilner couldn't see his face clearly. The shocking part was the loving care with which the killer was now stroking her hair. It had a hypnotizing effect.

Before Wilner could bark out an order to freeze or just fire his gun, the killer's head snapped up and he pounced with incredible speed and surprise, throwing his whole body at Wilner as the gun went off. The bullet flew wide and high and the killer's momentum bounced him off the larger detective, springing him down the hallway.

Wilner, stunned, shook his head clear, took one more quick glance at the body on the bed and followed the killer.

He raced down the hallway after the fast, agile man but as he came toward the front door of the apartment he ducked a chair that flew at his head.

The polymer chair fractured into a few large pieces on the wall just above Wilner's head. Holding one piece like about, the killer swung hard and knocked Wilner's gun to the old, rotting hardwood floor.

Wilner twisted and threw a low kick into the man's leg, then grabbed a piece of the chair himself and aimed at the killer's head. Instead, he struck the man's shoulder, the jagged edge ripping his old cotton shirt and drawing blood.

The killer sprang back, turned and darted down the hallway to the stairs.

Wilner stood up, a little unsteady, scooped up his pistol and stumbled as fast as he could toward the stairs. By the time he was out the front door he saw Besslia pulling up on his Hive-cycle.

He stepped out to the front of the porch and froze.

At the bottom of the steps the woman who had directed him to the second floor lay on the ground, now still in a soaking wet dress, her arms and legs poised neatly along her body. He saw the blood mixing with a puddle next to her neck. She had the same kind of wound as the woman upstairs.

This bastard was quick.

Besslia was off his bike and running toward Wilner when an old pickup truck thundered from the rear of the building, blasting through the front yard of the apartment building and bumping over the curb into the street.

Wilner raced to his car in seconds. As he jumped in he shouted, "Call it in, Steve. Two dead. Chasing old truck, I don't know the make. Prewar for sure." He didn't wait for a reply.

The tires of his hive screeched as soon as they made contact with the street. He flicked on his concealed blue lights and siren. Not that there were many cars to chase out of his way. In fact he had not used the lights in more than a year.

It took a minute to catch up enough to see the truck's tail-lights as he headed south. He got on his V-com as he tried to close the distance with the ancient, gas-powered pickup truck.

"Dispatch, this is UPF 536. I'm in pursuit of a suspect headed south on Highway Six." He checked to make sure he had called out the right road. He knew it used to be called U.S.-1 years ago but now it was just called the "Six."

Wilner hoped the call would go to the National Guardsmen on the quarantine border. He figured that was where this guy was headed. With Besslia staying at the scene, there would be no UPF backup for miles around. Wilner's right arm ached where the killer had struck him with the broken chair but it wouldn't help him escape. The UPF detective was pissed.

The truck took a hard right turn, almost flipping on one side. Wilner took the same turn. Just as the truck was coming up on one of the checkpoints manned by the military, the killer swerved hard along the canal. The door flew open and the killer jumped out of the moving truck and rolled into the wide canal.

Wilner slid up behind the truck and hopped out.

National Guardsmen were already firing from their checkpoint on the bridge into the water with their assault rifles, making artificial waves with the volume of fire.

Wilner scanned the surface of the canal, not wanting to get too close to the bullets piercing the water. He saw no sign of the fleeing man. Just the water ripped by rifle fire.

After a minute of sustained fire he heard a sergeant calling, "Cease-fire, cease-fire," to the six guardsmen who were still pointing their weapons in the direction where the killer had last been seen.

Wilner stepped up to the edge of the canal, his pistol hanging in his right hand, pointing down at the ground. All he saw was the dark, muddy water of the last canal in the southern United States with no clue to the fate of the killer he had just chased.

TWO

Detective Tom Wilner held his badge up high and had already holstered his pistol as he approached the National Guardsmen on the bridge.

A young Latin sergeant stepped down to meet him. "We heard the chase over the general frequency. We were ready."

Wilner said, "You don't usually shoot at people going into the zone, do you?"

"Nope, not unless it's something like this. These boys needed to cut loose."

"Ever see him surface?"

"No, sir. But after the fire we laid down, I don't think we ever will. We had to puncture his lungs and stomach. He'll be dragged by the current until something eats him." The younger man turned his dark eyes up to Wilner. "He really stab some ladies?"

"Looks like."

"That's probably why we were okayed to fire. With the new transplants coming in from up north and the Midwest they don't want no mention of this kinda stuff. They got us really cracking down on Quarantine Zone violations too."

Wilner nodded. "Makes us look like the Wild West. They want people to feel safe."

"Safe in Florida? I have a couple of guardsmen who say they've seen more action here than they did in Syria."

Wilner chuckled. "I doubt that."

"How do you figure?"

"Any of them asking to go back?"

Tom Wilner shook his head as he pulled up to the apartment building where the chase had started. Someone had at least placed a sheet over the woman's body in the front of the building. Steve Besslia sat on the stairs to the building speaking to another uniformed cop.

As he came closer he heard the unmistakable voice of the UPF district commander.

"Willie, what happened to the killer?"

"Hey, boss," said Wilner, turning to meet the shorter, fifty-year-old man who had run police operations in the Northern Enclave and Lawton District for the past eleven years shortly after the tax revenues had forced all the police departments to combine and form the state's only law enforcement agency.

"What happened?" His years as a captain in the army in several different wars showing by the impatience in his voice. The thick burn scar on his left cheek was a testament to the combat he had seen.

"I answered the call. Saw a man with the body upstairs. We fought a little and then I chased him."

"What'd he look like?"

Wilner shrugged. "I didn't get any kind of look at him. Shorter white guy. I might recognize him if I saw him again."

"When did this woman die?" He pointed at the sheet-covered body.

"During the chase. The guy was fast, boss, real fast."

"Coming from you that means something." He rolled his fingers in a hurry-up motion. "What happened to this creep?"

"He bailed out in the canal next to the Quarantine Zone and the guardsmen laid down a sheet of fire."

"They got his body?"

"Nope."

"You sure he's dead?"

"Nope."

"Why not?"

"Because I've seen too many guys slip away from firefights. I never think it's over until I see a body. I just wanted to check on things here, then I was gonna take Besslia and start searching the canal on both sides."

The commander nodded. "I even brought out crime scene on this one."

Wilner stared in surprise.

"The new policy is to make it at least look more like regular police operations. They figure with more people, tax revenues will increase. They don't want people scared off."

Wilner said, "I'm gonna take a look around before I go search for the killer's body."

"You're the detective on this so you can take charge. I'll send Besslia and a couple of patrolmen to look for the body now."

Wilner nodded and started to walk through the scene. It wasn't like the crime scenes he had watched on old video broadcasts or movies. There was no yellow tape to keep people away.

There were hardly any people to keep away. No one wanted to get mixed up in a UPF investigation and no one wanted a criminal mad that there might be a witness. There weren't many cops either. They were spread too thin over an area that used to cover five counties and seven major cities. The climate change and a couple of terror attacks had shifted most of the population north. Away from the borders and as far from the dreadful Miami Quarantine Zone as possible.

The first thing he did was stoop and peek under the sheet at the woman who had flagged him down. She was about thirty, with a pretty face and short brown hair. He knew where the wound was. He touched her cheek and moved her head to see the single puncture wound in her neck. It had to go deep to kill her in those few seconds the killer had to act.

A patrolman stepped up behind him and said, "Did you get him?"

"We'll know in a little bit." The patrolman wasn't squeamish seeing the dead woman. All of the UPF cops, even the women, had been in the service and most, like this guy, had seen combat. A single, clean corpse didn't do much to spook him.

Wilner started checking for witnesses and other evidence inside the apartment building. He positioned a second patrolman at the front of the apartment, which held the first victim. Wilner took a few minutes to see if he could figure out why she was a victim. It looked like she lived alone. He found an identification card for the district hospital. She had been an emergency room nurse. Wilner looked at the photo and then stepped into the room to see her face. He recognized her. He'd seen her in the hospital several times over the last year and remembered her smiling, happy to see cops coming inside, a safety blanket added to the second-rate security guards.

Her sleek, pale, nude body held no clue to her bright personality. This was one of the few murder victims Wilner had ever known as a cop. The poor woman's delicate face looked almost peaceful. Wilner wondered how she had been unlucky enough to fall victim to a killer like this. Had she known him? Where had she met him? Perhaps the hospital.

If Besslia found his body it wouldn't matter, the case would be closed and he'd be told to move on to something else. But if his body wasn't recovered Wilner needed someplace to start.

He gently pulled a comforter up over her body. The crime scene techs, if they showed, wouldn't be too thorough. They wouldn't care if he moved something like that. He just didn't think it was right to leave her so exposed.

He looked through the rest of the apartment but found nothing. Just outside the door he saw the remains of the chair that the killer had almost managed to crush Wilner's head with. He looked at the piece he had used to strike the killer. He bent down and picked it up. Even though DNA wasn't used much anymore due to the cost and the degraded database, there might be a fingerprint or something they could use to identify the killer. It was all he had right now.